Gilmore House Mysteries

Flight Plan

Brian R Lindsay

Printed in Canada

ISBN 978-0-9948042-3-5

Second iteration

FIN 08 11 2016

Disclaimer

This is a work of fiction.
The town of Westport is a real place as are some of the local businesses mentioned in the story but I have taken the liberty of rearranging some of its geography. I have added some buildings and businesses, all of which are fictional, as are all the characters.

Also by Brian R. Lindsay

Old Bones - A Gilmore House Mystery

Acknowledgements

As before, thanks are due to a great many people.

Thanks again to Jennifer Sallans of Volumes Publishing for helping me through the process.

Thanks to John Mader for aircraft information, to Bruce Penniston for still more boat and boating information and to Mary Jones for the loan of information books.

Ideas had evolved that had no place in *Old Bones,* but which I did not wish to discard so I had begun, in very basic terms, to write *Flight Plan* before *Old Bones* was even in print. Later I was spurred on to get busy with this book by not only friends and relatives but by readers of *Old Bones* who went out of their way to comment and who, for the most part, said they had enjoyed it and were waiting for the next one. Thank you for that encouragement.

Thanks for editorial assistance to Bruce in Lake Erroch, Grace in Thornhill and Erin and Chase in Smiths Falls. Thanks to Marg and Bruce in North Gower for editing and for canal information and to Mike in Kitchener for editing and some law-related information.

Thanks to Bruce Lindsay, Jo Meilenner, Nikki Everetts-Hamond and Mike Lindsay for vetting the recipes.

As always, thanks to Nikki Everetts-Hammond and Mavis Fenn. We three are still a "critique group", continuing to meet once a month, sharing and critiquing our writings. Mavis and Nikki, both published writers themselves, have been listeners, readers, editors and critics. They continue to be friends and mentors and their input has been invaluable.

And thanks again to Jane, who continues to be computer teacher, early reader, sounding board, researcher, editor, purveyor of insights and ideas (and recipes) and more.

Dedication

For Jane, with love.
As before, this would not ever have been finished
without your help.

And for Michael and Erin

Southeastern Ontario Road Map

Topographical map of Gilmore Island

This is a copy of a topographical map found among the stored Gilmore family items at the Westport Museum. It is thought to have been made by Alexander Gilmore, the youngest son of the Gilmore family. There is however, no way to verify this.

It is a very accurate representation of Gilmore Island.

Landmarks and labels have been added as none were found on the original.　RJH.

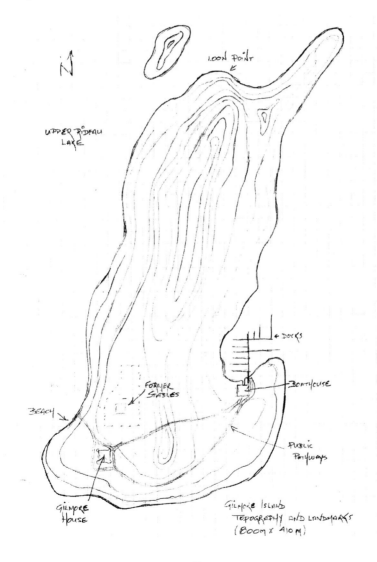

House Floor Plans

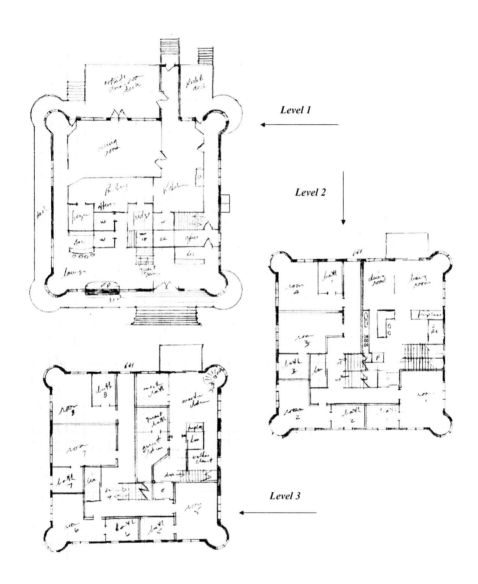

Level 1

Level 2

Level 3

Chapter 1

Winnstar Technologies Messenger   account wtim0001

New Message   **Thursday**   **10/07**

From : Jason Murdock CEO

To : Valerie Owens CFO, Richard Washburn COO, Suzanne Ellis President, Harvey Donaldson Senior VP R&D, Dianne Jones Senior VP Marketing

Jason – Hope you're all going to be ready on time for a change. The car will be around, starting at 7:00.

    Valerie – Yeah. Don't worry about us. Don't forget your underwear this time.

Jason – Not going to let me forget that, are you?

    Harvey – Where are we going, again?

Dianne – The Gilmore House Inn. It's on an island in eastern Ontario.

    Harvey – Should I be bringing fishing gear?

1

Richard – Up to you. Remember we have to get all the stuff into the back of the plane, so don't get too carried away.

    Jason – And remember that this is partly a business trip, not just a vacation.

———————

Winnstar Technologies Messenger   **account wtim0043**

<u>**New Message**</u>   **Thursday**   **10/07**

From : Hotrod

To : Spider

Hotrod – After all the planning this is finally our chance to get rid of some excess baggage and take control of the company. We'll see how business is after this trip.

    Spider – I hope this Gilmore Island place is totally boring.

Hotrod – It is. Don't worry. Nothing but a bunch of rubes – no-one there to get in the way of the plan. We'll have two weeks to make it all happen.

    Spider – If we follow the plan everything will work out and we'll be rich.

Hotrod – We'll be retired to our respective lives of leisure and they'll be gone. Too bad they were too stubborn to sell.

———————

At the Gilmore House Inn the rest of early summer passed much more quietly than had the earlier part of our opening year.

There were no more skeletons found in attics, the Gilmore House Inn's or anyone else's that I knew of. The excitement surrounding the news that a local man had been responsible for the death of a former town resident had faded fairly quickly given that he had elected to be killed rather than be arrested. Hence there was no sensational trial to prolong the interest. His nephew, a local business owner, had had some rough weeks once the story became public but that too seemed to have abated and those injured during the event were mostly all recovered.

High summer brought lots of new guests to Gilmore Island and we had our hands full dealing with them all. The staff, though still fairly new at the inn-keeping game, handled the pressure very well and became more and more a team that could be counted on to always do their best for their guests.

My name is RJ Harrison and I'm new to the inn-keeping game, too. I'm a fifty-something forced retiree with a sometimes wonky knee, a souvenir of my last case as an insurance investigator. My wrongful-injury pay-out from my former employer provided me with money enough to buy an island, with a stone-built, three-story Victorian house, partially converted to an Inn, in Upper Rideau Lake.

Upper Rideau Lake has the highest water elevation on the Rideau System between Ottawa and Kingston. It is surrounded by treed hills and at its far western end is the village of Westport and, near Westport, Gilmore Island. Here I was to have a safe and peaceful new life. Sure.

My first year has not been without its challenges. The Inn was a disaster when I took it over but, with many months of hard work and lots of help, Gilmore House Inn was ready to open in the late spring. It opened with a bang.

Not long before we were due to open I found the skeleton of a woman in the attic. So, instead of being able to concentrate on being host and chief cook for my Inn and its guests, I, along with my new friend OPP Sergeant Mike Grant, spent the ensuing couple of weeks trying to solve the mystery of her presence in my attic.

We managed to solve the mystery; well, two actually, and I fondly hoped that I'd finally get my safe and peaceful new life.

―――――――

About ten o'clock on a Friday morning in mid-July, we were pretty much ready for lunch hour and were organizing food for dinner. Bud, my right hand man in the kitchen, was preparing all the necessary ingredients and vessels needed to cook fresh Rainbow Trout Almandine, one of our specials that evening, and Frankie was peeling and cutting potatoes which, as super-fluffy whipped potatoes, would accompany the other special, Chicken with Tarragon, a gently sautéed seasoned chicken cutlet flavoured with white wine and fresh tarragon. The tarragon, and most of the other herbs we use, is grown in our own herb garden. A small mountain of fresh Ontario green beans covered one corner of the main prep table and a sink full of small cylinder beets rested in cool water at the side.

The conversation in the kitchen was spirited. We three were debating whether or not the Blue Jays would ever win another World Series and anyone who ventured in from the dining room joined in the discussion briefly.

"Frankie. Please turn on the oven. I need to roast some beef bones for making stock tomorrow."

"Sure, RJ. What temperature?"

"400°, please."

"Ha!" said Bud.

Frankie and Jeany both looked at Bud, who smiled a wicked smile and pointed a finger in my direction.

"Despite my best efforts, RJ continues to use Fahrenheit temperatures in the kitchen. Celsius is so much easier."

"I'm trying but I keep slipping back. Comes of growing up during the transition. I use Fahrenheit for cooking and Celsius for outside temperatures. I use metric for lengths and Imperial for measures."

Bud looked at the other two again.

"See what I mean. Totally messed up."

"Well, Bud, you have my permission to keep picking away at me about it. Eventually I'll get it. Frankie, *200°* please."

We continued to work and chat until our voices were quite suddenly drowned out by the roar of an aircraft passing low overhead. It faded slightly then changed pitch. We all went to the one small window and looked along the only unobstructed corridor between the Inn and the lake. An amphibious Twin Otter touched down on the water on the west side of the island, kicking up two giant rooster-tails of water and foam, before disappearing behind the trees that line most of that shoreline. I thought it odd that the pilot would choose to land on the west side of the island then taxi around to the docks on the east side. It was a long way to go. Maybe those in the plane just wanted to see what the island looked like. I hoped he would look out for rocks as he rounded the north end of the island.

We all returned to our work but the topic of conversation had changed. Bud and Frankie speculated about who might be arriving in such a flashy manner. I already knew. We finished up most of the dinner prep and I didn't feel bad about having to leave a half hour later.

"You guys are going to have to excuse me for a few minutes. I stopped to talk to Gwen on the desk one day a few weeks ago and she told me about her conversation with the person who made the reservation for the group that just landed out there. They're from a company called Winnstar Technologies, out of Winnipeg. They're going to be here for two weeks, our first booking of that length. Gwen said she got the impression that they might travel with enough stuff to be here for a month. The person making the reservation hinted that some members of the group always bring too much. Apparently they don't travel light. Oh well, they are staying two weeks, after all. They should be unloaded and on their way to reception by now so I'm going to have a look and play bell-hop if necessary – get them to their rooms with as little fuss as possible."

Bud watched as I took off my apron. "Better you than me. I'm allergic to those snooty types."

"I am too, to be honest, but they pay the bills and I put up with what I have to, within reason. Fortunately most of the guests we've had so far have been pretty decent over all. Most likely these will be too. Too early to tell. See you later."

I went out the back way and climbed the stairs to my suite. There was only a little dull throb in my knee as I reached the top. It was obviously improving. I grabbed a can of V8 juice as I passed through my kitchen, then I took the time for a quick wash and put on a fresh shirt before I went to greet the arrivals. I knew there would be no need for me to rush as the group from the plane would have been a while getting unloaded and to the Inn. I had already arranged that there would be some boathouse and dock staff there ready to help with the luggage so I took a few minutes to look over a couple of emails I'd received about buying some more boats for the Inn. A short while later I went downstairs.

The lobby, when I got there, was in chaos. Gwen had been right. It looked as though a couple of dozen people must be checking in, not just six, and maybe for a month, not two weeks. There was luggage everywhere, from one wall to the other, and piled in front of the stairs. I looked over as the main door opened. One of our young boathouse assistants had a trolley rolled up to the door having made his third, ten-minute trip from the dock.

"That's the last of it," he said quietly to me as he deposited another few cases on the now near-invisible hardwood floor. "I don't know how they got it all in that little plane."

"Twin Otters can carry a good load but even so this might have been pushing the limit," I said. "Whoever did the loading must be a magician." The young man left and I turned again to watch the circus at the desk.

Calm and efficient as ever, Gwen worked her way through the registrations, taking information and a credit card number and making room assignments. A fortyish man in tan Chinos and a yellow polo shirt did the checking in as the other five stood around chatting and commenting on their first impressions of the Inn. Soon the paperwork was done and the six new arrivals were ready to go.

"Is there someone to help with the bags?" asked the man as he put away his wallet.

Two of our dining room busboys double as porters, as needed. "We're here," said one of the two, eyeing the mountain of bags with some trepidation.

"And me," I added from the other direction.

Gwen piped up from behind the counter, "This is …." I cut her off with a shake of my head. No need to get into introductions just now.

"You can ride up in the elevator, four at a time at most, please," I said, "Or you can walk up. You're only up one flight – three adjacent rooms on the second floor."

"I'm for the stairs," said one of the women.

I grabbed a couple of bags and led the way. The woman, to her credit, picked up a small case and fell in behind me. The other five, seeing the example, each took a bag of some sort and followed along. The two some-time porters would load as much as was safe into the old elevator and send it up, walk up, unload and then ride down to repeat the process.

It was nearly a half hour later when all the sorting of suitcases, carry-ons, garment bags, backpacks, tackle boxes and fishing rods was done and the three couples had retreated, at least temporarily, into their rooms.

We three luggage carriers rode down in the elevator. "You two did a good job with that," I said as we reached the main floor. "I don't think I've ever seen that much baggage with so few people before."

"Yeah. It was definitely a load. At least they were decent tippers. The guy in the yellow shirt gave me three tens – one for each of us." He handed over a crisp new ten dollar bill to his buddy and to me. I handed mine back.

"You can give that to Gwen please. I'll see you later."

"Thanks, RJ. See ya."

The two young men paused briefly at the desk as they went back to their jobs in the dining room and I followed them as far as the front desk. Gwen was alone for the moment.

"Hi, RJ. That was some entrance, wasn't it?"

"Sure was. Quite the production. They seemed to be okay with the rooms once we got them up there and in. Have they made dinner reservations yet?"

"No, but I'd planned to give them a short while to get settled then give them a call and remind them."

"Good. Don't wait too long before you call. I heard one of them talking about going out for a walk to get some exercise after the plane ride. I'm going back to the kitchen. I'll be there if you need me."

"Actually, you don't need to go back. Bud came by a few minutes ago and said that all the prep is done and Jeremy will be here later for the evening service, so he can finish up any last minute stuff and you're off the hook for today. There, at least. Kim would like to see you sometime soon but not urgently, tomorrow morning would do, and there are two phone messages. Shall I just read them to you? Neither one requires a response."

"Okay, shoot." I leaned my elbows on the counter and watched Gwen as she delved into the debris on her desk and came up with two slips of pink paper.

"Andy Morrison called to say that the damages to the Picnic Boat were not as severe as originally thought and he'll have it repaired in a week or maybe sooner and for less than he quoted."

"Less is good."

"A secretary or someone at the Corbett Gallery called to say that Cameron Alexander was called away unexpectedly and would be unable to keep your appointment tomorrow. Ms. Alexander will call to reschedule in a day or two."

"Now that is unfortunate. Thanks, Gwen." I said. "And good job with that big group."

"You're welcome, RJ. And thanks for the tip." She waved the ten in my direction as the phone rang and she turned to answer it.

As I walked away I thought about the party boat. It was a Richardson Picnic Launch, about 22 feet long and built in 1939. I'd found it at a marina and had it brought to Gilmore Island. So far it was the only boat I'd personally supplied to the Gilmore operation. We used it for specialty cruises. One of the services we provided was a lunch or dinner service for two or four – seriously cozy with six – out on the lake: a self-serve, all-inclusive picnic-in-a-basket. It's self-serve because we want the driver concentrating on driving, not playing waiter as well. The boat is equipped with battery operated lights so it can be used into the late evening if necessary.

Last week a visitor had lost control of his boat and rammed the Richardson. The fibreglass boat got the worst of the encounter but there was still some damage, so our picnic service was temporarily out of business.

I'd decided to rename the boat when I got it back. In fact, Andy Morrison was going to get a painter to do the change while it was still in his shop: *Lady Cam*. I hadn't yet mentioned it to Cam and I hoped she'd be okay with the idea.

Cameron Alexander and I had been spending time together fairly regularly during the past month or so. Cam was the early-forty-something owner/manager of the Corbett Gallery in Westport. At about one and a half metres tall and in good shape, she was a force to be reckoned with, always on the move around the town, around the country and around the world where she collected items to sell in her showroom. She had short dark hair, fine features and slightly olive skin. We'd seen a lot of one another recently and I was finding I was liking her more and more.

Chapter 2

Winnstar Technologies Messenger   account wtim0043

New Message   Thursday   10/07

From : Spider

To : Hotrod

Spider– I saw a couple on the dock as I was leaving the plane. Bad timing. She's someone I know from a former company. Don't know if she saw me or, if so, if she recognized me. If they're staying at the Inn I may have to deal with her.

So, no more work to do today. I'd thought I'd be in a rush later to make it on time to Rideau Lakes Golf Club. I had lunch and a round booked with my friend Mike for the first time in a couple of weeks. Since he and I had worked together in solving the Veronica Graham murder we'd tried to get out golfing once in a while. We'd played the very nice nine-hole course a few times but both of our schedules had got in the way recently. Now it was well into July and I hoped the breeze would be up out on the course. The afternoon sun would be blistering hot.

I decided to head right out and maybe hit a bucket of balls before lunch. I stopped off at my suite to change into appropriate clothes, slid three bottles of water into a small pack and then made my way to the boathouse. I found one of the boathouse attendants with nothing pressing to do so I had him run me over to the mainland.

The boat was a 1933, Port Carling Seabird triple cockpit runabout, about 21 feet long. It was one of a few boats acquired by a previous owner - he favoured boats from the thirties, for some reason - when he thought he was going to be here for a long while. The boats stayed but he didn't.

As we motored away from the island I turned back and glimpsed the old house through the trees and thought of the Gilmores who'd come here more than a century ago, to start their new lives. After years of construction, their stay here after finally moving in was all too short.

A worldwide flu epidemic in the early 1900s wiped out most of the family and those who survived returned to their former home - Kingston. One daughter of the family, Victoria, had departed in mysterious circumstances some time before the epidemic struck.

The island and the house were left to deteriorate for nearly a hundred years, with only occasional tenants. More recently a lot of serious upgrading had been done but work was not completed before I came on the scene.

————

Gilmore Island is actually closer to the golf course than it is to Westport and as we skimmed over the glass-like surface of the lake I could see a few golfers out on the course.

The view today was, as usual, excellent as we crossed the water: a long, sloping hillside covered with an infinite array of greens and browns, topped by a vast and cloudless blue sky. The lake water glittered as the surface was disturbed by the faint breeze.

In no time we were at the public dock at Westport. I told the boatman that I'd be ready for a return trip by four o'clock at the latest. In this heat we would not waste a lot of time playing the nine holes. He motored off into the open water again and I walked along Main Street to the place where I garage my vehicle.

Mrs. Samuelson's place backs onto the water and is a large, treed lot with a big old house, a big old garage and some sheds and other, smaller, outbuildings.

As always when I came here I stopped to see the owner. I'd need to make it a quick stop this time. Mrs. Samuelson and I had become friends and so we liked to spend time together whenever possible.

I rang the bell at the back door. After a minute or two I rang again but still received no answer. Perhaps she would be here when I returned from golfing.

I used my remote to open the garage door I'd had installed soon after taking possession of half of the building. As I crunched across the gravel driveway I recalled the time when I and my friend Constable Josée Allard had been nearly killed there. I had escaped relatively unscathed, but Josée, spending a long time recovering from her injuries, was still on desk-duty at her new assignment.

I got the Lexus Hybrid SUV rolling and drove out Main to Rideau then left on Concession. Concession Street becomes Highway 42 at the edge of Westport and it's only about a five minute drive before the turnoff, north onto the peninsula, to the Rideau Lakes Golf Club. The Golf World driving range was right on the highway near the turnoff. That was where I was headed first.

I parked and dragged my old golf bag with its attached rolling cart out of the back, put down the wheels and walked across the gravel driveway and up the small rise to the range. I left the clubs beside the path and went into the clubhouse where I rented a bucket of balls and then headed for the driving range.

Only a few others were fool enough to be out there in the 32 degree Celsius heat so I pretty much had my pick of spots. I went to the farthest tee and began warming up, stretching and swinging the driver with first one arm, then the other, then both.

I put down a ball and, starting off gently, swung through the ball, connecting with a satisfying whack. The first ball didn't fly very far but it went fairly straight. I put down another ball and repeated the process, increasing force a little at a time, with varying degrees of success.

I was about halfway through the bucket when I noticed the attendant jogging toward me. I guessed there must be some kind of trouble or he would not have been running in this heat.

Dripping perspiration and breathing hard the fellow delivered his message.

"You're Mr. Harrison from the Gilmore, right?"

I agreed that I was.

"I just took a call from the dispatch at Smiths Falls OPP. They tried you at the golf course and didn't find you there so they tried here. They said to tell you that Sergeant Grant won't be able to join you at the golf course for your game. Said he's headed to your island instead because there's some kind of trouble and he thinks you should meet him there as soon as possible – something about one of your guests being dead."

Well, damn.

Before heading out from the driving range I called ahead to the Gilmore to have someone sent with a boat as soon as possible. I didn't get into what was going on at the island, because I wanted to make as much speed as I could. I drove back to Westport quickly and was putting the Lexus into the garage when I heard a siren in the distance. I decided to not risk a possibly extended visit with Mrs. Samuelson. As soon as the garage door closed I cut out through the trees to Main Street and got to the public dock as fast as I could.

Three of us arrived there at almost the same time. The boathouse attendant was just tying up the Seabird when I started along the raised walkway. Sergeant Grant's unmarked skidded to a halt in the parking area seconds later. The flashing dashboard light and the siren both ended abruptly as the car stopped and the door popped open.

Grant took a large backpack from the back seat and locked up the car. With his jacket over one shoulder and the pack over the other he hurried down the slope toward the water and along the walkway.

Sergeant Grant was what I once heard someone at the Inn describe as the perfect cop. He was a little taller than I – something over two metres - and had short dark hair. He was lean and fit and had a well tanned face with a couple of small scars and what would be called a strong jaw. He was soft-spoken, intelligent and polite but you always knew there were reserves of strength and points over which he would not be pushed. Some tested those boundaries but, generally, only once.

We'd met, for the second time, earlier in the year when he'd caught the case involving the skeleton in my attic and we'd become friends.

"I was hoping I'd catch up with you before you left. The marine unit is tied up with a situation at one of the locks at Jones Falls. Some guy took a houseboat he didn't know how to operate properly into an already half full lock. Just when his mate was set to grab the drop cables on the side of the lock he threw the engines into full reverse instead of neutral. Dumped the crew guy headfirst into the water and crunched an antique Chris Craft and a brand new Sea Ray. They'll be there a while. So, how was your day?"

"Up until 20 minutes ago it was pretty good. Almost a full house at the Inn and my golf swing is improving. I need more practice but I'm thinking it was just as well we didn't get to play today. Too damned hot." Grant nodded his agreement.

We arrived at the courtesy boat and the attendant untied and was off again almost as soon as we were seated.

"So what's going on at the Island?" I asked quietly. Grant and I were sitting in the rear section of the old, triple cockpit boat, and it was not too likely that the driver would hear anything we said.

Grant, nonetheless, leaned close and spoke as quietly as possible given that we still had to hear over the engine noise.

"All I know is that a body was seen floating face down in some quite shallow and very rocky water toward the top end of the Island. It's just around the east side of the peninsula, from … Loon Point I think you call it. I believe you're familiar with that spot. It's just south, about a third of the way down the shoreline."

I flashed back briefly to a time earlier that year when I had nearly gone over the cliff at Loon Point. My adversary at the time had outguessed me, realizing that I'd found where he'd tied up his small boat on the rocky shore and believing, correctly, that I'd have to go looking for further evidence. He had tied a flexible green branch to another tree in such a way as to create a trap, concealing the release among the other branches. When I ventured into the open space at the top of the cliff I had to move one small branch as I passed. That movement triggered the release of the tied-back branch which hit me in the back, throwing me toward the cliff edge. It was a near thing but I managed not to go over. I returned to the Inn that day cut up and bruised and with a better sense of my adversary's capabilities, even though at that time I didn't know who it was that I was duelling with.

The boat bounced over a wake and I was jolted back to reality. "Yes. I remember that place all too well. The east shore isn't anywhere near as high as Loon Point but the water is just as treacherous in places. Do we know how or from where the person got into the water?"

"I don't know anything more than what I've told you already. As soon as we get there I'll start seeing about getting him - or her? - out of the water. After that it'll be up to the forensic types and the M.E. to do their thing. They're coming by road so we'll need to see about bringing them across to the island once they get this far, if the Marine Unit isn't freed-up by then."

"Speaking of coming by road, how did you get here from Smiths Falls so fast? I just got the call a few minutes ago."

"I wasn't in Smiths Falls. I had a meeting in Kingston and was on my way home to get ready for our golf game. The call came through when I was not more than 10 kilometres from Crosby. I came straight here."

Soon enough we were at the Gilmore dock and we quickly realized that the place was buzzing with, well, not exactly excitement, but suppressed energy and we were fending off questions as we climbed out of the boat. I made sure someone was going to be available to ferry passengers at least until dark. I had the driver who'd ferried us go back and wait for the forensic team and the coroner, just in case the police boat wasn't free by the time that group arrived at Westport.

Sergeant Grant went around the north end of the boathouse and headed directly up the eastern shoreline. I went into the Inn and straight to the office to see Kim. I thought some level of damage control might be necessary. I was right, but I didn't have to provide it.

As I approached the desk a tall bald man and a small grey woman were both talking at once to Gwen.

"You know," the man was saying, "when we heard that there had been a murder associated with the place already we thought 'Okay, so that could happen anywhere really' and so even though we didn't like the idea of the murder and all we thought we'd come anyway but now …"

"But now," continued the woman, "we see a pattern and we think there's some kind of curse or something and we could be next."

"Yes, well, I don't think that's very likely, Mrs. Mason," said Gwen, "but we wouldn't want you to stay if you're not comfortable."

"Just give me the bill and let us get out of here. I assume we can get away tonight?" said the man.

I nodded to Gwen, unseen by the departing guests.

"Oh, yes. The boats are still running. We won't keep you here. The bill reflects only last night and last evening's dinner and today's lunch. No room charges for today, even though it's well past checkout time."

"Well, I should think not. Dead bodies turning up all over and you expect people to respect the checkout time policy? *Really?*"

Gwen handed back the guest's credit card. "Bodies all over? And I'd thought there was just the *one*. My information system seems to be running slow."

That bit of humour fell flat. The couple captured the extended handles of their rolling bags and headed for the door. "You'll not ever see us again," said the woman.

"I'll call down to the boathouse and make sure someone's ready to run you back to the mainland," Gwen called after them.

The door closed loudly.

"Now that was very odd," I said. Almost too odd was what I thought. The Masons seemed to be making a much bigger deal about what was happening than was warranted. Could it be they were trying to escape rather than just leave?

"You're telling me."

I walked closer to the reception desk. "Only *one* body?"

Gwen looked somewhat abashed. "Curses? Bodies turning up all over? I just couldn't let that nonsense go by. I suppose I shouldn't have said anything."

"Probably not," I said, "but I can't fault you for it either. I'd have done much the same, I think. I'm going in to see Kim for a few minutes then I'm going up the path to catch up with Sergeant Grant and see how he's making out."

"Kim's not in her office. I haven't seen her for quite a while."

"Fine. I'll talk to her later. Call my cell if you need me."

"Will do, RJ. See you later."

It was still bright and still hot when I went back out the huge main door. A slight breeze now gently rustled the leaves of maple and birch trees along the path to the boathouse. I caught sight of the Masons trotting around a bend in the main pathway to the boathouse and dock. Not wasting any time making their escape.

A shadow of something overhead passed by on the ground and I looked up just in time to see a great blue heron drift silently over the trees.

I went along a secondary path that went across country, past the derelict stables, over the saddle of the island, and on to the east shore and then up the shoreline.

As I passed them I wondered yet again if there was anything I could do with the old stables. I wasn't interested in getting into the horse business – that would be more trouble than I needed – but the stables must be of some more use than just as an interesting photo op for the guests. Perhaps a party venue or something like that.

During the original construction on the island the Gilmores had had a dedicated crew, mostly local carpenters and labourers, working on the stables and the riding trails. Word was that people tried to talk George Gilmore out of all this extra expense but he had to have his horses.

Pathways were cleared through the trees and crushed rock and then soil was carried in to level and smooth the trails so the horses would be able to run without fear of injury. A hundred years of rain and wind and weather had washed away all the soil and most of the trails, though still visible, were overgrown.

The path I wanted, up the east side of the island was kept well maintained and I made good time. I knew that I was half way to the top of the island when I passed a seriously bent tree. Probably a wind-fall, now long rotted away, had leaned against it when it was young and green, leaving a great arc in its trunk. The place I was headed for was not far beyond.

―――――――

Several of our off-duty staff and a number of guests were lined up along the top of the sloping, solid granite edge of the lake, watching the scene not far below.

Gulls and cormorants, perched on half-submerged rocks, watched from the water side.

Sergeant Grant, moving quickly, had, while I was inside, come back from looking out over the north-eastern shoreline and had commandeered a rowboat and now had a couple of the boathouse people out in it, with a large wake board tied behind. The rowers manoeuvred the boat carefully, threading their way between sharp and barely-submerged rocks until they reached their goal. As we watched from above, Grant carefully hauled in the floating body, now obviously a small, dark haired woman wearing dark shorts and a pale blouse or tee shirt. Matted hair obscured her face.

She was pulled onto the board and the boat was rowed slowly away, with Grant and the other employee holding onto the wake board and its grizzly cargo.

Grant heard the voices above him and looked up to the top of the cliff. He saw me and called out.

"RJ, would you please clear those people out of that area - just in case she came down from up there? Leave someone there to keep watch until I can make other arrangements."

In the distance we could hear the sound of a siren as the OPP Marine Unit headed toward Gilmore Island from the direction of the Newboro Lock.

Chapter 3

Winnstar Technologies Messenger   account wtim0043

New Message   **Friday**   **11/07**

From : Geek

To : Spider, Hotrod, Flower

Geek – I hear they found a body floating in the water near the island. That could be a good thing for us.

        Spider – If it creates a distraction – that's good, but it could also mean cops sooner than we want them. We'll need to be careful.

———————

Something was poking away at the back of my mind as I watched the rowboat slowly make its way south, but I couldn't get a grip on it. Not an unfamiliar sensation for me.

I ushered the sight-seers away from the edge and asked one of the staff who had been among them to stay and do guard-duty for a while, making sure he understood that he was to stay put, stay away from the edge and not disturb the scene any more than it had already been, until the arrival of a police officer. I hurried back toward the boathouse, trying to beat the rowboat and its cargo there and clear a section of the dock so they could land without too much interference. I rounded up two staff people and we started moving any guests we encountered away from the outer section of the dock area. This is the area where the Twin Otter was tied up – it was set aside for amphibious aircraft and very large boats, not that we got very many of those. It had wider slips and lots of room for wingspan, and there were currently no boats around it, hence no excuses for guests or staff to approach.

The area was cleared just as the rowboat came across the last stretch of open water before reaching the docks. I waved them away from the more congested portion of the dock and they steered around the moored Otter to the spot where I was waiting.

My two boathouse staff who'd been recruited for the retrieval operation were looking a little green as the rowboat slid up against the wood of the dock. This sort of thing was not covered in their job descriptions.

One of them climbed out of the boat, looking at me with an expression I couldn't quite read. He tied off one end of the boat while I got the other, then stood staring at the water, somehow unable to process a next movement. I laid a hand on his shoulder and his head turned toward me.

"Go sit over there, please, Tim," I said, indicating one of several benches strategically placed around the dock area.

He gave no real sign of having heard me but did as he had been asked.

By the time I looked back to the boat the other young fellow, Jordan, was out and in much the same condition. I just pointed to the first fellow and Jordan went and sat beside him.

Sergeant Grant was still crouched in the rowboat, looking closely at the form on the wake board floating behind.

"Well, RJ, it looks like you have another body to deal with." He spoke without looking at me – knowing I was there.

"Terrific. Just what the place needs is more notoriety of that kind."

"Nothing you can do about it now. I hear the police boat. How close are they?"

I looked around to the open water. "Two minutes tops," I said.

"Good. I'll be glad to get out of this cramped position, but I don't want to let the board go until I know it's absolutely secure." He glanced over his shoulder.

"Your two boys there did well but they're a little shaky right now. Not surprising. You might have to give them some time off after this is over."

"Yeah. I'll see they're looked after. Couldn't have been much fun."

"No, but it could have been a lot worse. She hasn't been in the water long, whoever she is. No bloating or fish feeding or any of that sort of stuff that happens to bodies that are in the water a while. I'd guess we're talking less than an hour or two from the time she went in 'til someone spotted her and raised the alarm. The body didn't sink because of all the rocks in the shallow water." He hesitated a moment then added a disturbing thought. "I have to say I was worried as we approached her. For a minute or two I thought it might be Kim. It isn't, but the physical similarities were scary for a while."

Suddenly I realized that that was what had been bothering me up on the shore. The resemblance to Kim was indeed striking. Even from as close as I was now I couldn't have said for sure that it wasn't her without seeing the face, which was now turned away from me and still partially obscured by matted hair. This person was wearing denim cut-offs – very dark with wet and very short, a white tee shirt and white boat shoes. The last time I'd seen Kim she was dressed in a business suit and dark shoes. I would have to take Grant's word for it that the body on the wake board was not Kim. I wondered where she was.

Kim was the Gilmore's business manager. A thirty-something woman with short dark hair and slim build, Kim was very good at what she did and ran the Inn much more efficiently than I could ever have hoped to.

She was pleasant and polite to guests and staff alike but had a strength of character that I admired and which prevented her from being intimidated by … anyone, as far as I knew.

While I'd been zoned out the police boat had arrived. I snapped back to reality as the big cruiser arrived against the dock and one of the officers jumped out. I took the bow line from the helmsman and tied it off. The officer who'd already disembarked tied the stern line and the helmsman killed the engines.

My back was to the boat when I heard the voice, imperious, grating.

"You there. You there – with the Inn. We need some help here."

I turned toward the sound. "Yes, you. Come and get these bags. I hope you haven't given away our room. Now that we've been dragged back here against our will there'd better be a place for us to stay. A safe place. We don't want to become another of this island's casualties."

Gwen would be thrilled to see these two again.

I waved my arms around and got the attention of one of the boathouse workers who came to the docked police boat.

"Would you please take the Masons and their luggage to the Inn? Ask Gwen to check them back into their former room."

With much grumbling and grumping from the unhappy guests the task was accomplished and the bald man and the grey woman departed the dock.

I met the officer who'd been the helmsman as he stepped out of the boat. "When those two left the Inn not long ago they said they would never be back. They were quite emphatic about it, in fact," I said.

"Yes, well that's what they told us as well. They were unimpressed with the idea of coming back but we had to insist. Sergeant Grant had notified us that there was a possibly suspicious death here and we thought it best not to let anyone leave before we'd had a chance to talk to them."

"I *bet* they were unimpressed. My fault actually. I hadn't thought about you not wanting people to leave, so I let them go. By the way, what did you do with my boat and driver?"

"We asked him to stay there at the Westport dock and wait for the coroner. He should be along any time now. We called him before we left Jones Falls and he was free and able to come right away."

As we were talking we had walked along the dock to where Sergeant Grant and the body on the wake board were still floating.

Grant was still bent over the stern of the rowboat, holding the wake board secure. He moved only his head to look up as we approached. "'Bout time you guys got here. You stop for coffee on the way?"

"Next time we have a case of lift lock demolition derby we're calling you to sort out the winners and losers."

Grant laughed. "Sounds like more losers than winners there today." Then he was serious again.

"RJ, these are Constables Reynolds, who you met earlier in the year, I think, and Conroy." We shook hands.

"We need to get this board out of the water without disturbing the body too much. We can't do anything with her until the coroner has had his time with her, but we need to get her secured and I can't stay here in this position much longer."

I spoke up first. "It'll be easiest for me to get a change of clothes so how about if I get in the water on the outside of the board and you three can lift it. I'll keep it from tipping so much that she slides off."

Grant thought that was a reasonable idea. I continued with the plan. "Let's move the boat and the board along the dock to that inside corner there. That way each of the three of you can take one side and I'll have something solid to keep me in place while I lift from the water."

Without further debate we made the move. Where the dock made an "L" shape we stopped.

"We ready?" I asked.

"I think so," said Grant.

I held up a finger indicating that they should wait a moment and jogged over to where Tim was sitting on the bench. I handed him my watch, wallet and cell phone and slipped off my shoes.

"Keep an eye on these for me will you please, Tim?"

I went back to the waiting crew and slid into the water. It was refreshingly cool in the heat of the afternoon.

We positioned the rowboat at an angle to the dock corner with the wake board on the inside. I held onto the boat with one arm and steadied the board with the other. The two marine officers took a side and an end of the board each, kneeling on the wood of the dock and bending low to the water's surface. Grant was still at the stern of the rowboat. They lifted slowly.

We had one false start as I lost my grip on the board. I repositioned and we started over. This time the board with its passenger rose slowly and smoothly from the water and was deposited on the dock. One of the marine officers brought a light-weight plastic sheet from the police boat and laid it carefully over the body.

Grant, now up on the dock, reached down, took my hand and practically lifted me out of the water. I stood dripping and staring down at the covered figure and wondered who she was and how she had come to be there and what was next, for her and for us.

Again my daydream was interrupted, this time by the arrival of the coroner in our 1936 Dodge, double cockpit runabout.

The now calm water was disturbed only by the ripples of the gentle wake and the old boat and its elderly occupant appeared as a 1930s postcard. The Dodge bumped gently against the dock only a couple of metres from where we were all gathered around the body. The spell was broken. The two marine officers went to tie off the lines and helped the coroner to disembark. He walked toward us slowly, his eyes fixed upon the plastic sheet. Without looking up he said, "Evenin', Michael".

"Evening, Joseph," replied Grant.

"So what have we here then? Take the cover off please and let's have a look."

One of the marine officers lifted off the bright yellow plastic sheet, exposing the sad-looking form beneath. The coroner stood looking briefly, sighed deeply then knelt down beside the body and began his examination. Grant told him all he knew of the situation. After a few minutes the older man stood.

"I think that's about it for now. As you know, Michael, I can't make definite statements without a proper examination under proper conditions. However, for purposes of your investigation I will say this: I would be very surprised to find any water in her lungs. I don't think she will have drowned. I expect she was probably dead before she went into the water. She received a very severe blow to the back of the head, sufficient I would think, to be the cause of death. The whole back of her head is caved in. Something like a grapefruit-sized rock perhaps. Not something she'd have done to herself surely and judging by its position, not likely an accident, though one can not be sure. I'd say the young lady was most likely murdered. I'll have a better report for you tomorrow, Michael, all being well, but I expect that's enough for you to be going on with."

A few seconds of dead silence followed this pronouncement.

"Yes. I suppose it is," said Sergeant Grant.

"Oh, and Michael, she seems to have no identification whatsoever that I can see," added the coroner.

Grant nodded.

The body of the unknown woman was placed, with great care, directed by the coroner, onto a stretcher and loaded onto the police boat.

I stood with Sergeant Grant and one of the other officers, Frank Reynolds, as they discussed the next step.

"One thing's for sure. We're going to need more help here," said Grant. "This could very rapidly turn into a major nightmare for all of us. There are about fifty interviews to conduct – between guests and staff, plus any day-trippers we can still round up. Some, your staff, will be wanting to get home for the night and others, the guests, will need to check out soon because their vacations are over or they have plans elsewhere. Either way we're going to have to get the initial chats over with as quickly as possible, and hopefully know where to find all of these people later."

"I think we have one empty room at the moment," I said. "A guest checked out yesterday and the next one cancelled – emergency medical situation or something. So you can have that room for interviews for now. The problem for me will be when new guests are due to check in. I don't want to have to turn people with reservations away. That will just cause me no end of trouble."

I shivered, suddenly feeling chilled despite the warmth of the breeze.

"You'd better get back and change clothes or you'll be the one with the medical emergency," said Grant.

"Yeah, I should go. I need to get to Kim, if I can find her, and Gwen and Sue on the desk and see what we have available in the way of rooms in the next few days."

"You go ahead. We'll make a few calls and round up some more help and I want to close off the shore all the way from Loon Point to the dock, if possible, and relieve your employee. It may be too late for that to be of any use, evidence-gathering wise, but I'll do it anyway – keep the forensics guys happy."

Marine Constable Reynolds spoke up.

"I've had Conroy take the coroner back to Westport. After he's done what's needed there, he'll come back and the three of us can start with interviews. We'll have to return to our regular jobs tomorrow. You'll need to get a couple of replacements in the morning." Grant nodded then looked at me.

"Go get out of those wet clothes, RJ," said Grant. "I'll come up to the Inn soon and we'll start questioning people."

I decided that it was sound advice and headed off in the direction of the Inn.

I picked up my gear from Tim as I passed him and told him to take Jordan with him, check in with Kim and then head home.

As I left the dock area I saw one of the women from the Winnstar group walking away from the scene.

As I neared the main door the police boat cruised by on its return trip from Westport. I knew that there would soon be any number of unhappy guests as the police started the first round of interviews.

I pulled open the door and almost collided with Kim as she came tumbling out. Having expected to have to push hard on the huge oak door, her momentum carried her past me and I only just managed to catch her arm before she headed down the stairs onto the pathway below.

"Thanks, RJ. With that much momentum I think I might have ended up in the lake if you hadn't stopped me."

"Unlikely I think, but don't say that, even in jest. Have you not heard about our latest aggravation?"

"Of course I have. The place is absolutely humming. Gwen is back on the desk and has been fielding all kinds of calls from guests wanting to know 'a' if they're in danger and 'b' if they're going to be allowed to leave when they're supposed to. I was just on my way to find you to ask those questions." Kim frowned. "You're all wet, RJ."

"Really?"

"No need to be sarcastic. I would have noticed earlier but I'm feeling a bit harried at the moment. I'm expecting a call from my sister and she hasn't called. Obviously. She's coming for the weekend, or at least she's supposed to be. Not here, I don't mean – to my place. She's usually very reliable and does what she says she'll do and I don't know why she hasn't called. I'm rambling, aren't I? I'd better get back in there and help Gwen. Good thing it's Gwen and not some of the other desk people. Not that they're bad mind you, but Gwen's the best we have. I'm still doing it, aren't I? I'd better go."

Kim turned to go. I reached and pulled the heavy door open. "Don't you want your questions answered before you go back?" Kim stopped and looked at me, raised one eyebrow, but didn't speak.

"The party line is that this is an isolated incident and that there is no reason for alarm that we're aware of. Most likely it has nothing to do with the island or anyone on it. The police will be doing interviews of guests and staff as quickly as possible so as not to inconvenience anyone any more than is necessary. Those are my words, not the police's, but I'm sure it will be close enough for now."

Kim nodded and continued through the door. I called after her. "After I change I'm going to take a walk through the dining room and let the guests there know to expect to be meeting with the police later. Meanwhile you and Gwen can talk about room availability: the police will need one for the interviews."

Kim waved over her shoulder and kept on walking. As I went up in the old elevator I wondered about Kim's sister. I wondered if the resemblance could mean that it was she that we had just sent to the morgue in Perth. I hoped I was doing right in keeping quiet about my fears.

Chapter 4

I went up to my suite, quickly showered and put on fresh clothes and went straight to the dining room. I walked and talked to guests, attempting to reassure them that there was nothing to worry about and to expect to be asked questions by the police. I was also gauging reactions to that piece of news. Generally they seemed to be all right with the idea.

Most of the group from Winnipeg was there, enjoying dinner. I gave them the same speech I'd given at a couple of other tables. Jason Murdock, the CEO, spoke up for the group at the table.

"Our CFO, Valerie Owens is not with us for dinner. She went out for a walk after the long plane ride and has probably gone for a shower and a nap now. I expect she'll join us soon. I'll pass the message along to her whenever we meet up again later. You'll no doubt be able to find all six of us in the lounge later if we're needed." I recalled the other woman from this group. I'd seen her on the dock earlier, after we'd sent the mystery woman from the water on her way.

One young fellow at another table was perhaps more nervous than I would have thought necessary. He was half of a couple who were younger, hipper and flashier dressed than most of our guests and seemed a little out of place. I'd find out their names and mention them to Mike when I saw him next.

The Masons were, as expected, grumpy and unpleasant, wanting to know when they would be able to leave. They weren't any happier when I said it would be the next morning at the earliest. We weren't going to let anyone leave in the dark unless it was absolutely necessary.

The next table I stopped at had a middle aged couple, casually dressed and looking fit and tanned. I gave them the spiel and asked how they were enjoying their stay.

"Good so far," said the man. "We just got here yesterday."

"We want to get out on the water tomorrow," continued the woman. "We drove to Westport and we don't have a boat of our own. Do we have to rent a boat?"

"Not necessarily. Probably better if you take one of the tours. There are a few to choose from. They go in both directions from here, that is, once you get out into the lake a bit." I oriented myself toward the French windows at the rear of the dining room and pointed first one way then the other. Some other diners were watching and listening.

"If you go that way – that's north more or less – you go through the Narrows Lock first, then as many others as time permits. Eventually you'd get to Ottawa but time will most definitely not permit that for a single outing. The other way – south roughly – takes you through the Newboro Lock first then, as before, as many others as time permits. The drivers gauge how long it will take to go from A to B and back and that depends on traffic, weather, times the locks close, whatever. You get a two, four or six hour trip regardless but how far you go in that time will vary. We give you a lunch to take and you can get out and move around as often as you want to take pictures or whatever. Go to the main desk when you finish dinner and they'll set it all up for you."

"Thanks. We will," he said.

"There's also a river tour boat called the Rideau King. It runs out of Merrickville and you can get it for a day-long tour on Thursdays, I think. It takes you from Westport to Merrickville on the river and you get ground transportation back to Westport."

"That sounds great. It's beautiful country around here," she said.

Agreeing, I moved on to the next table.

———————

After doing the tour of the dining room I went back to the main desk.

Gwen, who should have gone home by now, was still there and still working, talking to guests who came in person and taking calls from guests' rooms. I silently agreed with Kim that it was a good thing that Gwen was on that day. Sue, who was coming on to relieve Gwen, was out in the lobby, mingling with guests and answering questions.

I had just arrived at the desk when Mike Grant came in through the main door, apparently finished his preliminary search for evidence along the eastern shoreline.

"Mike."

"RJ. The other two are not going to be far behind me. The sooner we can get the interviews going the sooner we'll be able to release some of your staff and guests. I'll look after the staff while the other two do whatever guests they can tonight. Do we still have access to that empty room?"

We walked together toward the office. "I think so. We'll know in a moment. If not we'll arrange something else."

We nodded a greeting to Gwen who was taking yet another call and passed on to Kim's office.

Kim was at her desk, her back to the door. Her hands flew over her keyboard. After a fast glance over her shoulder and a motion to give her a minute, she returned her attention to the computer. She would stop and look at the screen then frown and type some more, then write a note on the legal note pad at her left hand. She continued on for a few minutes and we waited patiently because we knew it was for us that the information was being compiled.

Quite suddenly she stopped typing, ripped the top sheet off the pad and spun her chair around to face us.

"Thanks for letting me finish. I think we may survive this – room wise at least – as long as the interviews don't go on too long." She shot a quick glance at Sergeant Grant to see if he had got the message. He returned the look and nodded slowly, a slight smile touching the corners of his mouth.

"I'll do my best. If you'll tell me which room we're to use tonight I'll get started now with the staff members who are supposed to be leaving."

"Room 201 is the only one empty at the moment. It will stay that way – we won't take any last minute bookings - unless we end up with an overlap between guests leaving – or not leaving as it were – and those arriving. Room 201 is right at the top of the first flight of stairs."

"Thanks, Kim," said Grant. "All right, RJ. Let's get organized and we can start to move your people through the first interviews."

I had our two bus-boy/porters take three folding tables, a set of tall, padded room dividers, some wide and some narrow and a couple of extra chairs from the basement storage up to room 201. We set up the dividers so as to make three interview areas. It would be crowded but hopefully not too bad for the short term.

Grant and I went on ahead to shift the large furniture – bed and dressing table – out of the way, but soon realized that it wasn't going to work, space-wise. The extra chairs, room dividers and tables arrived soon after and I had the guys disassemble the bed and take it and the dresser down to storage. After that we had the room arranged in short order.

That done, Grant started to lay out pads and pens and began making notes of things he had already observed, and a whole long list of questions to ask.

I went back to the main desk. Kim was not in her office but Gwen was still there. Her replacement, Sue, had arrived earlier and they were both hard at work. I went into Kim's office and tore several sheets off the legal pad beside the computer then rooted around for a marker. I'd almost given up. I carefully turned over the contents of the bottom drawer until I found a marker.

I glanced at the desk top and saw an application form lying there. It reminded me that I needed to grab some of the completed application forms we keep on file. I wanted to hire another person for the kitchen crew. I went to the file cabinet in the corner of the office and pulled open the top drawer where I knew to find what I was looking for.

I pulled the hanging files forward one at a time until I came to a file marked 'kitchen'. As I pulled it forward I heard a clunk from the back of the drawer.

I reached to the back of the last file and moved it forward.

There, lying on the bottom of the drawer, was something I was not expecting to find: an evil looking, gunmetal grey .22 semi-automatic pistol. Why would Kim have such a thing at all, let alone be keeping it in the file cabinet at the Inn?

I left the pistol where it was, closed the drawer and left the office, not knowing what to think and not wanting to encounter Kim until I'd thought this through a bit.

Out at the check-in counter I folded the sheets of paper and tore them into smaller portions. On each I wrote a number – one to 24.

Starting with Gwen who was beginning to look somewhat the worse for wear, I handed the numbered slips to all the employees I encountered. I was careful to give the lowest possible numbers to those who had been ready to go home when this all blew up. I spent a lot of time explaining why it was necessary that all the staff talk to the police before they would be allowed to leave the island. Reactions varied. Most understood the situation and accepted the restriction with good grace – though some with a perceptible resentment.

By the time I got to the bar, word of my mission had preceded me. Tomas saw me coming and stopped in the process of polishing a glass. As I approached, he stared, not at me so much as at the small stack of papers I still had left in my hands.

"Hello, Tomas. How are you doing this evening?" I asked.

He stood frozen. His eyes flashed briefly to my face then returned to the papers.

"No! You cannot do this. I have done nothing."

With this he put down the glass, folded the towel and set it on the bar. Then, before I could react he vaulted over the bar and ran from the room.

Staring dumbfounded I heard the outside door of the dining room bang closed. Tomas was gone. I debated briefly about going after him right away but decided I'd better get things here rearranged first. Getting coverage for the bar should only take a few minutes. Tomas couldn't go far in that time. He'd certainly have to stay on the island. The police were not letting anyone leave. I hoped I was making the right decision.

"What the hell was that about?" said a voice from behind me. I turned to find Sammi, one of our lounge servers, standing at the end of the bar with much the same expression on her face as I had.

"I have no idea," I said. "I didn't even get a chance to tell him what I was doing. He just stared at the papers I had in my hand and then bolted."

"Nice leap over the bar, though," continued Sammi. "I heard he was once a pretty impressive athlete in his home country, Hungary or Bulgaria, or one of those Eastern European countries, I think."

"Seems to have been true. I couldn't have done that from a standing start, even without my wonky knee."

"But why'd he run away?"

"No idea," I said. "Sammi, you've taken the bartending course, haven't you?"

A little hesitation. "Yes."

"Okay. I have to get out of here and after Tomas as quickly as possible so I don't have a lot of time to get things organized here. I'm going to need *you* to take over behind the bar for now, please. I'll have one of the dining room servers come in to cover your place on the floor. Can you do that, Sammi?"

"I guess so, RJ." Then "Yes, RJ, I can cover the bar. I may not be as good as Tomas but I can do it."

"That's what I wanted to hear. I'm sure you'll do fine. Just take it slow and easy. You'll be great. I'm going to find a replacement for you. Back in a minute."

I headed for the dining room. As I rounded the corner I glanced back. Sammi was slicing a lemon, a look of serious concentration on her face.

I don't know how it works but news travels very quickly around here. All the dining room staff and half the diners at the late seating looked up as I entered the room.

A quick scan told me there was only one good replacement for Sammi in the lounge. I needed a person with some serious experience to cover the position. Drinkers can be problematic if they're not looked after as quickly as they think they should be, and on top of that there was the general sense of uneasiness because of the body being found.

Only one of the current servers had the stuff, even though she would be out of practice with lounge work. I knew she didn't want to work in the lounge but I had little choice.

I waited until she was alone at the coffee station in the corner then approached. Michelle, seeing my reflection in a coffee pot, turned to face me. "I saw Tomas making his hasty exit, so I guess Sammi is tending bar for the rest of the night. You're not really going to make me go work in there, are you, RJ?"

I stopped a metre or so away from her. "No, Michelle, I'm not going to *make* you do anything, as I hope you know." She sighed expressively but said nothing. "I'm going to *ask* you to go work in there, though. Hopefully it'll only be for tonight. You're the only one here who's got any lounge experience." I could see she was softening so I pressed on. "I could put one of these new folks in but you know that that might not end well. I could do it myself …"

That was as far as I got. "You're kidding, right? You as a cocktail waitress. I'd love to get that on film." Another big sigh. "All right, RJ. I'll help you out, and Sammi. Can't leave her without *some* real help."

Now it was my turn to sigh.

"Give me a few minutes to organize my tables and I'll be in."

"Thank you, Michelle."

I went back around to the lounge and found that Sammi had everything well in hand for the moment. I was still watching from the entrance when one of the party from the plane called rather too loudly for a refill. I was about to respond when a black and white blur passed me and went toward the large group. "You're going to owe me for this, RJ."

"Keep an eye on that group from the plane. I've already been hearing from staff that some of them are none-too-pleasant to deal with."

"You are *really* going to owe me."

Chapter 5

Now I had to find Tomas. I felt sure his sudden panic had something to do with his past and not with the present situation, but I wanted to get to him before the police got wind of his disappearing act.

Tomas was our head bartender. He knew his way around a bar better than most anyone I'd ever seen, and controlled the inventory of alcohol for not only his own patch but for the kitchen as well. Whenever I needed a wine or whiskey or whatever for a recipe I'd get it from him. I didn't have to maintain a stock of my own.

We knew little about Tomas' past in – damn – still couldn't remember where he was from – but rumour had it that it had not been pleasant. He was somewhat taciturn, though not unfriendly when you got to know him. Getting to know him however - that was the hard part.

I knew Tomas had gone out through the dining room door to the deck but I needed to make a stop at the office before going searching. He was almost certainly hiding somewhere on the island since all the boat staff had been told, in no uncertain terms, that no-one was to take a boat from the island until it was cleared with the police. I didn't know how good a swimmer Tomas was, but probably not good enough to swim to the mainland. I hoped.

I had to talk to Kim and I hoped to be able to do it without letting her know that I'd found the gun. That was a conversation for another time. She was in the office but on the phone, so, rather than wait, I scratched a quick note telling her about Tomas and that she would possibly need to find coverage for the bar and/or the lounge service position for tomorrow. I slid the note in front of her as she talked and left the room.

I went out the main door and down to the stone pathway then around back to the dining room deck. One of the servers was out there and I hurried up the steps to talk to her before she had to go to another guest.

"Hello, Marissa. How are you doing tonight?"

"I'm fine, RJ. You?"

"I'm well, thanks. I'm trying to find Tomas. Did you happen to see which way he went when he came out that door?" I asked, nodding toward the French doors leading to the main dining doom.

"He went toward the beach, then maybe up along the shoreline toward Loon Point. I couldn't tell for sure. I hope everything is all right." I said I hoped so too.

I was making my way carefully along the shoreline path, hopefully in pursuit of the disappearing bartender, when my cell buzzed.

I stopped and sat down on a large piece of driftwood and opened the phone. "Hello, Cam. What's up?"

"You called me, RJ. I assume you wanted to talk to me about something?"

"Right. I called you. Why did I call you?" There was silence on the other end as I tried to remember why I'd called her.

A pair of ducks made a low-level pass over the edge of the rocky shore and out into the gathering darkness.

"Sorry, Cam. I'm in the middle of something kind of weird and ... oh, I remember now. I got an email from an association I belong to – IHIAC – the Independent Hoteliers and Innkeepers Association of Canada. This is my first year as a member. The email was an invitation to attend their annual four day convention. This year it's near the end of August, in Whistler. I thought that that was an odd time for people in our business to be having a convention – in the busy season. I was told that it's only the busy season for about half the members, the others being busy for skiing and such in winter. Their compromise is that they have an event every eighteen months – first in summer then in winter."

"Sounds like a reasonable plan," said Cam.

"I wondered if you'd like to go along with me," I said.

"That sounds like a lovely idea, RJ. There are lots of antique shops and galleries in Whistler that I'd like to see. Let me check my schedule for that time period and I'll get back to you. Can you get me the exact dates?"

"Yeah. They're in the email. I just don't recall them right now. I'll call you later."

"Okay. I have to go. Have a good evening."

"Thanks, Cam. You too."

My day had just improved considerably.

The call had slowed me down and it was now getting quite gloomy under the heavy tree cover. Up the western shore I walked a little further, then stopped. There was no point trying to go all the way to Loon Point. I'd go there tomorrow if I needed to.

I went through the bush a way, then followed a little-used path across the island then down the east coast, past the place where the woman's body had been found, to the boathouse. It was a long hike and it was getting darker. A police officer whom I had not yet met stood guard at the entry to the docks. I made no effort to go there and passed him with a wave, which he acknowledged with a nod but did not return. Behind him, out on the water, myriad circles formed and dispersed as fish rose to feed on insects flying near the surface. I continued on to the Inn.

It was now quite dark and further searching was a waste of time. I had covered a lot of ground quickly and probably not thoroughly enough, not wanting to be out on the trails in the full dark. Even with the welcome glow of a half moon floating overhead, it would soon be darker than the inside of a cow out here.

I guess I'd hoped to find Tomas wandering aimlessly or sitting on a fallen log, waiting to be found, but he wasn't. Wherever Tomas was, he was most likely not going to be found tonight.

When I got back inside I found a few staff members seated in the lounge. "What's going on here?" I asked no-one in particular.

Gwen spoke up for the group. "We've all had our interviews and we're just waiting for Bill to be done, then the police boat is going to take us to the mainland."

"Good. That sounds like progress. I'm sorry you all had to be held up tonight. I appreciate your cooperation."

At that moment Bill came down the stairs. "Sergeant Grant says we can go now. He's radioed the boat to take us to Westport."

The group rose, collected assorted purses, bags and backpacks and headed for the door. "Thanks again. Good night," I said. As they hurried out the door I added quietly, "If any of you see Tomas, please tell him to come and find me."

Time for me to knock off for the night too, I hoped. Waving a 'hello' to Sue as I passed the desk, I went up the guest stairs to the second floor and stuck my head in the partly open door of the interview room. Grant was still there, jotting comments in the margins of the notes he had made during the interviews. He sensed my presence and looked up.

"How much longer are you going to be at it tonight?" I asked.

"Not much longer now, I think. As soon as the boat comes back from dropping off your staff I'll head for home, get an early start tomorrow. I sent the other two home a while ago. We got initial chats done, I think; all of the staff who were going off shift tonight and a few of the guests. We'll get the rest of the night staff in the morning before they leave and we've convinced all the guests that it would be advisable for them to stay for the night. No unscheduled water journeys in the dark. I have a guy on the dock just to make sure. We'll finish with the guest interviews as quickly as possible in the morning."

"I saw your guy on the dock a few minutes ago. He's in for a long slow night. Well, I'm going to say good night. I plan to be up early to assist you any way I can tomorrow." I didn't bother to correct his misimpression about having talked to all the staff who were supposed to be going off shift tonight.

"Thanks, RJ. See you in the morning."

I went to the elevator and through rather than up, exiting the secret door at the back of the car into the second-floor hallway of my suite. I passed through the living room and put on an Oscar Peterson CD and went to the kitchen. I couldn't remember having had dinner but it was too late for a full meal now. I found a box of Raincoast crackers and a nice piece of Canadian brie from Quebec. Some miniature tomatoes and some mild kielbasa and a glass of Valpolicella rounded out my impromptu dinner.

I took my tray out through the sliding door to the balcony where I was greeted by a dark and starry sky and a breeze scented with water and pine. Loons called in the distance and I could hear faint sounds of conversation from late dinner guests lingering on the dining room deck below me.

I sipped my wine and ate slowly and thought about how quickly things can go from seemingly fairly normal to very messed up. This afternoon all I had to worry about was what to have for tomorrow's dinner specials and whether or not I could beat Mike at golf. Now I had a disappearing bartender, a gun-toting – well perhaps that was something of an exaggeration - office manager and another damned dead body. What next?

Chapter 6

Winnstar Technologies Messenger   account wtim0043

New Message   **Saturday   12/07**

From : Flower

To : Hotrod, Geek, Spider

Flower – I've been sounding out some of the staff and I'm hearing this RJ character – the owner – thinks he's some kind of detective. Caught a murderer a couple of months ago. Bears watching.

   Spider – If he gets to be a problem we'll deal with him.

Hotrod – Just be careful. We don't want to attract a lot of attention by leaving a string of bodies around the place.

Winnstar Technologies Messenger   account wtim0061

New Message   **Saturday   12/07**

From : Spider

To : Sailor Man

Spider – Things are progressing. The innkeeper may be a problem if Jason
talks to him. I'm trying to think of something to keep him busy and
out of our hair.

Sailor Man – Maybe I can help with a diversion.

The next day was Saturday and although I was off work at
the Inn that morning I was up early so I'd be ready to help
Grant if I could. I also needed to find Tomas before the police
realized he was AWOL.

I made coffee and threw together a couple of poached eggs on
toast. I sat at the counter of the kitchen island and filled in my day
planner. If I don't write things down I have no chance of
remembering to do the things I'm supposed to do. My staff
continue, from time to time, telling me I should get a BlackBerry
or something. Although I've been resisting, I seem to be
weakening. My record with computerized devices has been spotty
at best. Though I'd had to work with them as part of various jobs
over the years I've never been quite comfortable with them, in any
of their forms. I was not yet convinced that I wanted to trade in
the tried and true pen and paper for the new and unknown.
Maybe, though, it was time to rethink my position.

Coffee and eggs were ready so I sat and ate and wrote my
notes. Several mashed and mangled scraps of paper and napkins
had to have their messages deciphered before the correct
information could be entered into the planner. *'That wouldn't be
happening if you had a BlackBerry, RJ,'* I could hear Kim saying as I
shifted the papers around for a better angle of examination.
Maybe I'd better think about getting a better system.

Kim. I didn't write anything in my planner about Kim. The fact that she had a gun in an often-unlocked file cabinet bothered me more than anything else that was happening. Well, maybe not more than the most recent body on the island but a close second. It seemed so totally out of character, so wrong. The real problem was that I couldn't see any way to sort it out other than by flat out asking her about it. If she or one of the staff had found the thing lying around somewhere she'd have reported it. If she wanted anyone to know about it she'd have spoken of it, surely to me if no-one else. But she hadn't. I wasn't looking forward to that conversation. Possibly I was making more of this than was necessary. I should just ask her about it.

I finished breakfast and put my planner in my pocket, then cleaned up dishes and was heading for the door when the phone rang. Gwen, newly arrived at the desk and sounding a lot more chipper than I'd have expected after not having left here until after ten or so last night, informed me that Sergeant Grant and company were on the way from Smiths Falls and would arrive within the hour.

I'd have to get busy and find Tomas before they arrived.

I checked the thermometer outside the living room window. Already mid-twenties and not even eight o'clock. Another hot one on the way.

So, where would I go if I was trying not to be found by anyone on a small island with a hundred or so people wandering all over the place? Tomas, I knew, had spent some of his off hours exploring the island and would have a fair knowledge of the terrain and any good places to hide. I knew them too. The most probable place was a small cave off a side trail near Loon Point, a spot I'd not thought of last night.

Leaf-filtered sunshine cast dappled shadows on the trail as I worked my way along the edge of the island. The soft greens of spring in the forest had deepened into the vibrant and seemingly infinite range of rich high-summer greens.

About halfway up the western shore, on the way to Loon Point, a path, rough and weeded over, branched off and sloped sharply down to the left toward the water. I went down slowly. It was one of those trails where one wrong step can send you headfirst over the edge and into the lake. Also, slower meant quieter and I didn't want to spook Tomas if he was there.

The path, though narrow and rough, levelled a metre or so from the mouth of the cave. I stopped and listened, for what I don't know. Not likely he was going to be playing a radio or chatting on a cell phone.

I stepped closer, concentrating on the cave entrance, and as I did so I kicked a small rock which bounced over the edge and tumbled loudly down the cliff. It flew through the air for the last three metres or so then splashed noisily into the water.

As the splash died away I heard a rustling sound coming from the cave.

Another step brought me to the opening. "Tomas. Are you in there?"

Two black shapes exploded from the dark hole and launched themselves over the cliff. A couple of cormorants flapped madly to gain altitude then thought better of it and landed gracefully on the water below. It was a minute or so before my heart stopped racing and I was able to think clearly again. I peered into the cave, sure now that Tomas had not been here. There was no sign of anything other than birds having been in there for a long while.

I retraced my steps to the main trail and continued up towards Loon Point trying, as I went, to think where else I could look for Tomas. There were no other caves along the shore and the rest of the north end of the island was all rocks and trees. I could think of no other hiding places up this way. That left the south end of the island and that meant the boathouse, the remnants of the old stables, not that there would likely be any good hiding places there, or the Inn itself.

I decided that the boathouse would be my first stop on the way back so I could have a thorough look there before returning to the Inn. The overnight police guard was still there and was keeping awake by walking up and down the docks. His job was to prevent anyone who had not been interviewed from leaving the island by boat or floatplane and he really had no interest in the boathouse itself.

As I had the previous evening, I waved to him as I approached but turned off into the dim and draughty old building before getting to the dock. Swallows flitted overhead, chasing flies and mosquitoes outside then disappearing, under the roof overhang or into the building, to feed hungry young.

Although some of the antique boats were kept inside under cover through the summer, the space was now largely empty. A quick walk along the inside slips soon showed me that Tomas was not lying in any of the uncovered boats and as I took covers off the rest they proved to be empty as well.

Along the back wall there were three upturned boats, all raised on blocks. I went to them last. Again, no Tomas.

That seemed to leave only the Inn as a place for him to be hiding.

As I exited the boathouse my cell buzzed. It was Kim, letting me know that the police would be arriving momentarily. I thanked her for the heads-up and as I turned my gaze to the water I saw the police boat slide quietly up to the dock.

Grant was again in civvies – crisp beige slacks and a cream coloured shirt – no tie – and a navy sport jacket. Two other officers, similarly attired, whose ranks I could only guess at, disembarked and began offloading several bags and cases of gear. As the pile grew I grabbed a luggage trolley from its storage area and pushed it toward the boat. As I did so, the constable who'd been on guard duty overnight turned from his unloading and called out to me.

"Sorry sir. This area is off limits at the moment. No-one is allowed to leave the island without permission from Sergeant Grant."

I was about to respond when Grant spoke from behind the man. "That's okay, Mills. This is Mr. Harrison who owns the place. He's not trying to escape; at least I don't think he is. He's assisting us with the inquiries."

By the time Grant finished speaking I had arrived at the boat. I shook hands with the constable. "Will they be letting you go home soon? You've had a long night out here alone. Since what? Seven or eight?"

"That's about right, maybe a bit earlier," said Mills.

"Well, if you want coffee or breakfast before you head home please come into the Inn and get what you like."

"Thanks. I may just do that."

"Thanks for getting the cart, RJ," said Grant.

"No problem. Not likely anyone else is going to be needing any of them any time soon anyway."

We started to walk along the dock. "Now, RJ, don't be pessimistic. We could have this all wrapped up by lunch time."

"That would be great, Mike, but somehow I don't think it'll happen."

Grant shook his head slightly. "Neither do I, actually."

We walked on in silence to the Inn, the others trailing not far behind. When we reached the lobby, Grant's associates went straight up to the second floor room where the others had worked the previous evening. Grant and I went to the dining room and sat in a quiet corner. I asked for two coffees and for a carafe for the two upstairs to be ready when we left.

"So, what's your plan for today?"

"The overnight staff first and the rest of the guests, I would think. Definitely start with those leaving, or wanting to leave, today or in the next couple of days. If there are suspects among them I want to talk to them before they get away. Then move on to any staff who were here before noon yesterday, in case they saw anything before they went off shift," said Grant.

"I'll get Kim or whoever's on the desk to put together a list for you of whoever was on the early shift yesterday and I'll personally go around and let them know you'll want to chat. Smooth out any rough spots. It won't take me long. It's a really short list. There aren't as many guests left to be interviewed as you maybe think."

"A list will be good, RJ. Thanks." We were finished our coffee. "I'd better get on with it. As you say, there aren't that many more guests so we should finish up fairly quickly. If you'll round up that tray with the coffee, I'll take it up with me."

We went to the coffee station where we found the setup all ready to go except for putting the coffee in the carafe. I did that and Grant left the dining room with his tray. I went to have a quick word with the breakfast cook then went to the office to start someone working on the new list. By 9:30 Grant had his list. I'd found that some of the guests had got an early start and were already out touring the island. Mike and his crew would have to get to them later. And there were still some staff left to talk to.

Now I could start to look for Tomas again and hopefully find him before Grant or one of his people realized he was missing. We'd been lucky so far but... .

I went to start a systematic search of the inside of the Inn.

The reception area was first. There was Kim's office and the reception area plus a large cupboard. All were empty at this hour. I had sent Sue, the overnight person on the desk, to the dining room to have a coffee while I looked around. I waited a couple of minutes until she returned, then went to the lounge. No luck here either. All the fridges were too small for a man to hide in and there were no enclosed storage areas. The guest washrooms adjacent to the lounge were similarly deserted. I thought as I walked away from the lounge that it was pretty unlikely that anyone would be hiding out in a fridge, especially a tiny bar fridge. Not likely the big walk-in in the kitchen either but you never knew.

As I left the lounge I could hear the sound of a vacuum cleaner. The housekeeping crew was finishing up the lobby. I waved a hello to them and went into the dining room, to the corner where there was a large storage area and bussing station. The bi-fold doors were unusually closed. Taking one door handle in each hand I slowly opened the cupboard. A badly stacked pile of folded table cloths tumbled out at me. I jumped back. No missing bartenders leaped out from behind the cover of falling linens. As my heartbeat returned to normal I looked around to see that no-one had taken notice of my activities. No-one had. I picked up the fallen table cloths, discarding those that had actually touched the floor into the soiled linens bin. I went to the main entrance and from there up the stairs to the second floor.

I needed to get the second floor storage areas searched before Grant and his crew realized what I was up to. I didn't want to have to explain to any of them why I was rooting around in cleaning supply lockers and laundry rooms.

I'd just finished the last of the second floor storage areas when I heard one of the police officers heading toward one of the guest rooms. I ducked into the elevator and went down to the main floor. When I got there I found another of the police officers stationed at the main door. I said a quick hello to the officer and to Gwen at the reception desk then went into the office.

I would have to leave the checking of the third floor storage areas and the attic hatches for another time.

It had occurred to me that I should have Kim try to reorganize the kitchen schedule, if that was possible, and get me out of working there for a few days so I could concentrate on the other more pressing problems now occupying my mind. I wrote a note to that effect and left it in the centre of her desk, glancing as I did so at the top drawer of the file cabinet which contained the gun. No point in looking at it again. I would deal with that later. Much later, maybe. As I was turning to leave I saw one of our mail-out brochures face-down on the desk. It had a strange-looking square symbol on the back – a seemingly random pattern of thick and thin lines all joined together. I knew I'd seen things like that before but decided I'd better ask Kim what it was and why there was one on our flyer.

I then left the office area and went to the top floor and repeated my search pattern, and again the storage cupboards and laundry rooms yielded nothing.

The only place in the building left to search was the basement – unless I really believed that Tomas did have a helper.

Not much happened in the basement except laundry. Several heavy duty washers and dryers and lots of shelving take up almost half of the useable space. The rest is storage for spare bedroom and dining room furniture, along with a couple of large freezers and a stock of firewood which is brought in through a storm cellar-type entrance at the side of the Inn. I don't know why I didn't think to look there earlier. It's a perfect place to hide, having dark corners and lots of stuff to hide behind and with little traffic.

Before going downstairs I went outside to check the lock on the storm cellar doors. These two large, almost horizontal doors should not have been used since the renovation. Large appliances such as the auxiliary freezers and the washers and dryers had been put into the basement through these, which was much easier than it would have been by way of the interior stairway. Since this entry is seldom used it quickly accumulates a covering of dust and leaves and other debris from on and off the island. I've sometimes found KFC or McDonald's wrappers, styrofoam cups and occasionally newspaper pages, dropped here after a day or two of high and dry winds.

The double doors were locked and had their usual coat of refuse. They seemed not to have been opened recently so I went back inside and down to the basement.

One light was on in the stairwell and another in the laundry room – its door hung open. Water sloshed around in one of the washers and a dryer hummed. No-one was in the room. I backed out, shut off the light and closed the door. I could still hear the quiet hum of the dryer as I went to the next door.

It squeaked as I pushed it open and stuck on the slightly uneven old basement floor. I shoved hard and the door popped open, my momentum propelling me into the darkness of the firewood storage room. I was too far in to reach the light switch and I fumbled along the dark interior of the door frame to find it. The room lit up reasonably well after I found the switch and as my vision adjusted to the light I saw that the room was almost empty. Nearly all the firewood had been used up and there was very little left. I realized that I'd have to get someone working on refilling the room before fall. I also realized that there was nowhere in there for Tomas or anyone else to hide. Another dead end.

The door was now stuck open so I left it and went to the last door in the hallway.

In the dim light of the hall I could see that there was a light burning in the storage room. Another perfect place to hide. There were beds and chairs and easy access to the kitchen for midnight raiding – surely Tomas must be getting pretty hungry if he hadn't eaten since his hasty departure from the bar last night. I went on, passing the locked door of the elevator maintenance room.

This door opened more quietly than the previous one had and I walked in slowly, taking in as much of the room as possible as I went. An overhead bulb near the door was lit and there was another light somewhere in the recesses of the large room.

I moved quietly forward, taking care to look behind and under things I passed. A row of dining room tables stacked one on top of another was followed by stacks of matching chairs. Several mattresses and box springs in plastic wrap leaned against a wall and shelf units held dining room and kitchen equipment, as yet unused. I rounded a shelf unit holding a spare coffee maker and a stack of stainless steel bowls when a sound came from ahead of me. The faint light I'd noticed upon entering the room was brighter now. Another sound startled me – boxes being moved. Then there were footsteps.

I realized that I was being foolish creeping around in the half dark. I should call out to Tomas and put an end to this nonsense. The footsteps came closer and suddenly the light went out. I froze where I was and was promptly ploughed into by a person about my own size, carrying a heavy load. We both crashed to the floor amid a cascade of wooden salad bowls and stainless steel teapots and a couple of boxes of spoons which split open, sending their contents skittering across the stone floor. In the dim light I recognized my assailant.

"Frankie. What the hell are you doing down here?"

I helped Frankie pick up his load which, as it turned out, was for the dining room staff. Most of them didn't like to go down to the storage area alone so they had prevailed upon Frankie to make the trip for them. He was only too happy to escape from the kitchen for a little while and readily agreed. It wasn't the first time he'd helped them out but I guessed it was the one he'd remember best.

After I left Frankie at the kitchen I was going to carry on with my search but a series of small problems and interruptions got in the way and I soon found that most of the morning had evaporated and I still hadn't found Tomas. I was beginning to worry that maybe something had happened to him.

When I could get away again, I went out the door and turned right, moving along the full length deck toward the back of the Inn. As I rounded the corner onto the dining room deck one of the men from the airplane group came dashing up the wide, wood stairs, breathless and sweating and looking very upset. I recognized him as the one who had been making the payment for the group when they checked in.

"My girlfriend is missing," he said. "I've been looking everywhere for her this morning already. I can't find her anywhere."

"Okay. Slow down a minute and catch your breath. Tell me your name first, then when and where you last saw your girlfriend."

The man plopped down into one of the outdoor dining chairs, tipped his head back and closed his eyes. "My name is Jason Murdock. I'm the CEO of Winnstar Technologies. It was yesterday afternoon when I last saw her." He sat up straight again. "Not long after we checked in she said she wanted to go for a walk around the island. Said she might go for a swim too, maybe. I needed a drink so I went to the lounge. Spent a couple of hours there. Around dinner time I went back to the room to see her and she wasn't there. We'd arranged to have dinner with the rest of our group so I went back to the dining room, figuring she'd join us. She didn't so I thought maybe she was just tired from her walk or her swim and had fallen asleep.

"After dinner we went straight from the dining room to the lounge and spent the next hour or so there. One of the other women, Dianne, decided she needed some fresh air before going to bed so she left the other four of us there.

"It was probably near midnight when the rest of us went up. Val – Valerie is her name – she wasn't there. I was going to go to the other rooms to see if she was around when Harvey came to ask if Dianne was in *our* room. We decided that they must have hooked up and gone outside again for a while.

"Anyway, I went to bed and when I woke up this morning she still wasn't back so I started looking."

"Was the other woman – Dianne? – was she in her room this morning?"

"I ran into Harvey - that's Harvey Donaldson, our senior V.P. of Research and Development - and he says she's there. He left her sleeping when he went out for his run."

"So no-one has seen your girlfriend – Valerie ? – since late yesterday afternoon. And no-one was concerned enough to report her absence to the staff?"

"Well, we all thought we were just missing her, like I said. She's pretty independent, goes off on her own sometimes, and we kind of don't get too carried away checking up on her 'cause she gets kind of pissed when we do."

He stopped for breath and looked absently around the empty outdoor dining area. I watched him. He made a visible effort to collect himself but said nothing. His eyes were a little glazed as though he was not quite all there somehow. Or perhaps some self-medicating was going on. I decided to prod a little and see what reaction I'd get but he started again before I could.

"I heard that a woman's body was pulled from the water near the shore of the island yesterday afternoon?" he asked. "We heard about it but we never even thought it could be her. We didn't think she was missing at that time and, like I already told you, she gets cranky when we check up on her."

I was getting annoyed. "Tell me what she looks like. I helped you up with the luggage yesterday so I have a memory of the three women. Which one was she?"

For some reason he had to think about that. Again the idea that he was a bit vacant drifted through my mind.

"She's about five-eight or five-nine, maybe one-twenty-five or so. She'd tell you she was one-eighteen probably but I know better. She has short dark hair – you don't really think it could be her do you?"

I wasn't sure how to respond to that. I knew that it wasn't possible. I wondered how he could not know the same. It couldn't be the same woman unless she'd dropped out of the plane, and surely Mr. Murdock would remember that, and that she had checked in with the rest of the group. What was his problem?

"What was she wearing when you last saw her?" This required even more thought.

"I think she had on shorts and a top ... with no sleeves, or maybe short sleeves ... I don't know what colour ... light I think ... and runners and those really short socks women wear with runners. I think. Maybe the top was white? She wasn't wearing that on the trip but she changed after we got to our room. I don't know."

Close enough. Shorts, light coloured top and runners. I decided instantly that the next order of business was to tell Mike about this and let him deal with this guy. Maybe he'd just heard the description of the girl from the water and, in the confused state he seemed to be in, transposed the two.

Then I had another thought.

"Didn't the police ask you and the rest of your group about the body that had been found yesterday?"

"Yeah."

"And somehow while you were being asked about one woman you all got amnesia suddenly and could not remember that one of your party hadn't been seen for several hours. Why?"

The vacant look was back. He said nothing as he sat staring at the empty table. I guessed I'd get the same response as before, anyway: 'we didn't think she was missing'. One minute Murdock seemed to be perfectly rational and the next, confused and lost.

My cell phone rang and the caller ID showed that it was Mike Grant. He was calling to fill me in on the morning's activities so far. I stood back a bit and watched my guest as I told Grant about my conversation with Jason Murdock.

Grant said he'd take over as soon as he got to the island. On his way he would make some calls and start to organize a thorough search of the island. He asked me to keep an eye on the guy until then. Something was definitely weird, he said. His other two officers had interviewed all three men and all three women from that group. They'd been told by one of the women that she hadn't been feeling well and had skipped dinner and that she was going back to her room to bed. We both wondered how Murdock could think she had been missing since the afternoon when the police had talked to her in the evening and if she'd gone to their room right after? It made no sense.

Despite all the time I'd spent on the phone, Murdock was still staring at the table.

I took Murdock to his room and left him there. He said he hadn't slept well and was going to lie down for a while. I went to the main desk and asked Gwen to be sure to let me know if Murdock came down again before either I or Sergeant Grant was able to talk to him.

Chapter 7

I was back in the kitchen by mid-afternoon. Bud was off that day and I was working on dinner prep and then doing the dinner service. The prep was fairly straight forward that day but baked beans were on the menu for tomorrow night and they had to be put together and then had to cook for about six hours. I would put them into the walk-in tonight and they'd be nice and mellow by dinner time tomorrow.

As I set the nearly half-metre wide colander over a prep sink, to drain the water in which the beans had been soaking since early this morning, I ran through my list of strange happenings of yesterday and today. I went to the walk-in fridge to get onions and garlic. Somehow the thought of dealing with a murder and an on-the-lam bartender bothered me less than having to confront Kim about the gun in her filing cabinet.

Tomas would have to turn up soon. There were only so many places on this little island for a person to hide, and I'd already looked in quite a few of them.

I peeled a half dozen local Spanish onions and took the skins off about fifteen large cloves of nice fresh Ontario garlic.

The murder, assuming that the floating woman had been murdered, had to take top priority for the time being. Yesterday and this morning I'd helped Grant organize the interviews with all the current guests. The staff interviews had mostly been wrapped up yesterday evening and this morning. That was *two* headaches mostly out of the way, but time was running short for me to find Tomas.

I turned on one side of the big flat-topped griddle and while I waited for that to heat up I went in search of the rest of the ingredients for the baked beans.

Grant had gone back to the mainland for a while. Hopefully he would know the identity of the woman in the water by the time he got back. Knowing who she was would focus the investigation. People who had never seen her or knew nothing about her could be eliminated from serious suspicion more quickly. Those who knew her or knew of her, less so. If any did.

A little olive oil was hot on the flat-top and the onions started to sizzle quietly. I turned down the heat a little. The objective here was to cook the onions gently until they were translucent, not very browned. The tiny pieces of onion would all but disappear among the beans, leaving only their flavour and aroma deep in the heart of the finished dish.

I oiled a huge baking pan and preheated the oven to only 275°. A long slow cook would ensure tender beans and a big, rich flavour.

I had no information about the woman in the water so I decided to put it aside. Mike had left a message at the desk saying he'd found Murdock spiny but just believable enough he had authorized a search of the island. Additional help was on the way. Finding Tomas had to be my priority. It was, after all, a small island and finding a man, even one who did not wish to be found, just should not be that hard. I would be able to go search a bit more if I left the other cook to carry on with the prep after I got the beans into the oven. I dumped the softened beans into the oiled baking pan and added the cooked onions and garlic, then most of the rest of the ingredients – some Bourbon, soy sauce, chilli sauce, mustard, ground ginger, pepper, brown sugar and maple syrup and a little of the beef stock I'd made the day before.

A gentle but thorough mix and it was ready. I covered the pan with a sheet of plastic wrap and a tight foil cover and put it into the oven.

With that out of the way I had two hours to kill. I set a timer in the kitchen and another on my phone.

I was crossing the main lobby toward the front door when Grant came in, meeting the two plain clothes officers and a couple of my early dayshift staff as they came down the stairs from the interview room.

"Hi, RJ," said Grant. He sounded okay but looked tired. The staff people went on their way.

"Sergeant," I replied. "Have you had lunch yet? I could have a word with one of the servers and let them know you'll be in, if you're ready for lunch."

"Lunch sounds good, RJ. I'll let the guys take a few minutes to stretch their legs and grab some fresh air before we eat then I'll get on with the last of the interviews. We're nearly done. Still a couple of your staff to go, I think. I'll do them first, then the last of your guests. Hopefully they'll be back to the Inn soon. These two," he said, indicating his constables, "will join the search team. I managed to get some experienced help from regional emergency services and Kim gave me a couple of Gilmore staff who could be spared. The search of the island is going on now. No dog yet but we'll have to make do."

I thanked Grant for the quick response and told him that I had some jobs to do and that I'd catch up with them later, then went to the dining room to organize one of the wait staff to look after the police officers.

Unless Tomas had somehow managed to get off the island I was determined to find him and I didn't have a lot of time to do it. Now there was a possibility that the search team would find him instead. Getting off the island would not have been easy since all our boats were under the watchful eyes of the police. I wondered again how well Tomas could swim, or if he was desperate enough to try it.

I was fairly sure that he wasn't inside the building so I decided to check the boathouse and maybe the cave again. If he'd been inside the Inn surely someone would have seen him and let me know. I had a pretty good rapport with the staff and was sure they would realize that I would not do anything to bring trouble to Tomas. I just wanted to find him and move on – whatever that meant.

A police officer was still stationed at the docks but otherwise there was no-one about. I hadn't bothered with stealth the last time I was looking around out here so I decided on a change of approach this time. As I entered the boathouse I slipped off my shoes and proceeded as quietly as possible into the dim interior.

Water lapped against the piers and old wood creaked and groaned in the light breeze. These sounds blended with any I made walking along the ancient planks of the boathouse, making it unlikely that anyone who was there would hear me.

There was only one place he could be and I'd looked there yesterday but perhaps not as thoroughly as I might have. Three upturned rowboats still stood on raised frameworks of wood against the back wall. They were a half metre or so off the floor and I could see under all of them just as I had the day before. This time I would be more thorough in my inspection.

I moved slowly, crouching low beside each one in turn, looking up under the gunwale into the dark interior. As I looked into the second boat I heard a groan and a creak of wood emanating from under the next one. I froze and waited. What sounded like a quiet curse, in a language I was unable to identify, was followed by more groaning and creaking. Pay-dirt.

"Tomas," I said quietly but firmly. "You must be getting awfully cramped and hungry in there. Why don't you come out and we can talk about whatever is bothering you."

I waited a moment. "Tomas, I know you're there. I'm not going anywhere until you come out and talk to me." Again I waited.

"Come on, Tomas. I don't know what it was that spooked you but whatever it was can be rectified. Come out and talk to me and we'll sort it out."

There was another brief silence then the sound of boards moving. A foot lowered slowly to the deck, then another and a figure in green and black lowered itself to the wood and began to crawl out from under the boat. A moment later Tomas, looking rather the worse for wear, stood before me, stone faced and silent.

"Are you all right, Tomas – not injured in any way?"

"I am well enough," he replied. "Stiff and a little hungry but otherwise I am satisfactory. So, now you have found me what will you do to me?"

The choice of words jarred me. "I will not be doing *anything* to you, Tomas. I've been searching for you because I was concerned when you ran off without explaining. Let's talk while we walk back to the Inn."

"That was some jump you made over the bar last night," I said as we left the boathouse.

Tomas flinched as we encountered the bright afternoon sunlight, probably the first he'd been exposed to in the past twenty-four hours or so. He shaded his eyes and we continued walking.

"So tell me why you felt compelled to disappear. I don't believe you had anything to do with that woman's death but you sure had something bothering you."

Tomas looked up toward the sound of a boat passing the docks and saw the police officer on guard duty. I waved to the officer and he waved back but otherwise showed no interest in us. The breeze stiffened and made the flag on the dock flagpole flap noisily and sent an occasional leaf flying past.

"The police fellow there seems to not be interested in me," said Tomas.

"Why would he be?" I asked.

"No reason. I panicked when you came to me with the papers." Suddenly it was all tumbling out. "It wasn't so much the papers as what they represented. You were sending us all to the police. To be questioned. To be questioned by the police is not such a good thing where I come from. Many people go to be questioned but not so many return, and some who do return wish perhaps they had not. There is suspicion and distrust and once interrogated and released sometimes you are no longer trusted – thought to have informed perhaps. Better maybe to not return at all."

We walked in silence a bit. Tomas looked over his shoulder in the direction of the police officer guarding the dock. He was looking out to the water, paying no attention to us at all.

"I can't really imagine what it must have been like to live under those kinds of conditions, Tomas, but surely you know that those kinds of tactics are not used in Canada. Here the police have rules to follow regarding how they do their work and for the most part they do follow them. People who go for questioning generally come back as they went – unless they are really guilty of something. And your friends here are not going to treat you any differently tomorrow than they did yesterday just because you were questioned and released – they all were, too."

"Yes. I know all this, RJ. I do really. But sometimes it is not so easy to put away the fears of the past." Tomas exhaled deeply. "So now I have made a fool of myself and have made the police suspicious of me as well. They will be wondering why a man who has done nothing wrong runs away and hides."

"As to making a fool of yourself – I think probably not. I think you'll find that even though they don't know any more about your past than I do, they will assume, as I did, that you were reacting to what you thought to be a dangerous situation. That even has the benefit of being true. Also, you've earned a lot of respect from your co-workers here in these past few months and I don't think you'll find them treating you any differently."

"Thank you, RJ. But what about the police?"

"As far as I know, they're not yet aware of any problems with their interviewing of the staff, and if we move quickly we can keep it that way. If you'll trust me and do as I say for the next hour or so we may get through this just fine. I have a plan."

Ten minutes later we were in my suite. I expect that some of the staff may have seen us heading for the Inn but no-one approached and we didn't meet any police.

"All right, Tomas, you need a shower, some clean clothes and something to eat, then you can go back to work." I pointed in the direction of the guest bathroom. "Shower's in there. Throw your clothes out into the hallway then take your shower. There's no big rush now. I'll leave a robe on the bed. Come downstairs to my kitchen when you get out of the shower."

Tomas had something of a glazed look. "Okay, RJ. I will do as you say."

I looked at my watch. My time away from the kitchen was rapidly running out. I'd need to get back there soon. I loaded

Tomas's clothes into the washer then thought about what I would give him to eat.

Not much more than fifteen minutes later – I was just finishing making a rather large sandwich – Tomas walked hesitantly into the kitchen, scrubbed and wearing the robe I keep in the guest bedroom. He was looking at the food.

I heard the buzzer of my washer, signalling the end of the load.

"Feeling better?" I asked. He nodded. "Come and sit at the counter. I hope you're okay with this," I said, pointing at the sandwich. "I didn't have a lot of selection so it's just smoked ham and old cheddar with some mustard and lettuce and tomato. Nothing fancy but I guess it will serve. Sit." I'm sure he heard my voice but I knew his entire attention was now on the meal before him.

He sat. I pushed the plate across the counter to him. "What will you have to drink?"

For the first time since entering the kitchen he looked at me. "Just water now, thank you. And maybe coffee after, if I could. I haven't had a cup of coffee since yesterday afternoon and I would like very much to have one, please. And, RJ; thank you for this."

I set a glass of water on the counter beside the plate. "You're welcome, Tomas. Now eat. I'm going to put your clothes into the dryer." Before I left the kitchen I put on a pot of coffee.

A short time later Tomas was fed and dressed and ready again to face the world, though perhaps some parts of it less enthusiastically than others.

"All right, Tomas, now we see what you're made of." I led Tomas toward the back stairs where we could descend without being seen and get Tomas into the Inn where he was supposed to be. "I know that it's only a matter of time until Sergeant Grant figures out that neither he nor any of his people have talked to you or even seen you since yesterday. We need to head off any question of your not wanting to be interviewed. We're going right from here to the room where they're doing the interviews."

Tomas almost fell headfirst as he stopped suddenly on the stairs. I caught him by the arm and pulled him gently on down. "Don't worry about it. I'm going to tell Sergeant Grant that when I was handing out the numbered slips of paper I did not give one to you and so you were not interviewed. Grant will probably assume that you went home when the other staff went last evening, not realizing that anything was not right. Now you're back and I brought you along to be interviewed like everyone else who was here the day the body was found."

Tomas stopped again as we reached the bottom of the stairs. "You would do this for me - lie to the police."

"No, Tomas. I would not lie for you to the police or anyone else, especially if I thought for a minute that you were in any way involved in the death of that woman. What I'm going to tell Sergeant Grant is not a lie, though I am being deliberately vague with the details. You were not given a paper to tell you to come for an interview, you were gone since yesterday afternoon and now you are back for today's shift. All true, in the very broadest sense only, maybe, but still true."

"But surely he will see through this. Will he not have questions about where I've been and why I wasn't here earlier?"

"Tomas, he will have no reason to ask you about anything other than if you knew the woman or if you saw her at any time yesterday. Answer those questions truthfully. You'll be out of there before you know it."

I don't think he believed me. We went along the hallway behind the kitchen and outside to the deck and back in again to the kitchen. Glen and Frankie were working there and both looked up as we passed but neither spoke. We went out through the dining room and the lounge and around to the public stairs. Just as we mounted the first step the main door opened behind us and a voice called out.

"Well there you are, RJ," said Sergeant Grant. "I've been looking for you."

Tomas continued on up the steps and I stopped to talk to Grant. "I was just bringing Tomas up to see you. We missed getting him in for an interview earlier."

Grant listened politely as I gave him the prepared script. "Okay. Better late than never I guess. Thanks."

He left me standing in the lobby and jogged up the stairs after Tomas. "All right, Tomas. Let's get this over with."

With that they both disappeared around the corner and I heard the door of the interview room close.

I felt bad about trying to slip one past Grant. I hoped I'd never have to explain it, though, after the fact, it likely wouldn't seem such a big deal as it did now.

I stopped and leaned against the wall of the main lobby around the corner from the bottom of the stairs, trying to regroup and figure out what to do next. I turned to the stairs and was about to take the first step up when two voices drifted down to me from the hallway above, bouncing off the walls of the otherwise silent stairwell.

"Keep your voice down, will you? Do you want the cops in that room there to hear?"

"Those cops in there were asking a lot of questions about a dead dark-haired woman. I don't like it."

"They were asking about that other woman – one they found floating in the lake. Just keep yourself under control. We're in the clear."

They had stopped at the landing, midway down the stairs. The second voice went on again. "But somebody's going to notice she's not here."

"Well yeah. When we all go to dinner again tonight and there's still one empty chair, there will be a major blow up. That's the idea, right? Then the cops get involved and we sort of help point them in the right direction. His world will start to come unglued and we'll be there to pick up the pieces."

"Right. Right. I know. I'm just a little nervous, that's all."

"Keep it together," said the other.

I heard them start to move again, down from the landing now. I stepped back and to the left, trying to get into a position where I'd be able to see who these two were, hopefully without them seeing me. Almost there.

Just then several people came in through the main door and some of them hurried directly to the stairs and up, momentarily blocking the progress of the two men. I had to move aside to let the new arrivals pass.

One couple stopped mid-lobby, squared off and started pushing one another and shouting something about plumage and neck rings or something. The disagreement escalated very rapidly and suddenly the woman hauled off and took a swing at the man with her back pack. She connected solidly and the man came careening across the lobby at me. I caught him before he fell over a chair and sat him down.

"Are you all right?" I asked.

"Oh yes, thanks. I'm fine. She just gets quite passionate about things sometimes. You know birders." He stood and began to follow the woman up the now empty stairway.

The two men were gone.

Chapter 8

My shift in the kitchen was still on and it was almost time for the dinner service to start so I had little time to think about what I'd heard. I went around to the kitchen entrance and jogged up my back stairs – something I could not have done a few months ago - and did a quick change of clothes, then I went back down to the kitchen.

Glen and Frankie were there with a new dishwasher we'd just recently hired.

"You got Tomas all squared away?" asked Glen as I put on my apron. All three were watching me.

"I'm not sure I know what you mean. Tomas is up having his interview with the police now because he missed having it yesterday and will be back at work later. He seems a little tired for some reason so he may work a short shift then go home and rest. I'm fairly sure he'll be back to normal tomorrow."

A moment of silence followed.

"Well I'm sure glad the worst is over," said Glen. "As long as the interrog – no, the interview goes okay?"

"Yes. We'll have to see how that goes, but I don't think there'll be any problem." I wanted the subject to disappear. "So, is there anything I need to know for this evening's service?"

Glen thought a moment then said "As far as I know there are no problems. All the prep is done and there's lots of stock of all the mains and plenty of fresh sides. You'll have to get the re-stuffed baked potatoes made. They're all cooked and ready to go. Oh, and there's a pan of rolls in the walk-in all ready to go into the oven."

"Sounds good. Who's on with me tonight?" I asked.

"Gil George," said Glen. "He'll be here in a half hour or so."

"Thanks Glen. I'm going to work at the desk for a few minutes. Let me know when you two are leaving, please."

I went to the kitchen desk which is around the corner of the pantry, slightly hidden from the activity and noise of the kitchen itself. I turned on the computer there and spent a few minutes inputting some orders Bud had left, scanned some orders we were expecting to receive in the next few days and tentatively allocated them against planned menus.

Time passed quickly and I was startled back to reality by Glen's voice. "We're off, RJ. Gil's here and he's getting the potatoes started. He's never actually made the re-stuffed potatoes before so you'll have to show him, and probably soon, so they'll be ready for the dinner service. And you have Sam on cleanup tonight. He'd just started a few minutes before you came in."

"Okay, Glen. See you tomorrow."

"Aren't you off tomorrow?" asked Glen.

"Yes, I am, but I'll be around to help out Sergeant Grant, if he needs me."

"Right. See you."

I got moving right away. Glen had stirred the baked beans a couple of times since I'd put them in the oven but they needed to be finished off. I wondered how things were going upstairs in the interview room as I pulled the heavy pan from the oven.

"Gil, I see you've assembled the ingredients for the re-stuffed baked potatoes. We'll do them together this time and you'll be able to handle it yourself after that."

Steam billowed out of the bean pan and a rich aroma filled the kitchen as I peeled off the foil cover and the plastic wrap. I stirred the brew and then tasted it. No salt had been added earlier in the cooking process. Salting beans too early can make them tough. I added a little salt now and stirred, then put the cover back on loosely, this time without the plastic. In a few minutes I'd taste again and add more salt if necessary.

"You'll need one of those small oven gloves to do the next part of the job, so keep them handy," I said to Gil.

In a couple of minutes I tasted the beans again and decided they were good to serve. I always go lightly with the salt in what I cook. Guests can always add more if they want to at the table. I had Gil taste the beans as well for future reference and then dropped the pan onto the work table and covered it with a solid lid. They'd need to cool some before going into the walk-in.

"Okay Gil, let's work on the potatoes. First thing is to lower the temperature of one of the ovens to 150° and turn off the convection, please. We want to keep these warm but the steam table would make the potato skins soggy. Grab that big stainless bowl from the shelf over there and a soup spoon and a long, serrated knife."

While Gil was collecting the gear I heard the kitchen door from the dining room open. I turned to find Tomas standing there, looking tired but calm.

"I am on my way back to work in the bar, RJ. Sergeant Grant has said we are done. Thank you."

"You're welcome. Have a good rest when you get home tonight. See you tomorrow. I'm sure Sammi will be happy to hear that you're back."

Tomas went back out the dining room door and I turned back to the prep table to find Gil standing there with a smile on his face and a large knife in his hand.

"I'm glad that worked out well," he said. "Should we start on these potatoes?"

"Yes. You can start by cutting each potato in half, using a serrated knife because sometimes a smooth blade rips the skin instead of cutting as cleanly as we want. Best give that knife a rinse when you're done. The potato will harden like concrete very quickly."

Despite the approach of the dinner rush, which always gets my adrenalin pumping a little, I felt myself relaxing. I hadn't realized how tense I'd been about the Tomas thing.

Soon enough Gil had finished cutting the potatoes.

"Okay, here's the deal," I said.

I talked as Gil worked, scraping the contents of each potato half into a large bowl, adding the additional ingredients: butter, sour cream, chopped chives, roasted red pepper, shredded cheddar, roasted garlic, salt and pepper. He mixed carefully so as to maintain some of the texture of the potatoes then re-stuffed the halves with the new mixture.

Now that Tomas was back with us and since I had nothing to do with the floating woman I hoped that the Inn would get back to normal, whatever normal was around here.

Gil had already shown that he had a good feel for food handling and, although he had had little practice before we hired him, he learned fast. Before long he had all the potatoes re-stuffed.

"Now they go on a sheet pan in the oven at a very low temperature to stay warm. We'll put them under the salamander for warming as we serve them."

Gil found a pan and arranged the filled potatoes on it.

"Good. Now you can slide the pan into the warm oven and we'll get on to the next job."

"What's that going to be?"

"Eggplant Parmesan – the vegetarian selection for tonight."

"Okay. Let's do it."

We headed for the walk-in and came out loaded with fresh, local vegetables: four large purple skinned eggplants, four young firm zucchini, a couple of bags of baby spinach and a large red onion. Already on the work table were bunches of fresh herbs: basil, oregano and parsley from our herb garden.

"You sure do manage to get great looking fresh produce, RJ. What's the secret?"

"Almost all of our produce comes through a distributor in Kingston but a large portion of it is grown locally. I met with the distributor many times before this place opened and he understands what I will and will not accept. My basic parameters are these: local first always – vegetables, eggs, meats, fruit – Ontario next – Canadian third and international as needed – stuff like avocados and bananas and such. He wanted to always get me the best price and could do so by going farther afield but I told him I was willing to pay a little more in order to get as much as possible, as close to home as possible. I could get cheaper tomatoes, for instance, from Mexico, in July, than I can get locally. But I don't. Won't.

"If outfits like Gilmore House buy local it makes the local producers stronger. They can turn some of their profits into better production methods – raise more chickens or cows or corn in the same amount of space, or for less cost, or both. Eventually that means better prices for me and a stronger local economy."

Gil was staring at me.

"Probably a longer answer than you were expecting, I think."

"Yes, but not a concept many people think about, I'd bet. Food for thought, so to speak."

"Right. Okay, you can wash the vegetables and round up some knives and three small flat pans while I sort out the rest of what we'll need." I got olive oil, flour, eggs, some dried herbs, bread crumbs, marinara sauce and a white cheese blend.

We sliced the eggplant, zucchini and onion and chopped the spinach a bit to make it lie flatter. The three flat pans got flour, egg wash and seasoned crumbs respectively and the cooking began.

The eggplant slices were run through the three pans then placed in the oil on the hot flat-top and browned on both sides.

While Gil cooked I went over what I knew about the woman who'd been found in the water. I was sure now that she was not a guest – surely her absence would have been noticed by now – and I also believed she was not a day-tripper. No-one had reported a missing person and there were no boats at the dock that were unaccounted-for.

The eggplant was done. Time to assemble the dish. Into a large roasting pan went layers of sauce, spinach, zucchini, eggplant, onion, fresh herbs and cheese. Then the same again. After the second layer, the last of the sauce and fresh herbs went on and a good amount of fresh grated Parmesan to finish. After that it was into the oven to bake.

As Gil and I cleaned up our prep gear and finished getting ready for the evening service I added a final thought about local food.

"And my distributor? He set up a tiny satellite operation in Crosby. Local farmers take their products to him and he distributes from there, and not just to us here. He's doing a bigger and better business too."

The dinner rush came and went with no problems and we got the kitchen cleaned up in record time. Good thing. With all my running around looking for Tomas and my encounter with Jason Murdock on top of a more than full shift in the kitchen, I was wiped.

We three from the kitchen parted company at the front desk, Gil and Sam left to go to the dock and I went upstairs to my suite. As I passed I checked out the room where the interviews were being conducted. It was dark and empty.

Chapter 9

The morning sun was clear and strong – it would be another extremely hot day. I had a quick breakfast and went downstairs. Sue should have already finished up her overnight shift on the desk but was still there, looking tired. She waved me over as I walked toward the main door.

"Still here, Sue?"

"Yes. Carole had a flat tire on the way. She'll be here soon. I have a message here for you from Sergeant Grant and Kim. They just left to go to the morgue at the Perth hospital. The police want Kim to look at the body from the lake the other day and see if it could be Kim's sister."

I was speechless. Obviously Grant and Kim had spoken and she had mentioned her lack of contact with her sister. I knew that Grant would have handled that nasty conversation as delicately as anyone could but I couldn't help thinking about how Kim must be feeling – wondering if it was indeed her sister lying there.

"RJ. Are you all right?"

"Yes. I'm fine. Just worried about Kim. How are things on the desk this morning?"

My clumsy effort to change the subject went unnoticed.

"Everything's okay, I guess. Quiet right now. That couple in 301 – you know – Mr. and Mrs. Mason – the ones who almost escaped then were brought back by the cops – they left just a little while ago. They were some ticked that it took the police until late yesterday to get to them for their interview. They say they're never coming back here. Never. Definitely. Can't say I'm too upset by that to tell you the truth."

"Just between us – I'm not either. I was just wondering if maybe Constable Brooks left them so long on purpose – because they were such a pain."

"He wouldn't do that, would he? No. Surely not. That would be very unprofessional. More likely it was their apparent desperation to get away that got Constable Brooks suspicious and doing extra thorough background checks on them. Those things take time, I hear."

I smiled at that. "Right. I'm going to make the rounds now. My cell is on. Please call me as soon as Kim and Sergeant Grant get back. And, Sue, what's the word on the last of the interviews? Did Sergeant Grant say?"

"Yes, the last guest interviews were done last night after one of the couples came back from an all day exploring trip of the island. He lifted the general travel ban in the evening but no-one was scheduled to go, except the Masons and their last interview didn't wrap up until after dark. All clear today."

"I think," I said, "that one of the things that was annoying the Masons was that other guests were being allowed to leave, if they needed or wanted to, after they had been cleared by the police."

I started to leave then thought of something else and went back.

"Sue, total change of subject here. I don't know how much time you'll be able to devote to this but I need some research done, please. There's no big rush. I'd like you, or Gwen or Carole, whoever is on the desk, to collect some information about smart phones, please. Perhaps put together a list of brands, features, that sort of thing. Also I need some consumer comments about ease of use, reliability. You get the idea?"

A look of disbelief appeared on her face.

"You're not really going to do this, are you? I can't believe it."

"Yes. I'm actually thinking about moving into the twentieth century, communications-wise."

"You do realize that this is the twenty-first century, RJ."

"One step at a time, Sue."

I went outside by the main doors and was greeted by a wave of heat. This day was, if possible, going to be even hotter than yesterday. I needed to walk and think and so, staying in the shade, I walked along the pathway toward the boathouse. It seemed to be business as usual there. Boats were coming and going and there were people all over the place.

Out on the lake I saw one of our oldest boats, a circa 1905, Fay and Bowen torpedo stern launch with a convertible top. This craft was used for slow, sedate cruises around Upper Rideau Lake. With a top speed of less than fifteen kph, slow and sedate was the only option and the four people on board looked as though they were enjoying it thoroughly.

The officer who had been on guard duty was gone since the restriction on departures had been lifted. The police had collected all the information they could from everyone who was here at the time the body was discovered.

Other than the Masons, who had been in such a rush to get away earlier, no-one had decided to check out because of the body. Today two couples were leaving as scheduled and another two would arrive. The rest of the traffic was guests and tourists making use of our daily series of tours of the waters of Upper Rideau Lake and some of the closer locks. I saw the couple I'd given the information to in the dining room heading out in one of our tour boats.

My cell rang. Grant. He filled me in on the trip to the morgue. It was not Kim's sister we'd pulled from the lake. They had left Perth and would be back soon. Kim was shaken by the event but okay.

The Rideau Canal was opened in 1832 and is a partially natural and partly man-made waterway over two hundred kilometres long. Along its length between Ottawa and Kingston it has almost fifty locks and over fifty dams and is the longest continuously operating canal system in North America. Unfortunately, being over one hundred eighty years old it has maintenance issues, parts are wearing out, and in recent years the federal government, which is responsible for its upkeep, has not seemed to want to spend the money to ensure its continued operation. It would be sad to see a World Heritage Site deteriorate. I hear now that there have been some new investments and things are looking up. Both Federal and Provincial governments are planning to put money into making repairs and improvements. Also, the lockage fees will be waived in 2017 in celebration of Canada's 150th birthday.

I've also heard some boaters complain that raising the rates and shortening the daily hours of operation was not the way to improve usage and thus, revenue.

Lots of tourists from around the world come to enjoy the Rideau every year and some of them stay at the Gilmore. I spent an hour or so in the area of the docks and the boathouse talking to guests about the Gilmore and the Rideau.

As I stood in the relative cool of the ancient boathouse, looking out over the lake, I saw two boats converging on the island at quite a good speed. As they drew nearer I was able to determine that one was the OPP boat bringing back Kim and Sergeant Grant. The other was quite a large yacht, at a guess perhaps some fifty feet or so - or about 15 metres for my younger staff. It was an old wood boat with two decks and a fly-bridge, bright white with lots of gleaming chrome fittings and a whole raft of small pennant-flags flying.

The police boat arrived first and by the time it reached the dock I was there to meet it. Kim and Grant were both standing on the open deck at the stern. I took the stern line from the Marine Constable and tied it off, then turned to help Kim as she stepped a little unsteadily to the dock.

"Thanks, RJ."

I gave her a quick hug. "Sorry you had to go through that but at least you know now that the person wasn't your sister."

"Yes. But I still don't know where she is. I've traded one worry for another. I'm going to finish up some things then I think maybe I need to take a little time off to work on this." She glanced quickly over her shoulder toward the boat. "Sergeant Grant is going to start looking, too."

I looked over at Grant and he just nodded once then went to talk to the driver of the police boat.

"You organize it any way you need to, Kim," I said. "Take whatever time you need and be sure to let me know if there is anything I can do to help."

Kim thanked me then walked away toward the Inn. I was about to go talk to Grant when the second boat arrived.

The yacht was old, built probably in the 1940s or 1950s, but looking as though it had just come out of the factory. It was bigger than I'd originally estimated.

As it approached the dock a couple of our staff went out to guide it to the longest available space which, as it turned out, was only just big enough.

The yacht was being driven from the fly-bridge and as it turned to enter the space between two docks I saw two people dressed alike, in what appeared to be uniforms – blue shorts – white tee's – white shoes - one on the fly-bridge and one on the bow.

The helmsman on the fly-bridge guided the large craft expertly to its parking place, touching the fenders gently against the wood. The crew-person at the bow was a young man. He tossed a line to one of the Gilmore staff then ran along the side deck to the stern and repeated the process, watching as the line was secured to the nearest bollard. There was a small wave to the person at the bridge and the engines fell silent. It was only then that I noticed that there was another person on board.

Standing in the centre of the stern deck in the shadow of the overhanging upper deck was an elderly man. He was perhaps eighty or so, deeply tanned and with thick white hair and a thin white moustache – sort of a Douglas Fairbanks Jr. look. Most of my staff wouldn't know who that was.

He was something under two metres tall, and lean. He wore a well-cut, light weight tan suit and a cream coloured shirt, open at the neck. He stood with his arms across his chest and with his feet spread for balance but wasn't holding onto anything throughout the landing.

I had approached slowly as the boat docked and was now fairly near. As I walked to the boat I'd glanced at the transom. *Serenity* was lettered there.

The crew person on the lower level of the boat moved to open the boarding gate in the gunwale. All eyes were on the old man as he stepped out onto the dock. His crew person stepped out behind him. Without turning around, the old man, in a firm and quiet voice said, "All right, Andrea. Let's go find whoever runs this place."

"It's Brent, sir. You remember Andrea's no longer with us."

The old man gave no indication that he had heard the statement but I saw something move in his eyes.

As they started to walk toward me along the dock I stepped in front of them.

"I can save you a walk. I'm the owner of Gilmore Island. My name is RJ Harrison."

"Harrison, is it?" said the man. He turned to the young man who had followed him off the boat. "Write that down, Brent. Harrison. ... RJ. ... *Owner.*" This last was said with a little more emphasis than the rest.

He stood for a moment, hands in pockets, gazing around the dock area, not looking at anything in particular, then he walked away. Brent followed.

I glanced over at Mike Grant who had been standing a few metres away. He walked toward me and gave a little shrug of his shoulders and raised his eyebrows. "Any idea who he is?" he said.

I was about to reply that I had no idea at all when a female voice from the upper deck of the boat answered the question.

"His name is Edward Xavier Smythe," said the second crew person. "He was once the owner of this island and has decided he wants to be again. You'd better go. He'll want you and he won't like to be kept waiting when he does."

Grant was quiet.

"Great. Just what I need. Well, I don't have time to follow around after him. I have guests to look after. I'm headed back to the Inn. Hopefully he won't cause too much trouble."

Grant looked at me. "I wouldn't take any bets on that if I were you, RJ. I'm headed back to the shop for the rest of the day. Let's be sure we each call the other if anything comes up relative to the case. And good luck with your new friend."

"Yeah. Thanks."

We turned in opposite directions, Grant toward the police boat and I toward the Inn.

Smythe. He had been the last actual *person* to own Gilmore Island which had since been in the hands of various development companies. Smythe had had a lot of major work done before he quit. And he'd left behind some nice old boats.

I went to the kitchen to work and found that Smythe had just left there, having wandered through without asking anyone. He and Brent had also walked through the dining room and the lounge, Smythe talking to guests and staff and Brent making notes.

Throughout the afternoon as I moved around the island various staff members came around with bits of information about Smythe's tour of the Inn. Apparently he'd been through all the public areas inside and out and had spent a lot of time asking guests what they thought of the place and asking staff about what they thought of me – how I was to work for – that sort of thing.

He made no effort at all to conceal the fact that he planned to buy the place back and left a lot of uneasiness among the staff in his wake.

Late in the afternoon he retired to his boat and stayed there, but he sent Brent back to invite some of my guests to come and have dinner with him on the yacht. Some accepted and the dining room was a little lighter than expected that evening.

By the time I got up to my suite that evening I was too wound-up to sleep. I spent a good deal of time replaying the day and wondering how I would deal with Mr. Edward Xavier Smythe.

I took a glass of wine out to the balcony to try to relax.

Suddenly the phone was ringing. Now what? I dashed into the living room and caught it just before it would have gone to voicemail. A low, soft voice purred at me through the handset.

"Hello, RJ. How are you this evening?"

"All the better for hearing your voice, Cam. I was just thinking about you. How are you?"

"I'm fine. I hear you're having a bumpy ride just at the moment though – another body, though not in the attic this time – owners-past coming back to haunt you."

I was thinking that she had remarkably good informants if she knew about Smythe already.

"Yes. Well, I will admit to having had better weeks. I'm looking forward to seeing you on Monday. Oh, wait a minute. That's tomorrow, right? I'm sure seeing you will help me get things back in perspective."

"Unfortunately I have more bad news to add to your already less-than-stellar week. I have to go to New York for a couple of days. I just found out today that a small gallery there is going out of business and they're selling off a lot of paintings and sculptures. I was there a couple of years ago. There's a lot of good stuff that I think I can sell here if I can get it. I leave here early tomorrow morning and will be back Wednesday evening. Sorry, RJ."

"Well, much as I'll miss seeing you, it sounds like a great opportunity. I hope you find lots of good pieces."

"Thanks, RJ. I'll call you as soon as I get back and we can reschedule. There's something else I need to talk to you about. Do you recall our conversation last week about your upcoming birthday?"

"Yes. I remember. I seem to recall saying that I didn't want to make a big deal about it."

"Yes, you did say that, RJ, but I've decided to ignore that request. I have a great idea and I know you're going to love it."

"Okay."

"I wasn't going to tell you like this – over the phone. I was going to wait until we were together next but since I have to go away the timing will be too short when I get back."

"Okay."

"There's a promotional event at the Hillsborough Winery, in the County, starting on Friday this week. You know what the County is, don't you?"

"Yes. Short for Prince Edward County. I've been a couple of times, just driving through. I recall a time, shortly after I came here, when I called it the Island, instead of the County. I've been educated."

"I ran into a rep from the winery not long ago and I mentioned what you had said about maybe getting all your wines for the Inn from one winery – you promoting them and them promoting you. Remember?"

"Yes. I remember." There was a brief silence.

"I thought maybe we could go. Together. Take off next Friday afternoon, all day Saturday and Sunday morning, even all day Sunday if we can swing it. It would be a good time to talk to the right people about supplying the Inn. The rep said he would set up a meeting with the owner for while we're there. If you'd like to go?"

I didn't hesitate. "Yes, I would. That sounds like a lovely way to spend some time with you. I'll get busy arranging coverage here. There's lots of time for me to find replacements."

"Great, RJ. I'll see you in a few days. Bye."

"Bye."

I hung up the phone and stood there staring at it for a minute. We seemed to be missing as many dates as we were keeping but the rest sounded interesting.

I'd need to get to Kim in the morning and tell her not to bother changing the kitchen schedule for right now. I'd need to have it changed to cover my time away.

I got a small snack and another glass of wine and headed back out to the balcony, putting on a Peter Appleyard album as I passed the music system. The sound of the vibraphone reminded me that I needed to search around for some more Appleyard, and Lionel Hampton as well. Always liked xylophone and vibes.

Outside, I listened alternately to the music from one side and the night sounds from the other and felt a little more relaxed by the time I went to bed an hour later.

Chapter 10

Winnstar Technologies Messenger   account wtim0043

<u>New Message</u>   Monday   14/07

From : Hotrod

To : Spider, Geek, Flower

Hotrod – Been giving Jason his new medicine since Friday as we planned. A little something in his drinks at night and in his coffee in the mornings. I'm building up slowly. He already seems out-of-it to everyone he meets.

Winnstar Technologies Messenger   account wtim0043

<u>New Message</u>   Monday   14/07

From : Hotrod

To : Spider

Hotrod - Keep an eye on Geek. He's a little skittish suddenly.

Spider – Right. Too soft for this.

Most of the next day went by in a blur. Except for the continued police presence, things on Gilmore Island were back to normal. Given recent history perhaps the police presence was normal, too.

After the breakfast service was done I decided that I needed to get away for a couple of hours – off the island. The fridge in my suite was almost empty. Time to stock up. I changed clothes and had one of the boathouse attendants run me over to Westport. This would be a good day to go get some fresh vegetables and eggs from local producers and maybe later hit a bucket of balls at the driving range. My last attempt at that had been cut short. I couldn't afford to be away too long but two or three hours wouldn't hurt.

As always I stopped at Mrs. Samuelson's house before I got my car out. I knocked on the door and walked around the house but she seemed not to be there. I got the car out, slipped in a CD of Gypsy Jazz by Django Reinhart, and went directly out of town, along Concession Street and out Hwy. 42. I'd stop at Kudrinko's on the way back.

There was a farm stand out Hwy. 42 which had all the fresh vegetables I needed and after visiting with the owner I carried on, going to an egg producer a little way down Hwy. 15 toward Kingston. Another visit there left me with no time for the driving range but the time away had been enjoyable nonetheless.

I stopped at Kudrinko's, a favourite with residents and visitors alike, for the last of my groceries and then at the LCBO.

After that I went to the Osgoode Bakery. I hadn't seen Sandi or Liz for a couple of weeks. As it turned out neither of them was there but the person in charge was a younger, though practically identical, version of them.

"Okay. I know you're not Sandi or Liz but you look like them. I assume you're related."

"Yup. I'm Sandi's daughter, Megan. You're Mr. Harrison, right?"

"RJ, please. Yes. You sure do look like your mother."

"So do my two sisters. There are three of us. Great, eh?"

Great. I left with a bag of butter horns and with my head spinning. Another set of triplets to deal with at the Osgoode Bakery.

Since I was close by I couldn't go home without spending a short while having a coffee and talking to Bernie at Cottage Coffee. It felt like a safe place to be – less like the twilight zone the bakery was feeling like. Besides the good coffee and good company there was the knowledge that there was only one Bernie.

After that I went back to Gilmore Island. My couple of hours had turned into three and a bit.

Smythe's yacht was still at the Gilmore dock and I assumed Smythe was aboard with his crew and not prowling around the island, so far.

I saw nothing of Smythe that morning but it seemed everywhere I went he was the main topic of conversation. I spent a good deal of time assuring my staff that I had no intention of selling the Inn.

———————

After I got rid of my purchases I went back down to the main level. As I passed through the lounge I saw a guest who was obviously quite loaded, hassling the young couple I'd seen in the dining room the other night. He was making some crack about their choice of clothing as I approached but I didn't become involved. Tomas was already on him and was removing him, with loud and derisive commentary, from the lounge. I nodded to the couple as I passed but they said nothing.

Tomas and I met one another near the main desk. He commented as he passed.

"He is a boater. Comes in wanting to drink but is always having had too much already. Is the second time I have removed him. Each time I call the dock to have them watch out and call the police if he takes out his boat when he should not. I don't know if they had to call the police or not."

"Okay. I'll check on that. Please let me know if he gives you too much trouble in here, Tomas. We'll involve the police if we need to."

He nodded and went on his way.

———————

Kim had not replaced me in the kitchen so I had been kept busy for most of the early afternoon, helping to prep for lunch and dinner. It was not until well after the lunch rush had ended that I was able to leave the kitchen and seek out Mike Grant.

I found him in the spare guest suite we'd set aside as an interview room. He was pouring over a page in one of his notebooks when I entered the room.

"Finally escaped the kitchen work for a while, did you?" he asked.

I pulled up a chair to the folding table he was using as a desk and sat down.

"Done for the day, I think. Unless something unusual happens."

Grant stacked his notebooks to one side and leaned his elbows on the table.

"Well, since unusual things *hardly ever* happen around here I'm sure you should be fine."

I didn't take the bait so he continued.

"We've been doing some digging into the six people from the aircraft. They're all senior execs with the same company: Winnstar Technologies Inc., from Winnipeg. They are an interesting bunch. All six work together in the same office complex. There are three couples in the mix. From what I can gather from their office staff, whom I spoke to by phone this morning, staff who are not averse to a little gossip about the bosses when they're away, the couples as they are now are not the same couples that they were previously, though they still involve only the same six people. It's all very confusing at the moment but I'll sort it out."

"Sounds almost incestuous," I said. "Has there been anything new on the missing one?"

"No. Not yet. It's really too bad we didn't know for sure that she was really missing before we let everyone go and took the officer off the dock. We would have had a whole new set of questions for some of the people leaving.

"I sent our vague friend on a trip to Perth to the morgue today to see if he can identify the body. Boyd took him. You know, I really don't know what to make of that guy – not Boyd, the other one."

"How so?"

"He suggested to you, and later to me, that our floater might be his girlfriend, the CFO of their company. But, timing-wise it's not possible. Later I got the impression, just before they left, that he knew that it wasn't going to be his missing girlfriend he was going to find there. For someone who's supposed to be a hot-shot CEO, he seems to be really out of it. Something's weird but I can't figure it out yet."

"You will. It's early days yet."

———

I'm not sure I accomplished much through the rest of the afternoon and the evening but I talked to a lot of staff and guests about Smythe and tried to reassure them all that I was here for the long haul. I hoped it was true. I also asked if anyone had seen the missing CFO. One of the dock staff thought he might have seen Valerie Owens as part of a group lined up waiting for a shuttle after the police had lifted the ban on leaving the island on Sunday. He wasn't sure.

Mike had had his guys talking to the rest of the group from Winnstar to see if any of them had seen Valerie Owens since their police interviews Friday evening. Turns out that Suzanne Ellis had been out walking with Valerie late in the morning on Saturday, long after Jason had given the alarm about her disappearance. Made Jason look even dopier.

On my way upstairs I stopped at the desk to ask Sue to please see if she could find a way to get a message to Mr. Smythe. I decided I wanted to meet with him and have him tell me in person what it was that he was up to. No-one was there at that moment so I stood at the counter and wrote a note. As I was dropping the note on the desk I noticed an oversized envelope marked simply "RJ - cell phones". I left the note and took the envelope.

I was in my suite having had a late dinner and it was almost ten when my cell vibrated. I turned down Oscar Peterson and answered the call.

"Hello, RJ? It's Sue."

"What's up?"

"I just got a call from someone on the big boat, not the man himself but one of his crew. It's not good, RJ. He said that Smythe had had dinner in our dining room earlier in the evening and was now complaining about being poisoned, something about bad fish or something. Anyway the caller says Smythe's threatening to call the health department, the newspaper and anyone else he can think of. Making lots of noise." She paused briefly. "Some of the staff are pretty upset about the whole thing."

She stopped for breath and I headed her off.

"I guess I'd better get back down there."

"Okay, RJ. See you in the morning."

Bloody marvellous.

I was out of the suite almost before I realized it. I forced myself to walk slowly down the stairs, calming myself. I decided I'd talk to my staff about what happened before I tackled Smythe.

By the time I reached the main level I was more or less back to normal, not relaxed exactly but determined to find out what had transpired and to deal with it.

There were a few people in the lounge as I passed through but the dining room was empty. I went into the kitchen and found a lot of my staff there. They were discussing the evening's excitement but silence descended in the room as I entered.

"So, who wants to start?"

Bud, who had been the main cook for the evening, took the lead as I expected he would.

"He had the Salmon en Croute. So did a lot of other people, with no ill effects. I did the whole thing myself; skinned the salmon, wrapped the whole thing in the pastry. The salmon was fine, as was the roasted asparagus, and the Hollandaise that was served with it. I did two salmon and almost all of it went. I had about a quarter of one left and we all had a taste after the incident and I saved the last bit for evidence, in case the Health Department gets involved. Same fish his portion came from. It's in the walk-in, RJ. I'll swear there was nothing wrong with the fish or any other part of the meal."

"I believe you, Bud. Seems like the rest of the crew does, too," I said as I waved a hand around at the group standing there, "or they wouldn't have let you feed it to them."

"Well, I think it was all a sham," said Michelle. "I served that table and let me tell you that guy's a real treat. He didn't have one good thing to say through the whole meal, about anything, and nothing was wrong, not with the food or the service. I think he started out being an A-hole to see if he could get me flustered and make me mess up so he'd have something real to complain about."

"His first mistake, I think," I said. "Don't believe I've ever seen you get flustered."

"Right. After that he settled for nit-picking about everything."

"Did he eat the meal?" I asked.

"Oh yeah. Three quarters of it at least. A funny thing about the meal? I heard him talk at least one of the other people at his table out of having the salmon. It was like he wanted to be the only one having it."

I digested that.

"Who were his dinner companions?"

"They were three of the people from the plane," said Michelle. "One couple and the guy with the missing wife or girlfriend or whatever she is. He doesn't appear too concerned about the fact she's been gone all this time, by the way."

"He's an odd one, all right," I said. "Were the other two from the plane there as well?"

"They were at a table for two, right beside Smythe's table."

"That's interesting. I wonder what got them together."

"Loads of money," said Michelle. "Having it, flaunting it and wanting more of it. I've seen it before. So have you, no doubt. Often they don't even seem to like each other but they gravitate to one another, each trying to one-up the next guy. They were the ones he had to dinner on the yacht."

"That's an interesting observation, Michelle. Was Smythe showing any symptoms when he left the table?"

"No. He seemed fine – his usual loud and annoying self. All six of them left together, though the one, the CEO, Murdock, seemed only half there. I think Gwen got the call about half an hour later – sat. phone from the boat.

"Another thing, RJ," added Michelle. "One, or maybe more, of the Winnipeg group seemed very friendly with Smythe, as though they already knew him, maybe."

I was quiet for a moment, thinking about how to proceed, then I decided it was best not to, at least not tonight.

"Okay, folks. That's enough for tonight. You all need to get home. We'll attack this again tomorrow. In the meantime please don't make any comments about the incident to anyone. Refer all inquiries to me. I'll deal with them. Now go home."

Bud hung back as the rest wandered off toward the door.

"I'm really sorry about this, RJ. I don't know what to say."

"Bud, I don't think you need to say anything. As far as we know, you didn't do anything wrong. Something is screwy about the whole thing. We'll get to the bottom of it soon enough. Don't worry about it. Go home and get some rest."

"Okay, RJ. See you tomorrow afternoon."

"Good night, Bud."

As Bud went on his way I stood wondering what was going on. I was sure Smythe was up to something. The challenge would be to determine what it was, exactly, and to figure out how to minimise the damage he could do.

My speculation was cut short as my cell again vibrated in my pocket. It was Sue. Again.

"RJ, I have a reporter from the *Review-Mirror* on the phone, wanting a statement about the food poisoning. What should I say?"

I thought a moment.

"You can say that the owner has no comment at this time but will release a statement as soon as the facts become clearer.

They won't be happy with that but it'll have to do for now. We'll need to look at the paper on Thursday and see if there's anything there about this. "

"Okay, RJ, I'll tell him what you said. You heading up for the night?"

"In a minute. Please give me the number that the call came from on the boat. I want to call Smythe."

Sue gave me the number and I keyed it in. A message said that Mr. Smythe was not taking any calls at this time. I saw no point in leaving a message.

I'd been walking toward the desk as I talked to Sue.

"Okay. I'm going now. Again. Good night."

"Good night, RJ."

I put the phone back in my pocket as I walked to the elevator.

When I got to my suite I tossed my phone on the kitchen counter, poured a glass of wine and took it to the balcony.

I sat in the near silent darkness, watching the stars, wondering what Cameron Alexander was doing right now, since she wasn't having a quiet drink with me. I hoped she was doing well in New York.

I was beginning to feel as though there were too many pieces to this puzzle I was involved with and too many people with things to hide. I needed help with information gathering and the sooner the better. I figured that if I knew more about the players I'd have a better chance of discerning their motives and possibly their future moves but this was info I wouldn't be able to get by myself and that would possibly take the police a long time to dig up. Time to call in the big gun.

Edwardo Castillo was a ghost from a past life. Long past.

He was a little younger than I and now lived in Waterloo, it being a major Canadian hotspot for all things cyber. He built and maintained his own computers, of which he had several, through which he could reach into almost any part of the world in a matter of seconds. It was rumoured that he sometimes bent the rules regarding privacy but as far as I knew he only did so in what he saw as a good cause, which was, by his definition, keeping governments and corporations honest.

We'd last actually worked together going on twenty-five years ago, but I'd kept tabs on him from time to time since then, making sure I could reach out if I needed to – not that I expected to. I watched his growth from a cold war listener and paper gatherer to an internet information harvester. One of the best.

He was also reclusive, seldom venturing away from his home. He didn't drive, shopped by internet and met with his various clients by way of a *Max Headroom* type interface on his computer. No-one – or almost no-one - knew what he looked like. It didn't matter. He had hundreds of clients; private, corporate and governmental, all of whom had sought him out because of his reputation for efficiency and for confidentiality. He was one of the world's pre-eminent information gatherers. He was also, I hoped, still my friend. Time to find out.

He had once bragged to me that there wasn't anything he couldn't find out. That was a long time ago. I expected he was even better now.

I went in search of my old address and telephone book. It was hidden away very carefully. There were secrets there, as there were secrets elsewhere in my past that I didn't want anyone finding out accidentally.

I had no expectation that he would answer his phone. He never used to.

I found the last number I had, keyed it and waited. After seven rings I disconnected, as I had once been instructed, and keyed in another number. A machine picked up. A computer voice requested that I leave a message.

"One of your claims to fame was that you never forget a voice. If that's still true see if you can find me and call me back, please."

Eddie could never resist a challenge.

I disconnected again and went to bed, hoping that he wouldn't call until morning.

Twelve minutes later the phone rang. No computer voice this time.

"Sorry to be so long getting back to you, RJ, but after I found your number, which was blocked, as you know, I had to put in a grocery order and email a couple of people."

"Always the smart ass, Eddie. How are you?"

"Great, RJ. You?"

"Good, Eddie. How long has it been? Eighteen – twenty years?"

"Twenty-one years, six months next week. Long time. You don't call, you don't write."

"Okay, Eddie. Enough. You're making me feel bad now, having to ask you for help."

"Like you said, always the smart ass. What d'you need?"

"I know you're always busy but I need help collecting some background information on a few people."

"Man, you know I could never be too busy to help you. You saved my life and my family's and there is no amount of work I could ever do that would ever repay you for that. You know this, right?"

I didn't respond.

"Yes. You know. So what's this about?"

"It's part of something I'm investigating."

"I thought you were out of that game."

"So did I, but things happen and somehow I wind up getting involved."

"Inn keeping not exciting enough for you?"

Guess he'd been keeping tabs on me, as well.

"As it is now it's plenty exciting. I'd like to have a little more peace and quiet. That's what I came here for. So far, no such luck." I waited a moment.

"How would you know that I was out of the game?"

"Maybe I look in from time to time."

"Right."

"So, give me the names you want researched and I'll see what I can find."

I gave him the Winnstar execs, Smythe, the Masons and the young couple who seemed out of place. I also gave him a brief rundown of what was happening – or what I thought was happening so he would have some context for his research. He said he'd get back to me tomorrow – or later today since it was now after midnight.

"Oh, RJ. If we're going to communicate you're going to need a better phone, one that can be more secure – for my peace of mind if not yours. I'm going to send you one tomorrow. It'll look like a regular smart phone but it'll have some special features already programmed: a note app, a camera, internet. I'll explain how to use them later. It's waterproof and I'll have it programmed with your existing phone number."

"Are you sure this is a good idea, Eddie? You know I do not deal well with technology."

"Still? Okay, don't worry about it. I'll help you learn how to use it. Bye."

I went to bed finally, not sure that I really felt better. I knew I could trust Eddie – he wouldn't let me down, but I wasn't at all sure I would be able to deal with the avalanche of information he'd dump on me very soon.

Chapter 11

Winnstar Technologies Messenger   **account wtim0043**

New Message   **Tuesday**   **15/07**

From : Hotrod

To : Spider, Geek, Flower

Hotrod – More of the good stuff for Jason. The cop thinks he's loopy but doesn't know why. Put the wrappers in the room for a maid or someone to find. Harrison's still prowling but I don't think he's got the stuff to figure out what's really up.

    Spider – I overheard Harrison asking his staff about Valerie.

Winnstar Technologies Messenger   account wtim0001

New Message   **Tuesday**   **15/07**

From : Jason Murdock CEO

To : Valerie Owens CFO, Richard Washburn COO, Suzanne Ellis President, Harvey Donaldson Senior VP R&D, Dianne Jones Senior VP Marketing

Murdock – We need to all meet to see if we can figure out what's happened to Valerie. I booked a corner of the dining room for this afternoon so we can meet.

Winnstar Technologies Messenger   account wtim0043

New Message   **Tuesday   15/07**

From : Spider

To : Hotrod, Geek, Flower

Spider – Poor sap still thinks he's running a company.

Early the next morning one of the guest couples checked out. They had been dining at the same time as Smythe and his party the previous evening and had heard later about the concerns regarding the fish, though they had not had it. The departure was two days ahead of schedule and there was no real explanation. Didn't like the place as much as they thought they would. Fine. Maybe true, maybe not. Not much I could do about it but it reminded me that I still needed to talk to Smythe about the incident.

I was on the breakfast shift that day and so went straight to the kitchen from the desk. The breakfast service was slower than usual so I took a look out into the dining room. There were a few empty tables, more than I'd have expected.

I finished the breakfast service and spent the rest of the morning and the early afternoon doing dinner prep and planning menus for the following week. I'd just about finished when Kim came hurrying into the kitchen.

"You'd better come, RJ. One of the boats sank with four guests and a driver on board."

I closed my kitchen computer and took off my apron, calling to Gil as I did so. He came out of the walk-in to hear what I was saying.

"I have to go. There's been a problem at the dock. I'll come back later and help you work on the prep." By the time I ended the sentence I was out the door and jogging toward the boathouse.

The day was only partly sunny and there was a stiff breeze coming off the lake as a small storm front moved through to the north. The temperature was down a few degrees from the previous days.

Whatever scene of chaos may have existed earlier, relative calm prevailed by the time I reached the dock. Someone on the staff had rounded up some beach towels which were draped around five very wet people. Several guests stood nearby, watching. I got along the narrow dock to the group as fast as the gathered observers would allow, without dumping any more of them in the water.

"I'm really sorry about this. Is anyone hurt?"

All five people looked at me. One man spoke.

"No. We're not hurt, and that's all that's preventing me from suing you for every nickel you have. We're wet and cold and that's all. More good luck than good management in that."

He shivered in the brisk breeze even though the temperature was still high.

"We were going to try to get lunch in a safe place on the mainland where we wouldn't be poisoned and we end up damn near drowned. We're going to get dry and pack then we're leaving, period. You'd better call the water taxi from the marina. We're not getting back into any of your old junk boats." The other three nodded their agreement.

With that the four guests hurried off, towels dragging and shoes squishing, to the Inn, leaving me alone with Des, the unfortunate driver of the ill-fated boat.

"Okay, Des. Please just give me a quick rundown of what happened then you can go get dried off."

Des adjusted his towel and took a deep breath. "I really don't know what caused the whole thing. We started out fine then there was a loud creaking noise from behind the passenger compartment – really loud - loud enough that we all heard it over the engine noise. We were still going fairly slowly and fortunately we weren't more than fifty metres from the dock. I looked around and saw that the whole back wall of the passenger compartment was pulling off the boat. I swung the boat around and headed it back toward the dock. Once it was pointed in the right direction I cut the engine and let it drift. I made sure everyone's jacket was done up right then just kept the wheel steady, pointed at the dock. By then others on the dock could see we were in trouble and Mark brought another boat out to us. By the time he got out to us we were all swimming. I guess you know the rest."

Now Des was shivering. "That's enough for now. Sorry to keep you here so long. Go get changed and we'll talk again later."

As Des went on his soggy way to the Inn I flagged down Mark.

"I just realized what I forgot to ask Des. Where's the boat?"

Mark turned to the water and pointed along the longest run of dock, the one that connected to the section where Smythe's boat and the aircraft were moored.

"It's out there, about thirty metres from the end of this dock in about three metres of water."

"Thanks, Mark," I said. I walked out the long dock to the end and peered out into the lake. There was no evidence of gas or oil yet. We'd need to move quickly to get the boat out of the water before it started to leak. I opened my cell and called Kim.

"Kim, I need you to call Andy Morrison, please. Tell him that one of our boats has sunk in about three metres of water and we'll need his salvage barge to get it up ASAP. Call me back and let me know his response, please."

"Will do, RJ."

As I stood staring out at the gently rippling water I heard a splash and turned to look. About twenty metres from where I stood, an osprey struggled to regain the sky, a large fish grasped in its talons.

Footsteps approached from behind me. I looked over my shoulder and saw my friend heading toward me. I turned back to the water and said, "I didn't know you were here today, Mike. When did you arrive?"

He stopped at the edge of the dock beside me.

"I think I must have been coming in the front door as you were running out the back. I went up to the interview room to pack up the last of my reports and notes, and I didn't hear about this," he waved a hand around in a vaguely all-encompassing gesture, "until a few minutes ago. Oh, and I told Kim you could have the room back. Thanks for letting us use it."

"You're welcome." My cell buzzed and I answered it. A moment later I ended the call.

"That was Kim. Andy Morrison is bringing his barge and a crew out right away to get the boat out of the water."

"Good. I wouldn't want to have to add to your troubles by giving you a ticket for polluting the lake."

We were both looking at the water so I couldn't see the smile that I knew was there. "Right. Thanks, I think."

Grant turned to go. "I've a couple of people to touch base with so I'll be around for a while. Buy me a coffee later when you get this all sorted out."

"Sure." Grant walked away. I waited for the salvage boat to arrive and wondered what would be next. As I waited I watched Smythe's yacht back out of its slip and move quietly away.

A couple of hours later I met Mike in the lounge.

Andy Morrison had come out, bringing a barge with a crane. They hoisted the damaged boat out of the water and took it away to the boatworks for repair. The waterlogged foursome from said boat had, true to their word, packed and left as quickly as possible. My involvement in the whole production had taken so long that Bud and company had finished up all the prep for dinner without me and I was off the hook for that. I related all this to Mike.

"So, what happened with our Mr. Murdock at the morgue in Perth?"

"He's a strange one, that's for sure. Of course the woman was not his girlfriend or his wife or whatever – he still hasn't confirmed that one way or the other. You and I both knew it wouldn't be, and I think he did too, but he insisted on going through the whole ordeal. He seemed only half here all the time he and Boyd were together. He also continues to insist that his girlfriend has been missing since the first afternoon but we know she was interviewed by Brooks late in the evening that same day, several hours after he says she disappeared. We had them all in, all six of that group, one at a time so they couldn't hear one-another's statements. Brooks and Emery were interviewing some of the guests – them included - while I worked through the staff."

I shook my head. "So, now we know she really is missing, but it can't have happened until sometime the following day at least, since Brooks and Emery know she was there in the evening and she was out walking with Ellis on Saturday morning. Murdock is the only one saying she's been missing since shortly after the plane landed. That seems to point to Murdock as, at the very least, a person of interest?"

"Yes. He's definitely wrong about when she went missing. They also say she wasn't wearing anything close to what he described. The question is this: is he mistaken or is he being deliberately obstructive? Maybe he's building an insanity defence?"

"It seems to me," I said, "that if he was going to make up a story he'd make up something a little closer to what the others were saying – haven't seen her since last night - or something."

"Yeah. You'd think. I'm going to see Mr. Murdock and ask if I can search their room. We'll see what he says to that. If he lets me search, maybe I'll find something worthwhile. If he won't let me search I'll have to see about getting a warrant."

"Good luck with that," I said.

"I had decided to release Brooks and Emery for other work but now that we have *two* possible crimes going here I'm getting them back to re-interview all your staff, this time with a view to collecting any information we can find on the whereabouts of the missing woman. Any chance we can get that room again?"

"Shouldn't be a problem. That room is still empty and there are three more now that those two couples we tried to drown and one who was expecting to be poisoned have left. We managed to rebook another empty room to a drop-in, otherwise we'd be at less than fifty percent capacity."

"We'll be as unobtrusive as we can be. There shouldn't be any reason to bother any guests this time around, with the possible exception of the group from Winnipeg, and we'll keep the disruption to a minimum. How's Mr. Smythe, by the way? I heard about the fish thing."

"He's holed-up on his fancy yacht, supposedly recovering from food poisoning. We haven't heard from him today. I've been trying to set up a meeting with him to try to find out what he's up to but so far he's been ducking me."

"Maybe he'll just go away."

"No. I think he'll be a thorn in my side for a while longer yet. I think he may be up to no good but so far I can't prove anything."

"Keep me in the loop on that. Well, I'd better get a little more work done tonight. Every minute I waste lets the trail, or trails should I say, grow colder."

"I'll come up to the interview room a little later and see how you're doing."

Mike headed for the stairs and I went the other way to the kitchen. Dinner service was about to get underway. Bud nodded as I passed through to my computer alcove. I went through the orders on the desk and entered them into our database. Kim would do all the ordering from this tomorrow morning, or make arrangements to have it done if she was unable to do so. I shut down the computer again and retraced my route back through the kitchen, this time stopping to talk to Bud. He told me he'd sealed and frozen the last of the salmon, as I had asked him to in case it was needed by the health department. I reassured him that there were no new repercussions from the incident and told him again not to worry about it. I'm not sure it helped.

I passed by the main desk and was handed a package. It had been delivered only a few minutes before. The return address was Waterloo.

Once in my suite I opened the parcel and took out my new phone. Eddie was right. It looked like a regular smart phone. I'd have to wait and see what the special features amounted to. I plugged it into its charger and bid it good night.

I supposed that my staff would be happy about my new acquisition, but I wondered if I would be.

A few minutes later, outside on the balcony, I sat in the dark, listening to the wind in the trees and the loons on the water and watching the fireflies floating by, until I felt ready to sleep.

Chapter 12

I had a fitful sleep and woke up feeling unrested. I had this vague remembrance of my new phone pestering me constantly, telling me to do things I had no idea how to do.

I was off that morning but would have to be in the kitchen at two o'clock or so to assist with the evening service prep.

Over an uninteresting breakfast I picked up my new phone and the instructions and tried to learn a few things – like how to turn it on, answer a call, basic stuff like that. I finished up knowing only marginally more than I'd known to start with. It was like reading a foreign language. I might as well have been reading the Spanish instructions for all the good it did me. Oh well. One step at a time. Right.

Breakfast done, I went down the back stairs and out into the herb garden. Perhaps an hour or so of weed pulling would help to refocus my mind. Unfortunately, the focus would have to be three-fold: the floater, for lack of a better term, the missing woman from the Winnipeg group and Smythe. With any luck Eddie would come through with something I could use before too long.

After about fifteen minutes of weeding, one of the boathouse staff came by. I had my back to the pathway and heard rather than saw him stop. I stood up slowly, tossed a handful of weeds into the pile I'd accumulated, and turned.

"Morning, Ben."

"Morning, RJ. I didn't mean to interrupt but I've overheard something I think you should know about. Maybe tell the police, too."

"Okay. Let's sit on that bench in the shade and you can tell me about it."

There are a number of old-style park benches at the edges of the stone pathway around the building and grounds for the convenience of the Inn's guests. We moved to the nearest one and sat. Ben waited a few seconds, organizing his thoughts.

"I probably should have come to you or Sergeant Grant earlier but I had to think a bit and decide if it was worth reporting. Earlier this morning, about eight o'clock, I was in the boathouse tidying up some tack before the day's rentals and such. I was in the tack room and as you know it's kind of secluded so I don't think the guys even thought to look for anyone in there. If they had looked and seen me they wouldn't have said what they did."

"And what did they say, Ben?"

"It was two of the men from the airplane group, the CEO and the second in command."

"Jason Murdock and … Richard Washburn?"

"Yeah, those two."

"Okay. So what did they say that bothered you so much?"

"It was Washburn who did most of the talking. The other guy, Murdock, seemed kind of out of it and didn't say much. There was a bit of small-talk as they came into the boathouse and I didn't catch much of that, but then, right out of the blue, Washburn asked Murdock what he had done with the missing woman, Valerie. He said she wouldn't just wander off and Murdock was the last one to see her. He said he could understand why Murdock would do it but that he'd picked a lousy time and place for it – on an island with only a small number of people around and nowhere to go." Ben stopped to regroup and I jumped in.

"Let me be sure I understand what you're telling me. Washburn actually accused Murdock of killing or in some other way getting rid of his girlfriend Valerie."

"Yup. That's what I heard, RJ."

"And how did Murdock react to all that?"

"He hardly reacted at all. He said 'no, he wouldn't do that – he loved Valerie – he didn't know where she was' – stuff like that. All real quiet and slow, like he was stoned or something. Oh, and the other guy said he should lay off the drugs – he was just drawing attention to himself and the cops would be onto him right quick if he kept it up."

"Did Murdock have any response to that?"

"He said he didn't do drugs – never did – then something about why did Washburn think he was using drugs. After that, Washburn said to forget it – if he wasn't going to own-up there was no point talking about it. After that they left –Washburn first, all pissed-off, then Murdock."

We sat in silence for a few minutes. A couple of guests wandered by, paying us no attention at all. I was vividly reminded of the bit of conversation I'd heard in the stairwell of the Inn. Two men. The same two men? No. Probably not. After a couple of minutes I broke the silence.

"Well, Ben, that's a hell of a story. And you were definitely right to tell me. You were also right that Sergeant Grant will need to be told. I'm sure he'll want you to tell him yourself rather than hearing it from me. You'll be okay with that, right?"

"Yeah. I guess."

More silence followed.

"All right. I think Sergeant Grant might be in the interview room by now. How 'bout we go together and I can set things up for you. You'll be out in no time. Are you supposed to be working this morning?"

"Not 'til eleven."

"Good. You'll be done by then. I'm sure Sergeant Grant will tell you this as well, but please don't repeat any of this to anyone at all until after this business is all wrapped up." Ben agreed that he would not say anything.

We left the bench and went inside, through the kitchen, the dining room and the lounge. As we rounded the last corner to start up the stairs we almost ran into Richard Washburn coming down. He blew past without even acknowledging us. Neither of us commented and we went up one flight to the interview room where I left Ben and Mike to talk.

I went back to my weeding and, having finished that, found a few other odd jobs to do. It occurred to me again that I would have to find another part-time maintenance person, since our previous one was now in permanent residence at a local cemetery.

I met Mike for coffee later. We sat in a quiet corner of the outdoor dining area; the sun was bright but not too hot and the breeze was light. We talked briefly about golfing again sometime soon and about the Blue Jays' season so far.

"I had a nice chat a few minutes ago with your guy, Ben," said Mike. "It's good that he trusted you enough to come to you about what he heard. I don't need to repeat the bulk of it, but there's one item of information that he forgot to tell you. He saw the missing woman, though he had no idea who she was specifically, other than that she was part of the airplane group which he remembered from the luggage moving session. She was walking on the dock near the aircraft about an hour or so after they all arrived. He described her as the tall, slim one with great legs and really short, dark, hair. Had to have been Valerie Owens, I think."

"Sure sounds like it. They're all three fairly tall and slim but she's the only one with short dark hair."

"And he's not the only one of your people who saw her that afternoon. No less than three others saw her in various places

– two significantly distant places on the island and one inside, in the lounge. And Saturday morning.

"She sure got around that afternoon, didn't she?" I asked. "I saw her too."

"Well, she's supposed to be an exercise nut and would want to move around some after the plane ride from Winnipeg. I guess it's not too big a stretch to figure she'd get around a bit. It is a fairly small island after all."

"Yes. It is. The problem is that it spreads out the possible area where she went missing to most of the island. She could be anywhere; in the building, on the grounds or in the lake."

Mike thought a moment then went on. "That's the one that worries me the most; that she went into the lake. We can search the whole island, inside and outside the buildings but the water will be much more difficult to deal with. The fact that we haven't had another floater reported says two possible things to me. One, that she went in the water after dark, either with or without help and was carried away by what little wave action there is in the lake, or two, that she was weighted down. No doubt there are other possibilities but those seem to be the ones that stand out to me at the moment. If she went in the water at all."

"I guess it's possible she got a shuttle to the mainland, though why she would, is anybody's guess. You've checked that out with Bascome's already, I expect?"

"Yes, and no luck there. The shuttle driver can't be sure of whether or not she was on one of his six runs that afternoon and evening. She could easily have been on one of them."

"It sounds to me as though you have to go after a warrant to search the individual guest rooms. You may or may not get the guests to agree to having their rooms searched. You know you won't get any flack from me about searching any of the rest of the island, including my suite if you feel the need.

Will you try for divers to check out the water around the shoreline?"

"I'll have to go to the brass on that. Warrants are hard to come by without a lot of good cause. I'm not sure we have it yet. Divers will be expensive. The powers-that-be will have to decide which they want to try first. I plan to ask all the guests today if they will allow me to search their rooms. It shouldn't be a big deal – not like I'll have to look in suitcases or peek around in the underwear drawer. You can only hide a body in so many places. If they all agree then we don't have to deal with the warrant issue."

"Whenever you want to start on the island, let me know. I guess your two guys can handle the Inn and the other buildings but there's a lot of ground to cover out there, despite it being a small island."

"I'm going to try for a canine unit and a few more guys for the outside search. Rick Spencer and his dog, Max, live in Lombardy so it won't be a big deal to get them here if I can get it authorized. I'll get a sample of Valerie's clothing from our vague friend Murdock. Actually, I think I'll start with him right now. If he refuses to cooperate it will give me more ammunition to use to get a search warrant."

"Okay, I'll let the office group know what you're up to and they can notify the rest of the staff to give your guys their full cooperation – unlock doors - whatever."

"Thanks, RJ." Mike was already up and moving. "I'll catch up with you later."

I gathered up the coffee things and loaded them on a tray. The sun was high, as was the temperature, but I didn't think it was as hot today as it had been the last few.

I passed by the reception desk on the way to the main door but the receptionist was talking on the phone so I didn't stop. I did stop to look at the bulletin board we have on the wall next to the reception area to see if there was anything new. What caught my eye was a poster for the annual Westport Music Fest, upcoming in August. I'd have to find out more about that, ask Kim what else we were doing to help promote it.

Chapter 13

The wave of heat that hit me as I went outside was less than yesterday's but still significant. I decided to go around back and make sure someone had remembered to water the herb garden, then maybe take a short walk in the woods before going back to the kitchen. Most herbs are pretty hardy but even they can only stand so much.

The herbs had been watered since I'd been there earlier so I continued on out the path that soon would split in two: one part going over the saddle of rock toward the boathouse and the other toward the centre of the island. A dense humid smell of warm cedar, pine and spruce wood and of leaf mould enveloped me as I moved away from the house and into the denser woods. Somewhere near there must be a hollow tree or a fallen log which was home to a hive. I could hear the droning but could not see the bees. What small breeze there had been out in the open disappeared and sounds of the outside world were muffled. Insects and a few birds flitted quietly around and I heard only my own footsteps on the stone path.

Until I heard the shout. "Fire!"

I turned and ran back along the path, out into the open space where the house is situated. I saw several of my staff gathered on the ground level at the edge of the dining room deck. A small trail of smoke rose near them but there was no evidence of flame. As I approached I saw that one of the wait staff had a fire extinguisher and had already made good use of it.

As I got closer I realized that the smoke was coming from a tall, narrow critter-proof trash container we keep at the bottom of the stairs to the dining room deck. It was next to impossible that anyone could have accidentally tossed something burning into the thing. My first assumption was that some careless smoker had dropped a live butt into the can.

"Good job here, you people. Thanks. No damage and it doesn't look as though any guests saw anything."

I decided I wanted to have a look inside, just in case there was another reason for the fire, but not right now.

Glen, from the kitchen crew, was among those at the scene. "Glen. Would you please do two things for me? Get a dolly and haul that trash can over to the boathouse. Put it inside and put a sign on it to say that it is not to be touched by anyone but me, and bring back a spare. Then take that spent extinguisher to Kim's office and let her know that it's there. She'll call the company to have it refilled. Oh, and a third thing please. Go to the storage room in the basement and get a replacement extinguisher for the dining room."

"Will do, RJ."

"Looks like the rest of you can go back to work. Thanks again."

I was no longer thinking about a peaceful walk in the woods. I wondered what more I could do with my trashcans than I already had: butt disposal containers and signs warning people to take care.

I stood a moment, looking at the Inn, wondering if it was possible that I could lose it, and my thoughts turned to Mr. Smythe.

I had already been aware, from the title search when I bought the island, that Smythe, now some eighty years old and still what

I would describe as lean and mean, was one of the previous owners of Gilmore Island; the most recent to actually do anything here before me. He'd had all the modern upgrades done to the kitchen and to the plumbing and electrical systems and had had new power and communications cables run from the mainland.

The rumour around town was that a downturn in whatever was his primary source of income had wiped him out temporarily and he'd abandoned the Gilmore project. It was sold to a developer who had plans to finish the project but did not. He left his old boats behind too, as part of the deal.

Several years after Smythe left Westport I bought the property and finished the conversion of it to a small hotel.

Suddenly Smythe was back, apparently having rebuilt his fortune, and wanting to retake ownership.

I'd put a lot of time and effort, not to say money, into the place and I was not interested in turning it over.

As I was thinking about Smythe I was walking toward the dock in the hope of being able to talk to him. I arrived there to find the boat gone so, unsuccessful again, I returned to the Inn.

A short while later I arrived back at the kitchen to help finish up the prep for the evening service. As I entered the kitchen my new phone chimed quietly and vibrated. I opened the screen and saw a text was waiting.

"Check your email ... found stuff. E."

Okay. But I had food to deal with first.

The specials were to be Garlic Lover's Steak and Rainbow Pickerel, the white fish served on a bed of spinach and with a topping of red onion, mushrooms, tomatoes and multi-coloured peppers – hence the name "rainbow". These would be served with local vegetables and potatoes or rice.

I began by making the compound garlic butter. I laid out a pound of butter to soften. As I grated the garlic I reran the events of the day as they had played out. We were no closer to finding out what had happened to the woman who'd been found among the rocks off the east coast, nor to discovering the whereabouts of Valerie Owens, the missing executive from Winnipeg. And, if the trashcan fire was something other than careless smoking, increasingly serious sabotage seemed to be going on.

The grating of the garlic went quickly. Yes, the cloves had to be peeled first and that added a little time initially, but after that it was a quick and easy job. This was going to be a seriously garlicky butter so I had about three tablespoons of grated garlic for the pound of butter.

I guessed I'd have to leave the floater – that seemed to be an unpleasant way of describing that unfortunate woman - to the police since I had no real involvement with the victim, nor did I have any information to go on. That investigation was ongoing. According to Mike there had been no missing persons report on anyone matching her description and none of the Inn or boathouse staff had recognized her from the autopsy photo the police had been showing around.

Valerie Owens was another matter. I'd met her – carried her luggage and spoken with her. I thought I'd seen her briefly as she went away from the Inn as she left for her walk. I was one of many who had. Seemed as though Jason Murdock was the only one who *hadn't* seen her.

I unwrapped the butter and dropped it into a bowl then added the grated garlic and a few coarse grinds of fresh black pepper. Several others of my staff said they had seen Valerie that first afternoon and evening, as well as the following morning, at various places around the Inn and the boathouse and dock. Then she was gone.

Using a small whisk I mixed the garlic and pepper into the softened butter. After I was satisfied that it was well mixed I turned it out onto a sheet of plastic wrap and formed it into a long, thin, log, about 3 cm. in diameter. This I rolled and wrapped tight and then placed in the freezer to firm up but not for long enough to freeze solid.

I couldn't have said why, but I was convinced that Valerie had not left the island – not willingly at any rate. I would have bet that sometime late that first evening, after the police interviews, something had happened to her, somewhere on the island. Tomorrow I would have to talk to all the staff who had seen her and find out how sure they were that it was Valerie and when and where they had seen her. Then I would have a better feel for her movements.

Glen came back into the kitchen and headed to the sink to wash up before starting to help with the dinner prep. "I took care of that stuff, RJ."

"Thanks, Glen. Now you're back you can finish the potatoes to go with the garlic steak. Jeany will be back in a few minutes to finish up the beans and the corn. I'll do the rice when I've cleaned up from the garlic butter."

I washed my prep dishes and began getting the assorted parts of my multigrain rice. As I worked I remembered that Glen had been one of the staff who'd seen Valerie Owens before she went missing.

"Glen, I hear you saw Ms. Owens the other evening. Can you please tell me when and where?"

"Sure. I saw her twice, actually. The first time was not long after the luggage production." He paused a moment, potato in one hand and scrub brush in the other, to recall the details. "I was called to the dock to help a guest bring some bags in from a boat and I saw her out on the farthest part, looking out at the water. She was wearing different clothes then from what she wore on the plane. I saw her again later but now I'm not sure if it was just before or just after I had my interview with the police. She was going up the stairs from the lobby toward the second floor."

He hesitated a second and seemed to colour a bit.

"What?"

"Oh, I just remembered that she had great legs ... and a neat little oval-shaped birthmark on the back of her right leg, just above the knee."

"That's a pretty thorough observation. They must have been really great legs. Don't suppose you noticed the colour of the clothing?"

"No. Sorry." He coloured a little more and shrugged, then went back to work.

We worked in silence for a few minutes. I was thinking about the movements of the missing CFO.

Soon the potatoes were washed and rinsed and were now headed for the pot to be parboiled. These were new Ontario potatoes, small and firm and would be cooked and served, slightly smashed and home-fried, with the skins on.

Jeany came into the kitchen and headed straight to the wash-up sink then to the prep table. "Sorry to be so long. I had to get my change of address done while Kim had time. The new place isn't much but it's a big step up from where we were before. Nice to have a full time job."

"Good to hear things are working out better for you. And there's no need to worry about the prep. Both veggies are quick and easy tonight."

Jeany started topping a large pile of fresh local green beans and I started the rice. My multigrain rice has four different grains, all of which add their own colour component but they have to be cooked separately to achieve the best end result. I got four pots of water going and started cooking the rice.

I went back to the subject of Valerie Owens.

"I don't suppose you saw Ms. Owens on the night before she disappeared, did you, Jeany?"

"No. Sorry, RJ. I was off. I didn't hear about all the excitement until I came in at two the next day."

"Right. Thanks."

I carried on with the rice, lifting a lid now and then to stir but mostly it was an excuse to be idle and think. I would have to spend a few minutes at my computer later and make a list of all the people I thought might have seen our missing woman.

I rechecked the walk-in for steaks and pickerel fillets and brought out the corn Jeany would be working on next. Glen had the potatoes parboiled and out of the pot to cool and the rices were almost ready; setting, resting, absorbing the last of the liquid without cooking any more. The last thing to make was the Tartar Sauce that would accompany the pickerel.

I'd have to remember to add Tomas to my list of people to talk to. He'd gone AWOL that evening but had been on the job when the group had first arrived and for a while after. There were also Michelle and Sammi from the lounge and Gwen and, later, Carole from the front desk.

As I gathered the ingredients for the Tartar sauce I remembered the conversation I'd overheard between the two unseen men in the stairwell. I was convinced that they were from the Winnipeg group: not Jason Murdock but perhaps the other two, Richard Washburn and Harvey Donaldson. That seemed likely somehow. I'd not had a lot to do with either of them but they were both close enough to the situation to warrant a closer look. I decided to seek them out, one at a time, and talk to them on some pretence or other and see if I could figure out if it had been them I'd heard.

As I was making the Tartar sauce two of the wait staff from the dining room came into the kitchen, one obviously prodding the other along. I'd already chopped a half cup or so of fresh chives and was in process of doing the same to a quarter cup of capers when they approached.

"RJ. Mary has something to tell you. Go on, Mary. Tell him."

Mary hesitated. "It's probably nothing."

"No. It is not 'nothing'. RJ, it has to do with the sinking of the boat. We were talking about it at coffee and Mary thinks she saw someone hanging around. Go on and tell him."

I looked at Mary and waited.

"It's probably nothing but I saw one of the crew people from the big boat hanging around that old wood boat that sank. She wasn't actually doing anything that I saw but she was crouched down at the back of the boat. When she saw me looking she got up and left – even waved at me. She had tools in her back pocket and a rag, but whenever I've seen her around she always has those."

"Yes, she does. I think she does the maintenance on Smythe's boat," I said.

"If I'd thought she was doing anything bad I'd have said something. I didn't really put it together until some of us were talking at coffee. Sorry, RJ."

"Nothing to be sorry about. Now that I know about this I can have a closer look. So, it was the woman?"

"Yes. I don't know her name. It wasn't Brent, the guy who's always following Smythe around, taking notes."

"I'll think about it. I'm sure I've heard her name. Thanks, Mary. You did good."

They returned to the dining room and I refocused on my Tartar sauce but with some new things to think about.

I put the chives and capers into four cups of mayo I had in a waiting bowl, then added two tablespoons of lemon juice, four tablespoons of sweet green relish and a quarter teaspoon of fine white pepper. I wondered why – Kaylee, that was her name – why Kaylee would do what I was suspecting she'd done. Perhaps I'd need to add her name and Brent's to my next list of things for Eddie to check out. I had no idea what their last names were and if Mike didn't either it would be difficult to run checks on them.

Another whisk was put to use to blend all the ingredients together and the bowl was covered and put into the walk-in.

I went to my desk to get my phone so I could call Mike and tell him what I'd just learned.

I decided I needed to go outside for a breath of air after I picked up my phone from the kitchen office alcove so I went out and made the call. It went to voicemail so I left a message detailing what I'd heard about the possible sabotage of the boat.

The wind was up and the temperature down some. Maybe a storm coming.

Chapter 14

Winnstar Technologies Messenger   **account wtim0043**

New Message   **Wednesday   16/07**

From : Hotrod

To : Spider, Geek, Flower

Hotrod – Took J to the boathouse to wring him out a little. Got an unexpected
bonus. One of the Inn staff was there and I padded the performance
for his benefit. Word will get back.

Winnstar Technologies Messenger   **account wtim0043**

New Message   **Wednesday   16/07**

From : Geek

To : Spider, Hotrod, Flower

Geek – Seems this RJ guy is more than he seems like Flower said before.
He's watching us like he suspects something. Tread carefully.

The evening service went well and was a little busier than the previous evening had been. Apparently some of our guests had decided to give us another chance.

We had handled it without incident and the food was a hit, apparently. Lots of good comments about the Garlic Lover's Steak with home fries and the Rainbow Pickerel with multigrain rice and the house-made Tartar sauce, that we'd served with steamed green beans or in-the-husk-roasted corn-on-the-cob.

We cleaned up in record time so the staff could get out and across to the mainland before the expected storm could prevent further boat travel.

When I got to my suite later there was a message on my answering machine from Cam. I called right away.

"I'm home, RJ. It took longer than I expected, but it was worth the extra time."

"That's great. It went well?"

"Excellent. I got some great pieces and for good prices. They're being shipped next week."

"I'm looking forward to seeing them, but I'm looking forward to seeing you more. I guess I'll have to wait 'til Friday though."

"Yes. It's too late tonight."

"If you say so."

"Are you all set for the winery trip?"

"Oh yes. I have coverage arranged so there should be no problems there. The investigations will just have to carry on without me for a couple of days."

"More than one investigation? Did I miss something?" asked Cam.

"Yes. We now have a missing woman, one of the group from Winnipeg that I told you about. She went missing a couple of days before you left, though we didn't know it at the time. I've been working with Mike, unofficially again of course, trying to figure out what happened to her. The woman we found off the east shore you already know about. That's still an active case but there's not much for me there. I have nothing to do with her that I know of, except insofar as she washed up on my shoreline. There's also the sinking of a boat – no injuries, gladly, and a small fire in a trashcan."

"Wow. Never a dull moment around there. How do you get any real work done?"

"I manage somehow."

"So, I have to get some work done tonight: paperwork for the gallery. I'd better get to it. Am I being pushy about the wine contract thing? Not really my business, I know."

"No. Not at all. And even if you were, sometimes I need a push."

"You're sure?"

"Yes."

"Okay. Do you mind driving on Friday?"

"No problem. What time do you want me to pick you up?"

"Two o'clock should give us lots of time to get there and still have time to get a good look at the place before dinner."

"Sounds good. I'll see you then. Bye."

"Bye."

After I disconnected I was still restless and it was still just barely light out so I decided to go for a walk to the beach and then, once I reached the shoreline I would turn north.

I could hear the ancient, but newly repaired, weather vane atop the tallest turret turning frantically, clattering loudly in the freshening breeze; definitely a storm coming. I walked along the path a short way, stopped for a moment then looked out over the water and then, thinking that I'd rather not be caught out in the rain, turned back toward the Inn.

I was almost past the trees, almost back into the open space of the beach when someone lunged at me from behind a tree. The blow caught me hard between the shoulder blades and I went hurtling through the air, over the rocky edge and into the water.

I am no swimmer. I have probably mentioned this before. Perhaps it's not such a bright place to live – on an island – when one is not a good swimmer.

I thrashed around briefly, alternately yelling and choking on lake water until I realized that I could touch bottom, at least in places. My panic subsided somewhat and I began to work my way to the shore, sliding off slippery rocks and submerging briefly a couple of times in the process.

I was almost to the edge when a couple of people, who'd heard me yelling, arrived. They were a middle-aged couple, perhaps day-trippers, not guests that I recognized. They climbed out and down, onto the rocks and reached to pull me up out of the water.

"Are you okay? Not injured? We could hear you but we didn't know where you were. It was hard to pinpoint the direction with the wind blowing," said one of my rescuers.

"There was someone else, jogging on the path, as we were coming along. Should have heard you but just kept going. Maybe had those little speakers in her ears. I didn't see," added the other.

"Thank you for your help. No telling how long I'd have been trying to get out of there without it."

"You're welcome. You'd better get in and get dried off. We'd best be going. Don't want to miss the last shuttle to the mainland. We're staying at The Cove tonight."

"Thanks again." They hurried off along the beach to the path to the dock. I stared after them for a minute then went the same way. Just as they were about to pass out of sight I called out.

"What did this woman ... this person look like?"

They didn't hear me. I didn't have the energy to run after them.

At that point I remembered having seen them in the dining room earlier. Hopefully I would meet up with them another day at the Inn.

I stopped briefly at the desk.

"Has it started to rain already, RJ?" asked Carole.

"No. It has not." I vaguely explained why I looked like a drowned rat.

As I leaned over the counter to talk to her I noticed the same brochure I'd seen earlier on Kim's desk.

"Carole. Could you please tell me what that square symbol is, there on the back of the brochure?"

She pointed. "This?"

"Yes."

"That's a QR code, RJ."

"Okay. So, what is a QR code and why do we have it there?"

"It's there so people can scan it with their smart phones."

"And why would they want to do that?"

"When they scan the code it takes them directly to the Gilmore House Inn website and then they can get information or make reservations – stuff like that."

"We have a website?"

Carole almost choked, trying not to say the first thing that came to her mind.

"Yes, RJ. We have a website. Did you really not know that? You're kidding, right?"

"Yes, I'm kidding. Kim had the website created before we opened but I just never gave it much thought. I'm not much for computers and such, as everyone around here knows. I barely get by dealing with what I have to do with the kitchen computer. And I've been kind of busy."

"Yes, but really, RJ." She shook her head ruefully. "You need to get out of the kitchen more often."

"Yes. I think I do at that. Good night, Carole."

The phone rang and she turned away to answer it.

I needed to get out of my wet clothes so I went up to my suite. It had been a long day and I wanted to sleep but didn't feel as though that was going to happen any time soon. I emptied my pockets on the kitchen island, spreading out the contents to dry and thankful that Eddie had thought to send me a waterproof phone. I had a quick shower, to warm up, and dried off. I was wound up about the disappearance of Valerie Owens and about my cold bath. I felt as though I was edging closer to making some progress but it was a slow process. I tried to see if there was a way to connect the dunking with either of the puzzles I was working on but couldn't, for the moment. I had no idea who had pushed me and even if I'd thought to get a description of the woman on the pathway there would still have been no way to prove that they were connected.

I got a small snack and was about to go sit in the living room with it and call Mike again, to fill him in about my plunge into the lake, when my phone rang. It was Mike returning my earlier call. I related both my conversation with Mary and my dip in the lake. I related my encounter with the couple who'd helped me, in case he might want to catch up with them at The Cove and see if they could give a description of the person on the path.

For the next short while we kicked around a variety of scenarios but finished up no further ahead. We were about to call it a night when he remembered the other thing he was going to tell me.

"I got the brass to spring for the use of the canine unit. I think I told you that we have a guy in Lombardy. He's going to come over and take a run around the island as soon as he can. I got some clothing samples from Mr. Murdock today so it'll be ready when the team gets here. All her clothes were clean and in the drawers – nothing worn – but it's the best I could get. Odd that we didn't find the clothes Valerie Owens was wearing for the plane ride.

"Hopefully this rain that's coming won't wipe out any trace of her. That's it, I think. I'd better get some sleep, RJ."

"Right. Good night."

I was about to head to bed myself when I remembered the text from Eddie. I opened my laptop on the kitchen island and got the email up.

I had not told Eddie my email address but he'd got it somehow. Maybe that sort of thing is easy, maybe it isn't. I wouldn't know. I was still baffled at what some people could do with computers, especially people like Eddie.

There were several pages of notes plus a lot of what looked like corporate documents – ones that I would have bet were not intended to be seen by people outside the company – from Winnstar Technologies Inc. and from a company called SmytheCo Investments. Not hard to guess who *that* outfit belonged to.

I read reports until my eyes started to blur and my brain got fuzzy. There was a lot of good info there but the two things that struck me most forcefully were that the Winnstar boardroom was not a happy place at the moment and that SmytheCo Investments was a shareholder in Winnstar Technologies.

As I drifted off to sleep later I wondered two things. Had the contentiousness of the Winnstar execs escalated to the point where some of them were trying to break up the company and to what lengths would they go to do that; and was there more to Smythe's appearance on the island than I'd been led to believe?

Chapter 15

New Message   **Thursday**   **17/07**

From : Hotrod

To : Spider

Hotrod – Old Jason gets the cops attention more all the time. All good. Did
she get rid of the clothes yet?

   Spider – Yes. Said she did. In the lake as planned. Same as I did. Be
   cool. I have everything under control.

_____

New Message   **Thursday**   **17/07**

From : Valerie Owens CFO

To : Jason Murdock CEO, Richard Washburn COO, Suzanne Ellis President,
Harvey Donaldson Senior VP R&D, Dianne Jones Senior VP Marketing

Valerie – Sorry to keep you all guessing these past few days. I've decided that I need a break and now seemed like as good a time as any. I got a boat from the island and caught a bus to Ottawa. I'm not telling you where I'm going from here but I'll be in touch.

Winnstar Technologies Messenger   **account wtim0043**

New Message   **Thursday   17/07**

From : Geek

To : Flower

Geek – What the hell ?

Next morning I was free of the kitchen so, after a quick breakfast, I went on a tour of the whole Inn, something I make a habit of doing as often as possible. I start at the top floor and work my way down slowly, looking in any empty suites, checking supply cupboards, looking at fixtures and furniture and the overall state of the cleaning and maintenance.

I found a couple of lights burned out and a squeaky hinge on the door of the cleaning supply closet on the second floor.

Again I was reminded that I needed to hire a part time maintenance person to handle all these little things as they arose.

Inside the supply closet with the squeaky door I located the mini tool kit. I keep one on each floor – pliers, knife, adjustable wrench and a multiplex screwdriver – so that unless it's something major I don't have to go to the maintenance room in the basement every time I have something to fix.

I took out a can of spray lubricant and a couple of sheets of paper towel and quickly eliminated the squeak and cleaned up the residue from the spray. The odour of the lubricant almost overwhelmed the faint smell of smoke that suddenly caught my attention.

I looked around but saw nothing. At the end of the hallway there was an open window and I wondered if the smell was coming from there. I went to the window and stuck my face up as close as I could get to the screen and was sure the smell was stronger but I still couldn't see anything.

I got down to the ground floor in record time, slowed somewhat as I passed through the lobby – no point in alarming the staff or guests – and went around to the dining room deck.

There, right up against the wall beside the dining room French doors, was another of our critter-proof trash cans. There was a small wisp of smoke rising from the top, drifting up and in the window above.

I tested the sides for heat and, finding little, I tipped the can slightly on an angle and rolled it to the edge of the deck then bounced the trash can down the wooden steps to the stone walkway. It had stopped smoking by now so I lifted the lid and found no indication of fire. I spotted a watering can in the corner of the garden and had a look inside. It was about half full so I took it and poured the water into the trash can, just to be sure. I was getting set to roll it away when one of the boathouse staff happened by.

"Bobby. I have a job for you. Go get a two-wheeled dolly please and take this trashcan to the boathouse. Leave it there with the other one that had the fire in it – it should still have a sign on it - and bring a spare here to replace this one when you come with the wheeler."

"You got it, RJ."

I stayed with the trash can, rooted around a little in the top of the trash to be sure the fire was out then left it sit. I sat on the steps and thought about who might be doing this. Either there were people around who couldn't read or chose to ignore my signs and weren't using the butt container or something more sinister was going on.

I wondered if the same person was responsible for the fires and the sabotage to the boat. Between those things and what I believed to be a phoney food poisoning incident, I was beginning to lean toward Smythe and his crew as possible suspects. If it was him, he was piling up a lot of little things that would, in time, hurt my business by making potential guests fearful of staying here. I had to put a stop to it somehow. I needed to meet with him soon.

Ten minutes later, Bobby was back with the two-wheeled dolly.

I smelled of smoke and garbage from having rummaged around in the burned trash so I went back to my suite to wash and change clothes. I'd have to get some laundry done soon or I'd have nothing to wear and nothing to pack for my trip to the County, tomorrow.

About nine I went out again, thinking I'd head for the dock and try to corner Smythe for a chat.

As I turned to go inside, Jason Murdock came running along the path. He looked as though he hadn't showered in days and his clothes were a mess but he had a big dopey grin on his face.

"She's okay. Valerie's okay. She's gone away for a while but I'm sure she'll be back."

I jumped in when he stopped to breathe. "How do you know this?"

"Here. Look." He pushed his phone almost in my face. Sure enough, there was an email from Valerie Owens, saying that she'd taken a shuttle to the mainland.

Murdock bounced off along the path. Mike was due here early today and this new information would be top of my list of things to tell him.

There was a stir of voices coming from the main lobby as I came down the stairs. I arrived at the bottom step to find a couple of staff and some guests all having a serious look at a fully uniformed OPP officer and a very large dog. Grant had told me the canine unit would be around sometime soon but had not specified that it would be today.

Now, given my recent conversation with Jason Murdock, the picture had changed. Maybe it was no longer necessary to have the canine unit work the island. I made a quick decision. Murdock's behavior was only a little less flakey now than it had been before and I was still not sure that anything he said could be trusted. I would let the dog do his job and hope that Mike agreed with the decision.

Fortunately the rain had held off, for now.

I approached the officer slowly and introduced myself as I went but did not attempt to shake hands, expecting the officer to make the first approach. He did.

"Good to meet you, Mr. Harrison. Rick Spencer. This is Max. Max and I are here to have a sniff around and see if we can turn up anything new. Sergeant Grant left me some clothing samples this morning. We'll use them and see if we can pick up a trail." Max looked up at me but had nothing to contribute to the conversation at the moment.

"I thought modern search dogs were not given stuff like clothing to work from. I thought they worked by finding and following unique scents."

"Most do, especially in large open areas or forests. Here there isn't likely to be any area where there is only one scent. People are all over. Everything will be overlapped. Under these conditions Max needs a specific scent that he can separate from all the rest, hence the clothing items."

"Good to know."

"Have you seen Sergeant Grant yet?" asked Spencer.

"No. I haven't seen him yet but then I've been busy putting out fires already this morning so I missed his arrival. If you happen to see him before I do, please let him know I need to talk to him, too."

"Will do. Come on, Max. Let's get started."

Constable Spencer and Max left to track the perhaps-not-so-missing woman. I went to the desk.

"Is Kim in yet?"

"In the dining room I think, RJ. She needed to check something."

I went around the corner and almost collided with Kim as she was returning to the desk.

"I was looking for you," I said. "How are you doing today?"

"Not too bad, I guess. I'm still not able to find my sister, but Mike – I mean Sergeant Grant - is helping with that. I was going to stay home today but there didn't seem much point. Here I'll be busy and not thinking about Karen all day long, wondering what's happened to her."

I nodded. There wasn't much I could say to make the situation better. "I'm sure Mike will do all he can. Make sure you take time off if you need it, okay?"

"Yes, RJ, I will. Why were you looking for me?"

"I just wanted to remind you that I'm going to that function at the Hillsborough Winery from tomorrow afternoon to Sunday. I know all my shifts are covered but you'll need to keep an eye on things when Bud's not here."

"I'll look after it, RJ. Cam's going with you?"

"We're going together, yes. Please keep that to yourself, Kim. I'm not sure yet how Cam will feel about having everyone know about our relationship."

"Actually, RJ, I expect most everyone already knows, and Cam knows we know. You didn't really expect to keep that a secret, did you? I know she didn't."

I just shook my head and walked away.

As I walked it occurred to me that it might not be a bad idea to have Eddie start looking into where Kim's sister might be. I realized also that I'd had an opportunity to ask Kim about the gun but had passed it up again.

I went through the dining room, which was practically deserted at that hour, and out onto the deck. I thought I'd better get to the boathouse and have another look at those trash cans – see if there was anything interesting to be found there. I had debated telling Mike about the first fire but figured he had enough on the go already. Besides, there was no reason to think that the trashcan fire was anything other than an accident. Now that there were two I'd have to let him know.

I'd just started on my way as my cell beeped.

Kim.

"I've just had Mark from the grounds-keeping crew in my office. You just missed him. He was doing his weekly routine of getting the trash ready to go onto the barge to the garbage dump. One of the trashcans from outside the Inn – not one of the ones you put the sign on - slipped out of his hand and tipped over. Amongst the trash that came out was a tightly wrapped bundle of clothing. It appears to be a very pale mauve blouse, a pair of dark purple shorts and a pair of sneakers all tied together with a narrow belt. That's all we can see without untying it. We thought we'd better not do that. Shall I call Sergeant Grant?"

"Definitely. I'll be right along. We'll need to get hold of Constable Spencer too. Mike will be able to get him on the radio if you don't find him first. And don't handle the bundle any more than is absolutely necessary, please."

Something about the clothing, the colours of the clothing in particular, bothered me, but I couldn't think why.

As it turned out, Constable Spencer and Max had covered a fair bit of ground in the short time they'd been gone so it was a half hour or so before they were able to meet us back at the Inn.

They had been using a sample of clothing from Valerie Owens, a sample given to Sergeant Grant by Jason Murdock, to see if Max could pick up her scent anywhere. Max was not having much luck because all of the clothes were freshly laundered. Spencer reported a couple of possible hits near the Inn but nothing to indicate a strong trail. But these new-found clothes provided not just a better lead for Max, but fresh evidence that all was not well with Valerie Owens despite the email I'd seen.

At some point earlier, while I was distracted, Mike had returned to the island but I had not seen him. He was just now getting the bundle of clothing from Kim.

Now that he had something new to work with, the dog handler started over. Grant had unrolled the bundle and bagged all the items separately. Now he gave one bag to Spencer who opened it just enough for Max to get a sniff, without actually touching the clothes. Forensics had not yet had their time with the evidence so it was important not to contaminate it any further.

Max's reaction was almost immediate. He seemed to be on the scent from the first second he put his nose to the ground. He began roaming, searching, following whatever invisible trail was there, around the lobby then to the main door. Constable Spencer and Max took the lead and Grant and I hung back a little so as not to be in the way.

At first the trail was straight and true: out the door and along the deck to the front steps and down to the stone pathway but suddenly Max did an abrupt about face and came back up the front steps and Grant and I had to scramble to get out of the way.

Max retraced his steps to the main door, then past it and along the side deck toward the back of the Inn and around the corner. He dragged Constable Spencer along through the outdoor dining area, beyond it and then back to the dining room door. Spencer opened the door and Max rushed through, continuing his search and causing something of a stir among some early lunchtime diners.

Quite suddenly he stopped at one of the tables and sat quietly, ears up, totally focused on the two women seated there.

There was silence in the dining room. The two women, the remaining two from the Winnstar Technologies group, sat stunned, staring first at Max, then at the rest of us.

Sergeant Grant was still carrying the evidence bags containing the clothes and shoes. He stepped around Constable Spencer and stopped beside Max. Max's attention did not waver. Grant held out the bags.

"Do either of you recognize these clothes?"

Both women glanced at the bag then back to Grant.

"No. Why should we?" said Suzanne Ellis.

Dianne Jones only shook her head.

Grant glanced briefly at Max then back to the women.

"My friend here seems to think they belong to one of you."

"So why should I care what the dog thinks? It's obviously wrong. I've never seen those things before."

"If I'm not mistaken," said Grant, "these look as though they're a good match for the clothes being worn by your associate when she went missing. She was seen in clothes very much like these right up until late in the evening the day you all arrived. You're sure they don't look familiar?"

I noticed a change in the two women. There was a loosening of facial muscles and a single deeper breath. Something Grant had said had caused them both to relax slightly at a time when you'd have expected them to continue to be tense.

"I really don't remember," said Suzanne Ellis.

"And you, Ms. Jones?"

"Sorry. I didn't pay any attention to what Valerie was wearing."

"Okay. Thank you. Sorry to interrupt your lunch," said Grant.

Neither of the women responded as Grant turned away. Constable Spencer called Max and the four of us left the dining room.

The outdoor dining area was deserted so we sat there and discussed what had just happened.

"I don't understand it. Max doesn't make mistakes like that – ever. He's been at this a long time and knows his job well."

"Don't worry about it," said Grant. "Whatever just happened in there I'm quite sure it was no fault of Max's. I think Max led us to the person, either Ms. Ellis or Ms. Jones, who was, at some time, wearing those clothes. They were both very surprised to be confronted that way."

"Yes, they were," I said, "but their reactions were slightly different. Suzanne Ellis was angry. Dianne Jones was frightened. They both recovered quickly and well. They're both used to dealing with high stress situations in business."

"You saw that too?"

"Yes. And I also saw that they both visibly relaxed at a point where they shouldn't have. I've no idea what that was about. I'm trying to remember what it was that you said just before that happened."

I looked through the glass doors of the dining room and saw the two women get up from the table and leave the room. I looked at Mike and nodded my head in the direction of the dining room.

"Must have lost their appetites suddenly," he said.

The constable stood up. "I think I'll take Max back home now. We'll come back again tomorrow if you like and have another go with the clothes you gave me first. It'll just confuse the issue if I start him tracking again today while he's still focussed on that stronger scent. C'mon Max."

We said our good-byes and Constable Spencer and Max left.

"Well, Mike, that didn't finish the way I thought it would but it produced some interesting results nonetheless."

"I wasn't just humouring Spencer when I said I thought Max hadn't made a mistake. Those two are not as innocent as they would have us believe. I think I'll assign one of the guys to do some more in-depth research into the executive team of Winnstar Technologies."

I wondered how I would start interjecting my information from Eddie – stuff that I probably shouldn't know and wouldn't want to have to explain. I did tell Mike about my earlier encounter with Murdock and that I'd made the decision to let Max do his thing without consultation. He agreed that, given Murdock's history with us, it was probably a good idea not to take what he said at face value. He also said he'd approach Murdock and get the number Valerie's email had come from and see if it could be traced if it was still turned on. I'd see what Eddie could come up with, too.

"I'm due in the kitchen soon but I'll give the encounter we've just had some thought through the evening. Maybe I'll remember the context of that inappropriate relaxation I saw." I rose from the table. "Oh, by the way, I'm sneaking away for forty-eight hours or so. Starting tomorrow afternoon. I'm going to the County to a winery."

"Cam going with you?"

"You too?"

"What? Just a question. Come on, RJ. Everyone knows you and Cam are an item."

Great.

Chapter 16

New Message   **Friday**   **18/07**

From : Spider

To : Flower

Spider – Really? What are you thinking? You kept the phone too, even after you finally got rid of the clothes? And the clothes in a trashcan instead of in the lake like we talked about? Come on. You are really starting to piss me off. We agreed that all the stuff was going away and we agreed that no-one would ever hear from Valerie again. You keep changing the plan and we're going to have trouble keeping a lid on this.

    Flower – Relax. I just thought it would be good to divert attention away from the island. Now that I've done that I'll get rid of the rest of the stuff.

Spider – Don't tell me to relax. You forget who's in charge of this operation. You do what I say, not whatever you feel like. What else did you keep? Not the wig? Please tell me you didn't keep the wig too.

Flower – I thought it might come in handy later. Don't get so bent about it. I'll get rid of both of them tonight or tomorrow – soon anyway.

Spider – I know there's a good place where the water comes close to the pathway just up from the beach. You can toss the rest of the stuff in the lake there and be done with it.

Flower – OK, OK. Probably tomorrow night, maybe the next.

Winnstar Technologies Messenger   **account wtim0043**

New Message   **Friday**   **18/07**

From : Spider

To : Geek

Spider – I need you to keep an eye on Flower while I'm away. She's getting out of control. Don't let her pull any more stupid stunts.

Geek – If you're going after the innkeeper, be careful. Rumours around here say he's tougher than he looks.

Spider – I can handle the innkeeper.

In the early afternoon we started the dinner prep. The dinner plan for that evening was one of the more straight-forward I could remember: spaghetti with meat sauce and baked lemon-thyme chicken.

I checked first to make sure that the chicken breasts – bone-in and skin-on - were thawed and the three ground meats for the pasta sauce were ready. Jeany and Glen were already there when I arrived and working on the salad to serve with the pasta and the potato and vegetable for the chicken.

As I browned the three meats – ground beef, chicken and mild Italian sausage meat – on the flat top, I tried to remember what was being said when the two women had suddenly relaxed a bit; not entirely, but some. Mike had been asking about the clothes that had been found in the trash, saying that the missing woman had been seen wearing an outfit that was basically identical. What next?

As I stirred the ground meats around on the flat top I finely chopped some Spanish onion, celery, some red, green and yellow peppers, mushrooms and zucchini. As the meats approached readiness I added the onions to the other side of the flat top, moving them frequently to be sure they didn't burn.

I thought back to my various conversations with staff; people who'd seen Valerie Owens that afternoon. They had all described the clothing in basically the same way, from late afternoon to late evening. If all those people had seen her in that outfit, why not these two? They'd been around the Inn at the same time. They hadn't flatly denied seeing her but said they couldn't remember or had paid no attention. Maybe. It might not be a bad idea to run that by Cam and get her perspective.

As the onions softened I added the celery to them and continued mixing.

"Has the garlic butter been made yet?" I asked no-one in particular.

"Did that as soon as I got in," said Glen.

I nodded in response and added the peppers to the mix.

While the peppers softened I grated garlic and chopped fresh herbs. While I had been distracted with my musings about missing women, Glen had opened a couple of large cans of tomato sauce and one of San Marzano tomatoes. I added grated garlic, the chopped mushroom and zucchini and a little salt and pepper to the vegetable mix on the flat top and pushed the browned meats to it.

The more I thought about it the better I liked the idea of getting Cam's opinion about the case, or cases. Maybe I'd call her tonight. If she wasn't too busy getting ready to travel we could spend a few minutes kicking things around.

The tomatoes and sauce went into a large stock pot. At the last moment I tossed the fresh parsley, basil, oregano and rosemary into the mixture on the flat top, tossed it around a bit then put the whole works into the pot with the sauce. Done for now. With about three hours of gentle heat and some judicious stirring the sauce would develop into something good. I dropped the lid onto the pot and went on to the next job.

So. What to do with three or four hours of available prep time with only one hour of prep to do?

"Glen. I'm going to head out for a short while. You have all the necessary instructions for the rest of the prep?"

"Right here, RJ," he said, indicating a small sheaf of paper sticking out from his shirt pocket. "I made notes from Bud's instructions. I'll have everything ready in lots of time. Jeany's here too, if I need help."

"Good. I'll be back in lots of time for the dinner service."

I was going to go to my suite and go over my notes about the missing woman but I didn't get there. Michelle, who'd been in the dining room setting up for the evening service, intercepted me as I was leaving the kitchen.

"RJ. There's a guy in the lounge who's behaving oddly."

"What kind of 'oddly', Michelle?"

"He's sitting at one of the small tables but instead of looking out from the wall seat as most people do, he's in the outside chair facing toward the wall. He's talking to himself – like he's rehearsing something."

"Did you hear any of what he was saying?"

"The one line I heard was something like 'and if I say she's been missing a week they'll ask why I didn't say something earlier and then what will I say?' Something like that anyway."

"Okay, I have a few minutes so I'll go and talk to Sammi and see if she knows anything. Thanks, Michelle."

I went around the corner into the lounge and passed the man in question as I went to Sammi who was in the far corner near the fireplace. I had seen him here before.

"Hello, Sammi. How are you?"

"I'm good, RJ. You?"

"Fine, thanks. Michelle just told me that there might be a problem with that fellow over there, facing the wall. What do you think?"

"I would say he definitely has some kind of problem, for sure. This is the third time he's been here in the past few days. Tomas and Gail refused to serve him both times because he was showing obvious signs.

"Today he ordered a drink – tequila – straight – but he hasn't touched it. He didn't seem drunk when he first came in or I wouldn't have served him. He waved at me and ordered as he was walking to the table. Now he just sits there talking to himself about a missing woman and what to do about her and about maybe calling the police. I was starting to wonder if this has anything to do with the woman you found floating in the water. Not that you found her exactly but, you know what I mean."

"Yes. Well, maybe I'd better go over and have a word."

I couldn't tell what he was saying as I approached. He sat, still facing the wall, head bowed, looking at his hands which were clasped before him on the table. As I sat in the chair against the wall opposite him he raised his eyes. He was fortyish, blonde and, I would guess, usually clean shaven, though not today. Maybe not this week even. His hair and clothes were a mess and his eyes bloodshot. There was a network of red lines radiating across his face and his nose was almost purple. He was way too young to look that bad.

"Are you the poleesh?" His speech was slurred.

"No. I'm not. Do you need the police?"

"Um, no. But ... wellmaybeIshould ... no, not now ... I don't think so ... but ... no." "Yes."

"'Yes' you would like to talk to the police?"

"I didn't really mean to hit her. Well I did, actually. I didn't hit her hard. Then she went swimming." There he stopped but only briefly.

"I picked up a newshpaper in Merrickville and read 'bout how you foun' a woman floating in the water. It was here? Gilmore Island?"

"Yes, this is Gilmore Island and yes, we did find a woman's body floating in the water here. That was several days ago."

"So she's here? She's okay? You foun' her floating. She's a good shwimmer ... floats good too." And after a brief pause, "I don't know what I'll do 'f I can't fin' 'er. We have t' get home."

We were interrupted by Geoff, one of the boathouse staff, running around the corner from the front desk. He skidded to a halt when he saw I was with a guest. I waved him over.

"Problem?" Now, why would I think that?

He moved in close and spoke quietly in my ear.

"Someone ran a thirty-two foot Sea Ray into an open slip a few minutes ago and just left it there – didn't tie it up – nothing. It was banging around between the two runs of dock and got the attention of a guest, who told me. I went and secured it. I think maybe I've seen it here a couple of times before. There doesn't seem to be anyone on board right now and there isn't any damage that I can see but there's what could be blood, dried up. It's on the floor of the aft deck and on the inside of the gunwale, under cover of the canvas top. Thought you should know."

"Yes. Thanks."

"*Lady G.*" This from my table mate.

"Pardon me?"

"*Lady G.*"

"Is that your boat?"

Geoff spoke up. "That's the name painted on the transom. '*Lady G'.*"

"Okay. Thanks again. You can go. I'll look after this. Oh, wait. On your way out stop at the desk and have whoever's there call my friend Mike. You know who I mean, right? Have them tell him what you told me. He'll get the idea. If not Mike himself – whoever answers. "

"Got it, RJ. Have fun."

I returned my attention to … whoever he was.

"So the *Lady G* is your boat. What's your name?"

"She just wou'n't stop. I tole her and tole her but she wou'n't stop."

"Stop what?"

"I cou'n't stand it 'ny longer. I cou'n't get away far enough not to hear."

"What was she doing that you didn't like?"

"She's a good shwimmer."

"Say again?" His speech was getting harder and harder to understand.

"We b'n t'gether ten years. Fin'lly cracked. No more."

"When did she go swimming? Where?"

At this point he looked toward the archway that was the end of the lounge and the start of the main lobby. While his attention was elsewhere I reached over and moved his glass of tequila a little further away from him. Of course, when he turned again, he noticed – reached to take it back. Before he could get there I put my hand over the glass and pulled it closer to me.

"I don't think so. Seems like you've had enough already."

"Who're you t' say what's 'nough? C'n *never* have enough tequila. There a liquor shtore here? My case 'zalmosht empty."

"No. And even if there was they wouldn't sell you any, any more than I will, in your current condition."

"C'mon, man. Just lemme have that one 'n' I'll get go'n."

"You haven't told me your name yet."

"Gimme my drink."

"No. Sorry but it's against the law for me to serve alcohol to anyone who already looks as though they've had … enough."

"Fine. I'll go back t' the boat 'n' have one. Then I'll go somewhere more frien'ly."

He hoisted himself up from the low chair and staggered off in the direction of the lobby.

"Bunch of unfrien'ly people 'round here anyway."

As soon as he was gone I got up and followed. As I was rounding the corner I saw two of the Winnstar group, Donaldson and Ellis, near the reception desk. When they saw me, they turned casually and left.

I heard the boater ask the receptionist if she knew where his boat was. She said she didn't. He continued on his unsteady way out the door.

As I passed the desk I called out to Gwen.

"I'm going after that guy. I'm not sure what I'll do when I catch up with him but I can't let him take his boat out."

"Relax, RJ. No need to rush off."

"Pardon?"

"He's not going anywhere – not in his boat anyway."

"Explain, please."

Gwen held up a key ring with several keys and a huge, bright orange floating fob.

"Geoff took these from the boat when he tied it up – didn't want it to get stolen or something."

"And you didn't see any reason to tell our drunken friend that you had his keys when he asked if you knew where his boat was?"

"Of course not, RJ. It didn't seem like a good idea, and anyway, he didn't ask about the keys."

"Damn right. Good work. I'm going to follow him anyway, just to make sure he doesn't fall in the lake or something."

"See you later, RJ."

Geoff was waiting for me when I arrived at the dock.

"You can hear him banging around in there looking for his boat keys. The cursing is incredible. Every now and then he gets quiet - maybe sucking back some more tequila."

"That was a very good idea you had about taking the keys to the Inn. You may have prevented something bad happening. Well done."

"Thanks, RJ. Oh, look there. The police boat's coming. That was fast."

"I think these guys must have still been close after dropping Sergeant Grant at the Westport dock. Lot of boats out there today so they're probably doing random safety checks. They may be thinking of opening an office here, they come so often. Maybe we should think about giving them a corner of the boathouse."

That drew a smile from Geoff.

"I should stay and meet the police but I have to get back to the kitchen – I'm cooking tonight and I have stuff to do. Wait here, please and, as soon as the boat ties up, point our friend out to the officers and then ask one of them to come inside and I'll brief him on what I think this guy's been up to. He'll make his own decisions about what to do."

Chapter 17

A short time later, as I was stripping fresh thyme leaves for tonight's chicken, Marine Constable Brooks came into the kitchen.

"Hello, Mr. Harrison. I'm told you have some information about a Mr. Phillip Matthews who owns a boat that found its way to your dock."

I related all I knew about Mr. Matthews based solely upon what he had said during our brief meeting in the Gilmore lounge. Brooks took notes.

"Thanks, Mr. Harrison. That clears up a few details that were being either omitted deliberately from his account of things or distorted by the alcoholic haze."

"So, how did you make out with our inebriated boater?"

"Let's say he won't be doing any boating, drunk or otherwise, for a while. He was still tearing the place apart, looking for his missing keys, when we arrived. We called out to him as we approached and identified ourselves. We don't generally board boats that are tied up unless there's some really good reason. He came out onto the aft deck and when he saw we were police he said he was glad we were there and would we help him search for his… keys. His language was quite colourful.

"Having been invited to look around we did so and found an empty case of twelve one litre bottles of tequila and another case with only one left and there were two bottles open that he was working on as he searched.

"We also found the blood on the aft deck that your guy reported. There was also what looked like dried blood up the inside of the gunwale and on the bottom of a small fire extinguisher that was hanging nearby. However it got there, no-one seems to have made any effort to clean it up. We called the forensics guys and they'll be here soon to go over the whole boat."

"Nice of him to invite you aboard."

"Yup. And because of that we got the whole enchilada."

"Meaning?"

"We found his spare set of keys. He'd been looking for a ring with a big bright orange fob. The spare keys were on a ring with a big bright lime green fob. They were hanging on a hook in plain sight in the galley but he was so far gone that he didn't recognize them for what they were. We made sure they were for the boat – fired it up. He had access to the keys so that put him in care and control of the vehicle. Since he was exhibiting behaviour that suggested he might be intoxicated we had the right to get him to blow. And we did."

"And dare I ask what the number was?"

"Point two zero two," said Brooks.

"What? How is he still alive?"

"No idea, but I'd guess he wouldn't have been for much longer if he continued like that. Not that he's going to get the opportunity."

"How so?"

"We felt we had sufficient grounds to detain him on suspicion of the murder of his wife, whose picture we found on board. It is a very good match for the autopsy photo of the body found off your shore. Now that we have a name, and a picture, the official ID should be easy enough. He told you that he hit her but he didn't say he'd done it with the blunt end of a fire extinguisher. He still contends that she dived overboard after he hit her but judging by the amount of blood on the deck and up the gunwale she didn't do any diving. I'm guessing the coroner will confirm that. She lay there on the deck for some time then was lifted up and put over the side."

I could think of nothing to say to that.

"Oh, and I don't suppose you will have heard yet, from Sergeant Grant, the latest about the woman in the water. The tox results on the victim show that she was in the same condition as this guy is – point one six-four. Hopefully the guy will come clean when he's confronted with all the evidence, if he can remember anything with all that tequila in him."

Again I was speechless.

"I'd better get going," said Brooks. "We need to get Mr. Matthews to Smiths Falls for processing. Thanks for your help, Mr. Harrison. No doubt you'll be hearing from Sergeant Grant about all this in due course. We'll get the boat moved as soon as the science guys are done with what they need to do here. Oh, I almost forgot to tell you. The reason why Matthews clobbered his wife? She wouldn't stop whistling. He says it went on and on and the more tequila she had, the more she whistled. He finally cracked."

With that Brooks left the kitchen. I stood staring at my pile of thyme leaves.

Glen and Jeany had finished up almost everything. I began to assemble the lemon-thyme chicken while Glen readied the garlic toast.

Despite the feeling that it should never have happened I was glad to know that that one mystery was resolved.

––––––––––––

Each skin-on bone-in chicken breast was seasoned with a little salt and pepper and set aside, a few at a time. It's never a good idea to salt meat or fish or poultry too far ahead because it draws out moisture. It can make the meat dry inside and wet outside which can prevent browning. A little ahead is okay.

It was good to know that one of our current mysteries was likely solved, a whole week after it had started. I hadn't caught up with Smythe as I'd planned to today. Hopefully soon.

Since these chicken breasts were too thick to cook entirely to order, a couple at a time were started as the dinner hour approached. Each was browned on both sides in a pan with olive oil then placed on a rack over a sheet pan, a good quantity of lemon zest and some fresh thyme leaves placed on top and a small squeeze of fresh lemon juice was added last. The rack went in the oven to finish.

I worked away at the chicken and Glen started to precook some pasta. Trays of thick sliced, garlic-buttered Italian bread were ready to go.

The dinner service went smoothly and we wrapped up at a decent hour. Glen and Jeany and the dining room and clean-up crews went off to the last shuttle and I was on my way upstairs when my cell phone rang.

It was Carole.

"RJ. I just got a call from Glen. He was leaving with the rest of the evening group when he saw Brent, you know, from Smythe's boat. He was hiding behind a tree at the edge of the path. Glen didn't know who it was at first. After the group passed the person started to move toward the Inn. When he did he came under one of the pathway lights and Glen was able to identify him. He says he's sure it was Brent."

"Okay, Carole. You keep an eye on the main door and let me know if he comes inside that way. I'll have a look around outside."

I went out the main door and along the deck to the back of the Inn. Brent was not there. It was more than possible that he knew he'd been spotted and had returned to Smythe's boat. For some reason I didn't think that was the case. I wondered what tonight's target might be. As I stood trying to decide where he might have gone I thought I heard a sound emanating from the north and west of me. The only thing in that direction was the derelict stables. It was a ways off and through some trees so whatever I'd heard must have been quite loud.

I mentally flipped a coin and went not up the path along the west side of the island but through the centre, the harder way but more direct. It was not a long walk and I went as quietly as I could over the rough ground.

Soon I came to the remnants of the split-rail fence which had at one time formed the perimeter of the corral. Twenty metres or so inside that was what was left of the stable, three of its four walls were damaged but still standing; the fourth had long since fallen in, along with a large portion of the roof.

The sound of pieces of wood being dragged around and banged against one another rose from inside the structure. I stepped over a downed piece of split-rail and continued on.

I peered around the corner of one of the standing walls and was astounded at what I saw.

Using a rough scaffold of boards, someone had been rebuilding a portion of the overhead structure of the stable.

Using existing roof joists, some of which were still in place on one end, someone was lifting them up and bracing them with other pieces of wood at the other end. A couple of upright posts with a flat board on top supported the joists. Whoever it was did not appear to be using a hammer or even glue to keep the planks in position. It could not possibly stay standing up for long. I looked at the amount of work that had been done, the number of unstable uprights and cross beams and joists and realized that it was probably not intended to stay standing. It looked very much like it was being set up to collapse on the first person who ventured in and touched anything. The games had taken a sharp turn; from not much more than troublesome to potentially deadly.

I still had not seen whoever was moving the boards into position, but was assuming it must be Brent. I heard a new noise from behind a wall, outside the building. Carefully I picked my way across the littered floor in the direction of the small door in the far wall.

Without warning a long thin pole was pushed through the opening of a long broken window. It connected firmly with one of the uprights nearest the wall and pushed it loose. The structure began to topple with me inside. I turned and ran as fast as I could over the wood-strewn floor.

The upright support post in the centre held in place just long enough. It toppled, bringing with it the last of the roof joists, crashing against the inside of the wall just as I tumbled headlong through the gap. Somehow I had escaped serious injury. I had a few new scrapes and bruises to show from my adventure but that was all.

I got up out of the dirt and leaves and stumbled around the outside of the building to see if anyone was still there. No-one. Whoever it was had gone and, I suspected, would not return. I'd be watching now and they would know that. But how had they known I would be there? Was the Brent "sighting" deliberately obvious, meant to draw me out? Probably not.

I went cautiously back inside and made sure there was nothing more that could cause injury to one of my guests who might happen by.

Satisfied that it was safe for now, I made a mental note to have the office print up some signs asking guests to avoid the stable.

As I returned to the Inn I knew that I was no nearer to pinning anything on Brent. He'd been seen near the Inn but I hadn't seen him at the stables.

I wondered if there was any point in reporting the incident immediately and decided against it. It would take hours to get police here and I wasn't sure there would be much they could do anyway.

Chapter 18

<u>New Message</u>   **Friday**   **18/07**

From : Geek

To : Hotrod

Geek – Picked up a communication from inside the Inn – someone spreading gossip about the boss. Harrison is going to a winery for a couple of days starting today – taking the girlfriend. Maybe something you can use.

     Hotrod – Definitely.

<u>New Message</u>   **Friday**   **18/07**

From : Hotrod

To : Spider

Hotrod – Geek somehow intercepted a text or something from someone working at the Inn. Says Harrison is taking a road trip. Winery tour.

Spider – How can we make use of that?

Hotrod – We follow and if the opportunity presents itself we take steps to see that he doesn't come back.

Spider – When?

Hotrod – Leaving this afternoon says Geek. I've ordered a vehicle brought from Smiths Falls. Cost a bundle to get it brought out here but necessary. Pack for a couple of days.

Spider – I'll be ready.

Another small storm front had passed in the night, this time dropping some rain and leaving a cool freshness to the air in the morning. There was the indication, if not the promise, of a sunny but somewhat cooler day ahead.

Kim had found coverage for me for the time I'd be gone and I didn't have to go to the kitchen this morning or on Sunday afternoon. I finished off the last of my laundry and got my packing done, then I set about making some notes to email to Mike.

Mike Grant was not expected to be around today. He was working at the detachment in Smiths Falls. There, he and others were slowly and steadily accumulating bits of information about Valerie Owens and the Winnstar gang. With the assistance of the Winnipeg Police Department and the RCMP, the file was growing.

I, however, did not have access to that file and would not. The next time I saw Mike he would bring me up to date and I would try to slip in some of the info I'd received from Eddie.

As much as I wanted to get away for a couple of days with Cam, I was nervous about leaving with so many things going on. Mike would handle whatever came along relative to the Winnstar bunch. I would finish putting together my notes on that so he'd have everything I had; facts and suspicions.

I still hadn't talked to him about the fires and my suspicions about them, the boat sabotage and now the incident at the stables. That was where my biggest concern was – the safety of my guests. I'd leave that in my notes as well, and maybe he'd even send someone to keep an eye on the Inn while I was gone. He'd be pissed that I hadn't told him sooner about what I thought Smythe was up to. I should have. He was the police after all. Oh well. I'd email him the notes and we'd discuss the fires and whatnot when I got back.

I was almost finished packing when the phone rang.

"Hi, Kim. What's up?"

"Hi, RJ. Sorry to interrupt your preparations but I thought you'd want to hear about this. One of the housekeeping staff came to me a few minutes ago and told me about something she saw in one of the suites when she was cleaning. There was a wig sticking partly out of a drawer, just a couple of inches. She remembered having heard that we all were interested in any information we could get in order to help the police find the missing woman, and she recognized an anomaly, so to speak."

"What anomaly was that?"

"She knew who's suite she was cleaning and knew what the woman looked like. She also knew that the missing woman, the one we were looking for was the one with the short dark hair. The wig was dark and was in the room of one of the other women, one who has short blonde hair. She got to wondering why and thought she should say something."

"That's a pretty good observation on her part and it sounds suspicious. It may mean nothing at all but, then again, it could have some significance. Did she touch the thing?"

"She says not. She left it hanging partly out of the drawer."

"Good. The suite she was in? Was it Donaldson and Jones?"

"Yes. Should I call Sergeant Grant? He's not coming here today, right?"

"Right. Yes. Make the call. I'm sure that even if he can't make the trip himself today he will want to send someone as soon as possible. He might need a warrant before he can do anything if the guests aren't feeling cooperative, and that can take time. Who is it anyway? Our staff person."

"Gloria Smith."

"Okay. Thank Gloria for me and tell her that Mike or one of his people will surely want to hear the story from her. Ask her not to talk about this to anyone else, please. And find out her schedule before you call Mike. Still no word on your sister, I take it."

"No, nothing. Mike has been gradually broadening the search, though I'm not sure what all that entails. So far no luck."

I had nothing helpful to say to that.

"You have my cell number so if anything happens you can reach me. Anything. Please keep an eye on the comings and goings of the Winnstar bunch and call me if they do anything weird. I'll be gone shortly and will be back Sunday afternoon. But you know that. I've sent Mike an email about the Winnstar thing and about the fires and stuff. Please make sure to talk to Mike if anything new comes up."

"Okay, RJ. Enjoy your time away."

I hung up the phone and closed my bag. I made sure I had all I needed then picked up the bag and a garment bag and headed for the door. I hadn't been entirely sure I wanted to go away but there was no way I could cancel on Cam now. I put the anxieties aside, one of which was Kim and the gun. Again this would have to wait.

Now I was feeling a little more comfortable about leaving now that Mike would have all my info and I was definitely looking forward to my couple of days away with Cam.

As I passed through the lobby on my way out I saw Jason Murdock sitting in one of the guest chairs in the corner turret alcove. He was sitting rigid with his head down and his hands on the arms of the chair. I went over to him.

"Mr. Murdock. Do you mind if I ask you a question?"

He didn't speak but looked up at me.

"Mr. Murdock, does Valerie Owens have a birthmark on the back of her right leg – an oval, just above the knee?"

He continued to stare at me, seemingly without either seeing or hearing me, deep in thought. I was about to go when he spoke.

"No. No birthmarks." He thought a moment then asked, "Why did you ask me that?"

"Just wondering."

I turned and left. I felt bad about leaving him there without having given him a proper explanation but I had to get going. I promised myself I'd add that to the list of things to tell Mike, then I tried to put the problems away for a while.

I'd come to this place to try to have a normal life and I needed to focus on that. Part of growing into that normal life was this weekend which meant, to begin with, being on time for a lady I hoped would be important to my future.

Chapter 19

I picked Cam up at the gallery as planned and we had a pleasant drive to the County. The fields we passed on the way had a parched look in a lot of places. The relentless heat of the past week had taken a toll. Some grain crops had ripened quickly and would have to be taken off soon or be lost. The corn season would have been shortened considerably without the benefit of last night's rain. Hopefully there would be more to come, but not too much.

When I made the turn at Hwy. 15, I remembered something.

"Cam, have you ever been to the Old Stone Mill at Delta? It's just a few minutes down Hwy. 42 there."

"Sure. I've been there a couple of times."

"Well, I just discovered it a few weeks ago. It's quite a place. Still grinding wheat and selling the flour in their gift shop. It's a National Historic Site, over two hundred years old. I'm going to get some of their brochures to put at the Inn."

"I was there last year in the spring and got some local maple syrup and again in October for the fall fair. I bought a lot more baked goods than I should have," said Cam.

"I bought some of their stone ground flour and got their bread recipe. I'm going to try my hand at bread-making again."

"Good idea," said Cam.

As we drove the conversation gradually turned to the investigations I'd become involved in. Cam had been on the outside of things when I'd become involved with Sergeant Grant and the body in the attic earlier in the year. Now we were spending a lot more time together and I wanted to get her impressions of what was going on with the missing woman from Winnipeg and the ongoing attacks on the Inn.

"I'd been inclined, when you first told me the story, to think that the police dog was wrong when he picked out the two women he did. But I've been thinking about it and now I'm not so sure," she said.

"How so?"

"The clothes that were found were exactly like those seen on the missing woman by several staff and by you. So the logical conclusion is that they belonged to Valerie Owens. But the dog disagrees. As a woman I would go out of my way to *not* have the same outfits that other members of my group had, so again the logical conclusion is that they belonged to Valerie. But the dog disagrees.

"I think the dog was right. I don't have any idea why it would be but, I now think that at least one and maybe both of the other women had an identical outfit to the one Valerie was last seen wearing."

I had to think about that. These were not perspectives I was familiar with.

"So if they had such outfits, why? Presumably one of these women at least was actually wearing the clothes or Max would not have behaved as he did. Why wear the same clothes?"

"To make people think that Valerie was still there when she wasn't?" said Cam.

"But, again, why?" I asked.

"Maybe Valerie did leave the island. I know she wasn't positively seen going but it's not impossible. Maybe she … needed a vacation … eloped with some rich old guy … I don't know. Maybe the others are covering for her while she gets away."

"A little far-fetched maybe, but, as you say, not impossible," I said.

"Here's one that's even more far-fetched," said Cam. "Maybe that weird husband, or whatever he is, did her in and they're covering up for him."

That idea got my attention.

"Maybe. Murdock is definitely an enigma. Supposedly a hot shot business type, with all that implies, but at the moment he seems as though he'd be unable to work up brain power to account for his behaviour or the energy to kill someone." Cam had no immediate response to that, so I continued.

"She's disappeared too completely. There's no proof that she left the island, despite some possible sightings around the dock area and that message she is supposed to have sent. But if she didn't leave, where is she?"

"And if she left she'd probably have taken at least some of her stuff with her," added Cam.

"I'm not convinced that we have the details correct but I think you're right that she's dead. Maybe he did it or maybe something else is going on that we don't know about yet. What if he's been planning to get rid of her, finally did so and is working on building an insanity defence with all this weird behaviour?"

I drove in silence for a few minutes then carried on.

"And here's another thing: is it my imagination or do all three of the women from Winnstar look similar? I don't mean they'd be taken for triplets but height, weight, colouring – all similar – all but hair."

"I never saw Valerie Owens or the others either, so I couldn't say," said Cam.

We put aside the discussion of the women of Winnstar and watched the scenery as we drove through Prince Edward County toward the winery.

We arrived at the Hillsborough Winery in good time and had a look around before heading to Sandstone, our Bed and Breakfast. It was a nice old place: two levels and lots of green around it, on the fringe of Wellington, a community of about 1700 people in Prince Edward County, just west of Picton.

Sandstone was on a side street that ran down to the lake. Our suite looked out over a garden and then the water with a view of a large sandy shoreline off to the east.

We checked in and unpacked what little we'd brought for this short stay. We didn't have a lot of time but wanted to see some of Wellington while we were here so went for a walk around the town.

We went up to Main Street and turned east, looking in shop windows as we went. After making a quick stop at Foodland for some snacks for later, we crossed at Wharf and spent a while browsing around the Sidestreet Gallery.

We went back toward the B&B walking on the north side of Main and stopped at The Tall Poppy for coffee and one of their famous scones.

Part of the event at the winery was a dinner both evenings so Cam and I returned to Sandstone with lots of time to change and get ready for dinner. We had so much time, in fact, that we had to find something to do.

"Be a shame to waste an hour just sitting here," said Cam.

"Would. Maybe we should test out the bed and see if it's comfortable enough for sleeping later. What do you think?"

"Fine idea."

So we did.

Later we headed for the shower, Cam first, then me; less chance of getting distracted that way. When I came out of the bathroom Cam had the TV on and was watching an old movie – *The Prisoner of Zenda* from 1932. It caught my attention and I watched for a few minutes. Always liked Ronald Coleman.

We dressed and went back to the winery. It wasn't far. We took a taxi, just in case either or both of us enjoyed too much wine.

Hillsborough was indeed set up to be an event facility as well as a winery. The banquet room was not large, perhaps space enough for 50-60 diners, fewer than that, if there was to be dancing at the event, but it was very nicely decorated.

Today the dance floor was set aside as a reception area for the event, with a bar and hors d'oeuvres table. We registered for the event and went over to collect a glass of wine.

A few moments later, as Cam and I toured the room, chatting with some of the other guests, I happened to look in the direction of the door and saw a couple I recognized coming in. I turned away from them and spoke quietly to Cam.

"If you look over my shoulder you'll see a couple just signing in. They're part of the Winnstar Technologies group. He's Richard Washburn, the COO and she's Suzanne Ellis, the President."

Cam watched a moment. "They look a little harried, as though they've been rushing to get here. I wonder if that would be because they got lost finding the place or if it was a spur-of-the-moment decision to come here? No doubt there could be other possibilities, too."

"Maybe they were doing what we were doing and lost track of time."

"Maybe."

Cam continued to peer over my shoulder. "They're definitely looking for someone. They're standing together but not facing one another and are scanning the crowd. I'd bet they're looking for you, RJ. Taking any bets?"

"I know better than to bet against you, Cam." I thought a moment and made a decision. "I want to be in control of the situation when I let them see me. I want to see their reactions when I pop up in front of them if I can manage that. I used to be pretty good at reading those sorts of unguarded reactions."

"In your former life?"

"Yes."

"Which one?"

"Not now, please. For now, let's see if we can work our way over to that side door and maybe get around the outside and come at them from behind."

Cam raised one eyebrow at me but said nothing.

Keeping my back to them, I walked toward the door to the patio and Cam fell in behind me. We found a sidewalk which eventually led around the building to the wide open main door. When we arrived, Cam walked across the entrance and looked in.

She stopped and turned at the far side of the door. "Now would be a good time."

Washburn and Ellis were both still where they had been, more or less, but each now had a glass of wine, and Washburn had a small paper plate with food on it. Both had their backs to the door.

We approached quickly and I signalled Cam to go to one side as I went to the other and we arrived abruptly in front of the pair.

"Well, Mr. Washburn, Ms. Ellis, what a coincidence running into you two here."

Washburn dropped his plate of food and looked quite taken aback. Suzanne Ellis didn't flinch but some of the other guests looked, then looked away.

I extended my hand and they both took it in turn, then I introduced Cam. Washburn's initial shock wore off quickly and he smiled and we three – Washburn, Cam and I - exchanged pleasantries. Ellis remained mostly silent, speaking only when spoken to. During those couple of minutes, every time I had occasion to look at her she was already looking at me, her dark eyes flat and hard.

A waiter came and cleaned up the spilled food and the four of us walked away toward the bar for another sample of the local wine.

We spent only a short time together, during which we asked how they had come to be at Gilmore Island, here at this event, where they were staying in the County – things like that. We received a lot of evasive talk, subject-changing and such and came away knowing little more than when we started. We parted company not long after and by the time the barbecue dinner was ready to be served they were nowhere to be seen.

Over our plates of prime rib and baked potatoes, corn on the cob and salad, Cam and I quietly discussed our encounter.

"I suppose you noticed that neither of them actually gave us a straight answer to any of our questions?" asked Cam.

"Oh yes. And they were very good at the evasion. It would be hardly noticeable if you weren't looking for it, I suppose. They just kept on talking about anything and everything until you couldn't really remember whether or not they'd responded to what you'd asked."

"I'm guessing they get lots of practice with their board of directors and investors and anyone else associated with their company," said Cam.

"Yes. Makes me wonder about how much of that went on during the police interviews. Not that I thought they had anything to do with the woman we found floating in the lake. The timing was wrong for that. I don't really know where I'm going with this but I just feel like something's not right with them."

"One thing's absolutely certain, RJ," said Cam. "Suzanne Ellis doesn't like you."

"She did give that impression didn't she?"

We continued to discuss the Winnstar execs through the rest of dinner and dessert and through the accompanying rounds of wine. After dinner we mingled, meeting the winery owners, some local business types and local residents. I had my first meeting regarding a limited association between the winery and my Inn. The evening wrapped up late and we caught our taxi back to Sandstone.

Late though it was, we did not sleep but rather talked and made love until the wee hours.

At nine o'clock in the morning we were just barely ready when the taxi returned for us, taking us to a day-long tour of the winery, with lunch and specially selected wines and dinner, also with wine and an evening's entertainment with yet more wine. At no point that day or evening did we see the couple from Winnstar.

During that day Cam and I had another meeting with the owners of the Hillsborough Winery. They had a remarkably complete selection of wines and the price was right. We finalized our deal that day.

What with the long day in the heat and the food and wine, by the time we returned to the B&B we were both too tired to get up to much. We fell into bed and were instantly asleep, comfortably in each other's arms.

Chapter 20

We woke late and packed slowly, then started on our way back to Westport.

We retraced our route along the 401 and up 15 toward Smiths Falls, stopping from time to time to look at scenery or to investigate a building Cam thought might house some antiques or artworks. The scenery up that highway is lovely and we were talking and looking until suddenly, as we were reaching the end of a long downhill run, the front right quadrant of the Lexus collapsed, sending us screeching, amid a shower of sparks, toward the gravel shoulder and the nearby rock-cut.

As we left the asphalt the broken undercarriage dug deeply into the soft, dry gravel. The car twisted, tipped, threatened to turn over but somehow did not. We came to rest, still upright, with Cam's door wedged against the granite rock face.

By the time I'd made certain Cam had not been injured by the airbag deployment someone was banging on my side window. He'd called 911 and wanted to know if we were okay. I said we were and he opened my door. I was pretty shaky and had a hard time getting out of the seatbelt. The fellow passed me off to someone else who'd stopped to help and went to work getting Cam out of the car.

I half sat and half leaned on the hood of a small car with Cam beside me, took out my cell and called Mike Grant. He answered right away and I told him what had happened. He said he'd get there as soon as possible but in the mean time to wait for the police and paramedics and do whatever they said: go to the hospital if it was thought necessary, whatever.

Several vehicles were stopped on both sides of the road by the time the police arrived. Traffic was moving, albeit slowly, past the scene when the paramedics got there soon after. They checked us both out and pronounced us both very lucky. A few bumps and bruises and minor scratches were the worst of our injuries. The medics said they'd take us to a hospital if we wanted to go but they didn't think it was necessary. They warned us that we'd probably be sore the next day where the airbags had hit us.

I was sitting on the back of the emergency vehicle having a bandage applied to a little cut on my forehead when I recognized the passenger in a car that was rolling slowly by. Suzanne Ellis. She didn't look happy. By the time I could react it was too late. The car accelerated as the congestion cleared and was soon out of sight. What had seemed a few minutes ago to be a freak accident now took on a whole new look.

Although I didn't voice my thoughts to Cam, I began to be firmly of the opinion that I was being targeted by the group from Winnstar. It sounded paranoid, even to me and I sure didn't want to have anyone else know what I felt. Maybe there was an element of déjà vu. It seemed as though a lot of people were intent on doing me harm, as one had a couple of months ago. I didn't know who had done what exactly, but I was quite sure that someone from the Winnstar group was responsible for the disappearance of Valerie Owens and that my investigation, or my involvement in the police investigation, was the reason that I'd been pushed into the lake and that my car had just been sabotaged. The other problems I'd had at the Inn, I'd been attributing to Smythe. Maybe I needed to rethink those incidents too and see if there was any way any of them could have been caused by someone from the Winnstar group. And I was going to have to force a meeting with Smythe. I needed to get a better feel for his level of involvement with the incidents of sabotage and with the Winnstar execs that he seemed so chummy with.

———————

We waited in the back of the police cruiser for a while after the emergency responders and the tow truck had gone. I'd told the officer about my call to Sergeant Grant and he volunteered to sit tight for a while.

When Mike arrived he spent a few minutes with the other officer and then moved us into his unmarked car.

"I can't leave you alone at all without you getting into trouble, can I, RJ? You okay, Cam?"

"I'm fine, thanks. More or less."

I wasted no time telling Mike about Washburn and Ellis, their mysterious arrival and departure from the winery, and the all too coincidental car wreck, though I didn't get too carried away about my suspicions. Mike called ahead and had the tow truck diverted to the police impound yard at Smiths Falls rather than the Lexus dealer in Ottawa, just in case.

After that we were a very quiet group for the rest of the ride back to Westport. I offered to have Cam come to the Inn with me but she declined. I didn't press. We said our goodbyes at her place and Mike took me the rest of the way to the Westport dock where the courtesy boat was waiting for me.

"I'll be out to the island tomorrow but not too early. Get a good rest and we'll go after this again."

"Thanks, Mike. Why don't you meet me for breakfast if you don't have anything else happening? Nine o'clock?"

"Sounds good. Oh, one other thing. I got your email about the Winnstar group. Thanks for that. There was also stuff about the problems you've been having – fires – sabotage. I appreciate that you think I'm busy – and I am – but I'd rather hear about things like that as they happen, not days later. Don't keep things like that to yourself."

"Right."

"We'll add Smythe and company to our discussion tomorrow."

"Good. See you in the morning."

I took my bags to the boat and got in the back. I think I could easily have gone to sleep there but for the growing pain in my ribs where the seatbelt and airbag had hit me. I hoped Cam was not having too bad a time.

After the ordeal of getting back to Westport and then to the island after the car crash I was wiped and ready for a long sleep. We'd managed to kill most of the day getting back from the County, and it was now early evening. I checked in at the desk to be sure there wasn't anything pressing that I needed to deal with right away then I started toward the stairs.

On the way there I realized I was hungry – I didn't remember eating since breakfast. I went back to the desk and dropped off my luggage then went to the dining room. It was not full and I was able to get a table right away.

Dinner was a subdued affair and I'm not sure now what I ate. I took my time over it, dulling the pain in my chest with a couple of glasses of wine.

Finally I felt as though I'd better head up or risk falling asleep at the table. It was not very late but had grown dark while I was having dinner. I retrieved my luggage from the desk and started up the stairs.

I'd just passed the first landing and was continuing up when I heard footsteps passing behind me on the landing. I stopped and turned my head just in time to see Dianne Jones disappear down the stairs. Suddenly I was wide awake again. No sleep yet.

I waited a moment then followed. I made it to the bottom of the stairs just in time to see her go out by the main door and turn along the deck toward the back of the Inn. I returned my suitcase to the desk and headed to the darkened dining room and stood at the French doors waiting for Dianne to pass. She came to the corner of the dining room deck and then went down the steps and along the path in the direction of the beach. She was hurrying and her large purse, slung over one shoulder, bounced against her hip with each step.

I waited a few seconds, then followed as quietly as I could, keeping to the centre of the path where the loose stone chips between the flagstones had been well packed. The night was cooling and a slight breeze rustled leaves overhead. A loon called in the distance.

The path was curved and I kept losing sight of her even though she was not far ahead. I slowed each time I came in sight of my quarry and wondered how far she would go and if I could remain hidden among the deepening shadows along the pathway. She never looked back, apparently giving no thought to the possibility of being followed.

I didn't have to go very far. There is a spot about fifty metres along from where I'd taken my splash earlier in the week, where the trees part briefly, allowing an unobstructed view of the lake. Here she stopped and moved to the edge of the path overlooking a similar kind of rocky shoreline to that where I'd gone swimming. It was higher and rockier, but with a more gradual slope to the water.

I crept closer as Dianne's focus was on removing something from her bag. She reached in twice but I couldn't see what the two things were that she took out. She threw the bag back over her shoulder and stepped carefully out onto the rocks that formed this part of the shoreline.

With incredible speed a figure in black darted out from among the trees on the opposite side of the path, just as Dianne raised her arm to throw one of the items out into the water.

I started to run toward the action. In the near silence of the forest I heard only the huff of suddenly exhaled breath as the attacker hit Dianne in the back – very like the way I'd been hit – propelling her out further onto the rocks.

One of the items from the purse flew wildly, fluttering as it was caught by the breeze, toward the water. I heard the other – something harder - bounce down among the rocks. It sounded like a cell phone being dropped on a hard floor.

The attacker made to go past the path edge and onto the rocks, maybe to be sure the job was indeed done, but must have heard my approach. She turned and bolted up along the pathway and was out of sight around a bend by the time I reached the scene. She. Yes. Dark though it was I was quite sure the attacker had been a woman.

Now I was faced with a choice: give chase or go down over the rocky edge and see if I could help the victim.

No choice really. I pulled my phone from its holster and called the Inn, telling the person on the desk what had happened and asking her to first call 911, then Sergeant Grant, then muster whatever help could be rounded up from among the staff still remaining this late at the Inn.

The rocks of this part of the shoreline are large and uneven and my progress was slow. I kept looking at Dianne who, though she had fallen to a spot quite near the bottom of the incline, had not gone into the water; she was not moving.

There was a lot of blood, visible even in the deepening darkness, on the rocks near her head. Her arms and legs were splayed out at inappropriate angles. She was on her back, draped over and between large chunks of granite. Her head was turned slightly to one side and her eyes were open.

She was very still but was, against all hope, breathing. I could see this as I got near. I moved to a position where I would be in her line of sight.

"Please don't try to move your arms or legs but, if you can hear me, can you let me know?"

"Hurts."

"I bet it does. I'm not going to touch you or move you at all except to try to stop the bleeding from where you hit your head, okay?"

"Okay."

"You're Dianne, right? You know who I am. I'm RJ." I took off my tee shirt and started to use it to staunch the blood flow at the side of her head.

"I saw that someone pushed you. Do you know who it was?"

"No."

"I've already called for help so don't worry. You'll be okay." I had no idea whether or not that was true.

No response that time.

We stayed like that for what seemed an eternity but was, in fact, less than an hour before serious help arrived. During that time some staff and guests arrived and left, some with blankets and warm drinks, some with no more than encouragement.

I had made a second call to the desk and had them keep an eye open for anyone dressed in black returning to the Inn and to get one of the boathouse staff to keep a lookout for anyone wanting to leave the island. I also asked the receptionist to find Harvey Donaldson and let him know what was happening,

I stayed right beside Ms. Jones. She didn't say much and I had the feeling that she was drifting in and out of consciousness. Occasionally she would mutter a few words.

Once there was something about spiders and another time about flying.

The hospital in Perth, the OPP and the regional emergency response crews together launched a remarkable rescue effort, finally getting my stricken guest away to the hospital. It was no easy task given the relative remoteness of the island itself and the awkward location – part way up a shoreline of large rocks.

At some point, Harvey Donaldson had shown up at the scene and basically got in the way. He tried to go with Dianne but was refused for lack of space. I lost track of him after that.

I had been standing, wrapped in a blanket, watching the rescue and in something of a daze. As the paramedics were packing up their gear I looked around at who was left there and found, to my surprise, Wil Bascome and Mike Grant, one on each side of me.

"Wil was shuttling emergency personnel across when I arrived at the marina, so he offered to bring me over himself."

"I figger'd ther'd be some as might be needing a ride back after all the excitement'd died down so I stuck around. You sure do lead an excit'n life, RJ. Car crashes and missing women, attacks in the dark and big flashy rescues. Excit'n I call it."

"Yes, well, I might have called it something else but I guess you're right. I think I could do with a little less excitement of this kind, though. Thanks for lending a hand, Wil."

"No problem, RJ. Happy t' help. Looks like the last of 'em are ready to go so I'll say g'night. Oh, RJ. That big ol' yacht's been out there on your dock a long time and I don't guess he's stayin' at yer Inn. I hope you're chargin' him rent for the docking space for that monster."

Mike and I said good bye to Wil and were left, standing alone in the silence, looking at the crime scene.

"You'll need to put a guard on this spot overnight, Mike. There are things to find down there. I thought I heard a cell phone hitting the rocks but I could be mistaken. I for one am not going down there to look tonight."

"Don't worry about it. One of the guys who are helping to carry gear back to the dock is going to stay here, on the scene, for a while. I've already arranged for someone to be here over night and the boat that brings him will take us back. Before I go, you and I have to get caught up on any things you might be remembering, now that the immediate excitement is over. A forensic team will be here early to see what there is to see. We both need to get some sleep before that happens or we won't be worth squat tomorrow."

"Right. I feel like I could sleep for a week. Let's go. We can go to my suite and get a drink and regroup."

"You know, RJ, Wil's right. Any other marina or whatever would be charging him a hefty fee for a boat that big. Why aren't you? Why don't you?"

"Actually, I hadn't thought of it, charging, I mean."

"The other thing to consider is that, if he becomes too big a pain, you can ask him to leave. It's private property, after all."

"Maybe. I just don't want to antagonize him until I know what he's up to."

We walked most of the way back to the Inn in silence but as we approached the building Mike asked, "I meant to ask you this before but we got sidetracked. Other than a real dramatic ending, how was your trip to the County?"

"Very nice. Very nice indeed. I have some more ideas to run by you about what went on there, in addition to what we already discussed."

Mike and I headed in through the door I'd exited, a very long time before, it seemed, locking it behind us as we went. The dining room was dark and deserted and we passed through and around to the stairs. I waved absently to whoever was on the desk – not really seeing who it was.

Carole called out to me.

"No luck with either of the things you asked about. The boathouse reports no boats leaving and no-one asking to be taken and I saw no-one, in black or otherwise, coming back into the Inn after you called. Mr. Donaldson said he was asleep and I woke him up. He went out a few minutes later. Your suitcase is still here."

"Okay, thanks."

Mike went around the desk and picked up the case, then came after me.

We climbed the stairs in silence and I recalled the start of this most recent adventure, which triggered another thought. I was quite sure somehow that the attacker on the pathway tonight had been a woman. It was dark and I couldn't be sure but … I was sure.

I wondered if it could have been Kaylee, from Smythe's crew. Given our suspicion that she was the one who had sabotaged the boat – and Andy Morrison had confirmed that it was no accident – was it possible that she was capable of more serious things? Maybe. She'd been seen prowling around the Inn at night. But I couldn't see a motive for attacking one of the Winnstar group.

If not her, who?

Although I didn't have any better evidence now than I'd had before, my thoughts returned to earlier that afternoon when I'd been sitting on the tailgate of the ambulance. I was leaning toward suspecting the last of the women from the Winnstar group, Suzanne Ellis. What reason she could have for wanting her co-worker dead I couldn't guess but she seemed a reasonable prospect. How Richard Washburn and Harvey Donaldson fit in, if they did, I had no idea.

Maybe I just needed sleep.

Mike and I sat and talked about the evening and the possible plans for the following day. We speculated about where the attacker had got to: into the Inn by some means we couldn't yet fathom, still outside and waiting for morning or gone from the island somehow. After a half hour Mike got a call saying that the boat was back, and he left for the night.

Sleep.

Chapter 21

Winnstar Technologies Messenger   **account wtim0043**

New Message   **Monday   21/07**

From : Spider

To : Hotrod, Geek

Spider – We have to regroup. Flower's done. We go on. Hotrod, you need
to ramp up J's medications. I'll rebuild the plan.

Geek – What have you done? Why did you do that to Dianne?

Spider – Suck it up, wimp. Stay focused or you're next.

――――――――

I awoke with a start, earlier than I'd have expected to, given
how late I'd gone to bed. The dawn was just starting and the
air was full of the sound of birds. I groped around in my
memory, trying to get a handle on what had woken me up.
Then I remembered. I'd had the two trash cans that had had
fires in them taken to the boathouse and labeled so that they
would not be touched by anyone except me. Now I realized

that another trash removal day had come and gone and I hoped that no-one had got overly industrious and disposed of the contents of those two cans with the rest of the week's garbage.

I showered and dressed as quickly as my sore ribs would allow, skipped breakfast for the moment and headed for the boathouse. I made a mental note that I'd need to call Cam soon and see how she was doing. Later. She was probably trying to sleep in.

I hurried out to try to get this job done before my breakfast meeting with Mike.

The lake, as I approached it, was knee-deep in pearl-grey mist and at the edge where it met the shore, cat-tail stalks danced, ghost-like, above.

The boathouse was deserted, as expected, but the first staff would arrive soon. Way in the back corner I found the two trashcans still with trash inside and with the signs attached.

I went to the storage locker and got a couple more trash bags then returned to the back corner. There was an old work table nearby so I dragged it into a shaft of sunlight. As I did so it occurred to me that maybe I shouldn't be doing this at all. Would this be considered tampering with evidence? No. I would evade that issue by trying to convince myself that all these odd things were just freak accidents. Bull.

Fortunately, both of the cans had been emptied not very long before the fires, so there was relatively little inside either one. I lifted the cans up onto the table one at a time, laid them on their sides and removed the tops then began slowly removing the contents. One was still soggy from the water I'd poured into it and the other had a residue of the foam from the fire extinguisher. They both smelled bad.

I'd brought along a handful of small plastic bags and some food-handling gloves. I wore the gloves as I dug through the trash and it didn't take me long to find the thing that, for the moment, stopped me going further.

This must be old movie week or something.

What I found was a timed incendiary device, straight out of a 1960's movie.

A match book had been opened and one match removed. The filter end of a cigarette was inserted behind the remaining matches and the book closed. The removed match was struck and used to light the cigarette and the whole thing dropped into the trashcan. The cigarette would burn down slowly until it came into contact with the remaining matches which would ignite, setting fire to the surrounding trash.

I repeated my investigation with the second trashcan and found the same thing there. Both had failed to cause serious damage or attract a lot of attention. The parts of the device from the first trash can were in decent condition though covered with fire suppressant foam. The second the same but soaked with the water I'd poured into the can. My memory of the movie was that the resulting fire there was much more impressive than it had been here. Good thing.

There had been a little smoke and a small amount of flame but thanks to a very observant staff member who was quick with the fire extinguisher in the first case and the convenient placement of the second can we had prevented either of the fires from doing any damage or being noticed by guests.

I now changed to fresh gloves, put the remains of each device in a separate mini-bag and photographed it together with the contents of the can from which it had come. I re-bagged the trash separately also and left both bags in the corner with the "Do not touch" signs attached.

If it came down to it we might be able to get DNA samples from the cigarette filters. That analysis might take weeks but in the end we could have a suspect. Maybe. I was all set to put the trashcans in the location where they could be put back into use as needed but stopped. It was even possible there might be fingerprints from the arsonist on the outside of the trash cans.

On my way back to the Inn I ran through a mental list of people who might likely remember a 1960's war movie well enough to reproduce this effect. One name stood out, maybe two. No doubt there were others but Smythe and Brent were at the top of my list again. And again without any proof. I'd need to find out if Smythe or either of his crew were war-movie buffs. I needed to get Smythe face to face, too.

Despite not knowing for sure who had set the fires I was now certain that they had been set deliberately and the fact that they were both set in outdoor trashcans said that the person doing it was perhaps more interested in creating mischief than in doing serious damage or in getting anyone hurt. Smythe again? If he was really interested in having the place back again he would want it in one piece. His objective seemed to be to make the guests uncomfortable enough that they would not return and would spread bad reports, things that could be blamed on my poor management and that would not necessarily reflect badly on the Inn itself.

Somehow, though, I didn't see Smythe as the one actually damaging the boat or setting the fires. He seemed more the type to have someone else do his dirty work for him. The observation by Mary, one of our wait staff, about Kaylee, Smythe's jack-of-all-jobs aboard the boat, made me decide to have a closer look at her. I'd emailed Eddie about her and Brent. Maybe there would be a response soon. I'd have to think of a way to identify them to Eddie, since I didn't know their surnames. Photos maybe?

As I walked back I thought about what sort of pressure might be brought to bear on a person who was willing to do the kinds of things I suspected. Last night, when we'd talked in my suite, I'd told Mike about what Mary had thought she'd seen Kaylee doing. He could look at her background and see if there was any previous record of this kind of behaviour. Brent too. If Mike turned up a criminal record for either of them he'd have a better reason for pulling them in for a chat than just my word or that of one of my staff. That alone would be enough – encouragement – for some people to confess what their boss had told them to do. Others would be less easy. And if no record was found we'd have to resort to other methods – or I would anyway.

I went up to my suite and changed out of my smoky-trashcan-smelling clothes. While I had a minute I put in a load of laundry then went down to the dining room for breakfast. Eggs Florentine with smoked salmon sounded good. As I waited for Mike to arrive I sipped my coffee and made notes on a paper napkin. I hadn't yet figured out how to make notes on my new phone. I also called the desk and asked them to try Smythe again and see if he would agree to a meeting. If he didn't respond I'd go pound on the side of his boat, see if that would get his attention.

Also, I'd need to tell Mike about what I'd found in the trash cans. That would add impetus to Mike's initiating the search for criminal records for the people in Smythe's employ, if that hadn't already been started. That should not take too long if he had last names. I needed to check what hospital Dianne Jones had ended up in then see if I could find out how she was doing. The sooner she could answer questions the sooner we would get some answers, if she could answer questions - if she would.

I was just finishing up my second coffee when Mike arrived. He had new information.

He ordered breakfast and we talked about the things his people had discovered about the group from Winnstar Technologies. They all had cell phones, naturally, and Grant now had all their home and office and cell numbers, not that we had any idea at the moment what good that would do us. Warrants were being sought for getting access to their phone records, finances etc. Those would be difficult if not impossible to get since we had no proof of any crime.

I thought about Eddie and wondered if he could do an end run around the rules and get the info we needed.

"Not to change the subject, but I have something to give you before I forget."

I reached for my shirt pocket and extracted the two small plastic bags containing the recovered timing devices. I told him what they were and where I'd found them and that I'd taken pictures of the whole procedure, which I would email to him later.

"Thanks, RJ. I'll see that these get into the system. Probably next time – if there is a next time – you should leave this kind of stuff to the forensics guys. If it came to a court case this would not be admissible as evidence."

"Yeah, I know. I just wasn't taking all this seriously enough at the time, hoping the incidents were all just nasty accidents, and also didn't want to bother you with it."

"You know better now?"

Mike continued with his story. The hobbies of the Winnstar group were interesting if probably un-useful to us. Dianne Jones was an avid gardener who raised orchids. Richard Washburn was a weekend racer – had half a dozen cars which he maintained and drove himself in a variety of events. He was also the group's pilot, though the plane belonged to the company. Suzanne Ellis was a climber who spent her off hours at climbing venues or on trips to whatever she could find to climb. She was fond of free climbing – no safety equipment. Harvey Donaldson was a techie who seemed to spend his time going to computer and video games events. He bought video and computer games of every kind. His only change of pace seemed to be that he liked fishing. We were still waiting for info on the other two.

"None of this helps us much so far but maybe something will fall into place later. We're still digging through their lives in Winnipeg, but as quietly as possible. With technology being what it is, it's possible that they might have safety measures in place that would let them know that we're looking at them and I'm not sure I want that just yet."

"One thing it tells us is that Richard Washburn probably has the know-how to have damaged my car. If he can keep race cars on the track, a bit of sabotage isn't likely to be beyond his capabilities. He might have had tools in the plane that he could have got access to before he followed Cam and me to the County, or he could have stopped at Home Hardware in town to get what he needed. Speaking of which, has there been any word on what caused my crash?"

"Not so far. They were wheeling the trailer with the Lexus on it into the garage as I was leaving there this morning, so maybe later today or tomorrow. I'll check out the hardware store. If I show a picture of Washburn around there someone might remember something. It's not that long ago, after all. I wonder when and how he found out about your trip. Only a few of us knew until the morning of. That's when word started to get around, I think."

"Nice to know my personal life is of such interest to everyone."

Mike raised an eyebrow at my churlishness but said nothing for a moment or two. He laid his open notebook on the table beside his coffee cup. I glanced at it briefly.

"Before I came in here to see you I went out to the scene of last evening's "excitement" as Wil would say. The forensic group was finishing up already. Other than a lot of blood under the spot where Dianne Jones fell – or rather, was pushed to – they found a wig – short and dark – and not one but two cell phones, eventually. One of the phones was very close to where Jones was lying but at first they didn't know about the other one. One of the guys got the bright idea, since I'd told them your idea that the second thing being thrown might have been a phone, to ring the phone numbers stored in the one we'd found. It worked - but only briefly. The other phone didn't really ring, just buzzed briefly then went silent but they got a general direction to search. It was, more or less, in the same location where the wig had been found. They found it in a hidden depression between some rocks and it was lying in a very shallow pool of water. They did recover it but it no longer works. The thought is that since the case and the glass were cracked and had allowed water from the pool to enter, the ringing and vibration destroyed circuits that might have survived if the phone had been able to be dried out thoroughly before it was used. Calling it had been a risk and the risk backfired. The phone near the body had a flower sticker on the back. An orchid no less. I'm guessing that what you saw just before she was pushed was her throwing the wig and the one phone into the lake, or trying to. Maybe."

"What number did the found phone call? Who's was it?"

"It was a Winnstar account number and there was no name attached." Mike looked down at his notebook as if to refresh his memory. I looked too.

"Given her hobby," I said, "it's a good bet that the phone with the flower was Dianne's. How long before the tech people can get into the phones, or at least the one that isn't dead, and get us something to work with?"

"No idea, really. They know it's a priority and they'll call the minute they have something. They'll probably get something from the phone with the flower but, despite what you see on television, the prospect of getting useful information off a phone that is by most definitions dead is not always good."

At that moment Mike's cell rang. He answered, listened and disconnected.

"That was the officer on duty at the hospital in Ottawa where Dianne Jones was transferred very early this morning. She was taken to Perth first but they decided there that she needed more specialized help than they were able to provide. She seems to be awake and the constable thinks the doctors might let me see her. I've got to go, just in case."

"Hopefully she'll be able and willing to give us some answers," I said.

"Maybe. In the mean time I'll find out about the background checks on Smythe's crew. First we had to come up with last names for them. While you were away in the County I got one of the marine guys to go to Smythe's boat and ask. The two helpers were not there but Smythe gave my guy their last names. Now we're good to go. Somehow I don't see them as being involved in this Winnstar stuff but you never know. I'll call you if I get something." He got up to go. "And I'll have one of my guys pick up the garbage bags from the boathouse."

"What were the names – Smythe's crew?" I asked.

"He's Smith, she's Jones."

"Sure they are. I'll keep picking away here. Oh, before you go – one more thing I keep forgetting to ask. The Music Fest is coming up in August. Cam and I are planning to go and I wondered if you'd like to join us. You have someone to bring?"

"I might. We should look at the schedule and see what's going to be happening."

"Sounds good."

Mike left for his drive to Ottawa and I decided I needed to get away for a short while before the dinner prep began –

maybe go and see Cam and make sure she was doing okay after the car crash. A brief change of scene might help to clear my mind. I went up to my suite and collected my reusable grocery bags and a wine-bottle-bag and headed out. I thought I'd have a go at catching up with Smythe as I went but, again, the yacht was gone.

I had one of the boathouse guys take me across to Westport.

As we cruised across the smooth clear water I took out my phone and called ahead to Cam. Not home or not answering. I emailed Eddie.

"Got # from a Winnstar phone. WTIM 0043. No idea what it means. Internal comms?"

One of the many odd tricks I'd picked up in past lives was the ability to read, very quickly, upside down. It didn't hurt that Mike's writing was very neat.

After the boat landed I walked to Mrs. Samuelson's place to get my car. I was almost there when I realized that there was no car there to get. It was in the police garage in Smiths Falls. I carried on anyway thinking that it had been a while since I'd visited with Mrs. Samuelson.

I had just reached her door when she came out, sweater draped over her shoulders and purse in hand.

"RJ. How nice to see you. It's been a while."

"Yes. It's been a busy couple of weeks. You're well?"

"Just fine thanks, RJ. You're having an interesting week, I hear. Missing women, floating bodies, fires, food poisoning. And now car crashes too. You're all right, aren't you, RJ? What next?"

"What next, indeed. Hopefully some solutions. That would be nice."

"I'm sure it would, RJ. Look. I'm sorry but I can't stay to visit right now. I'm on my way to a meeting and I don't want to be late."

"That's fine. I'm just going to walk over to Kudrinko's and pick up a few things. I'll see you next time I'm in town."

"Bye for now, RJ. Give my regards to that nice Mrs. Alexander for me, won't you?"

She hurried off to her meeting and I went up the block to the grocery store.

As I walked I replayed Mrs. Samuelson's parting statement. Something was wrong with it but I couldn't put my finger on what. I'd taken a couple of steps when it hit me. 'Mrs. Alexander'? What was that about? Now that I was thinking of Cam again I called her cell, deciding as it rang that I'd only ask about how she was feeling after the car crash, and leave the other for an in-person conversation. No answer.

Kudrinko's was very busy as it usually is during summer holiday season but my visit was quick and easy. I got what I needed and walked back to the dock. When I got there I tried Cam again but she was still not picking up.

Chapter 22

When I arrived back at the Gilmore dock there was a scene of frantic activity but it seemed to have no useful purpose. People, lots of them, were milling around, some looking into the boathouse and some out toward the lake.

As I stepped from the boat my phone rang. Kim.

I answered. She was standing at the far end of the dock.

"RJ, you need to get back here as soon as you can. Most of the canoes are gone – someone's stolen them."

"Who the hell steals a bunch of canoes? And I'm here." I waved both arms over my head. Kim looked around then came toward me.

"I've called the police and there are a couple of our guys out looking."

I stood, silent, gazing out over the water. What next?

Kim's phone rang. She answered, listened and disconnected.

"One of the guys found the canoes – well, some of them anyway. The ones he sees are well out along the lake, around the curve where the golf course is, just sitting there against the shoreline."

"Call him back, please. Tell him to leave the ones he's found if they're safe for the moment and go on further and see if the rest have also gone on that way."

Kim did as I'd asked while I went to one of the remaining staff.

"Let's go. One of your co-workers found some of the canoes. We'll go get them while he looks for more."

I called out to Kim.

"When you go back to the Inn would you please take my groceries to the kitchen and stash them in the walk-in? I'll collect them later."

We left the dock in a hurry in the Seabird runabout and headed out. In a few minutes we arrived at the large bay where some of the canoes had been left.

"Does anyone know how this happened?" I asked my companion.

"All anyone saw was a small outboard heading away from the north end of the docks with a string of canoes behind it. All the ones that weren't in use at the time. They were all in a row and strung out in a long line. No-one knew what was happening, really. They all just went off across the water and around the headland where the golf course is and were gone."

"And no-one recognized who was driving the boat?" I asked.

"Not that I know of. I heard it was a small, white outboard."

All the canoes we found still had their ropes attached so we slowly manoeuvered around and within a short time had all of the first six canoes tied together nose to tail. We'd just started to move out of the bay when another of the Gilmore runabouts, the Dodge, came into view. It was hauling more canoes.

As we got nearer, the driver of the other boat called out. "A guy from a cottage down the lake has the last of them. He'll be along soon." That last boat rounded the curve almost immediately.

Like so many wranglers with strings of unruly ponies we made our way very slowly back to the island. There were lots of people still on the dock and so there was plenty of help to get the canoes ashore without damaging them. I assigned one of the more experienced guys to do a thorough check of each one to be sure they were safe and sound.

"Did you get them all?" asked Kim.

"Yes, I think so. All we could see, anyway. Hard to know exactly how many were out there loose. Some are out on rental. We'll do a proper count later. Turns out they were more liberated than stolen. Whoever took them just untied them and left them to drift. Fortunately it wasn't windy. They'd have been battered on the rocks. Doesn't look like there's any damage."

I handed Kim a scrap of damp paper.

"That's the name and contact info of the cottager who helped us with this. Please send him a comp lunch voucher."

"Sure, RJ. This more of Smythe's work, you think?"

"I've no doubt about it," I said. "I just wish I could prove it." I looked toward the outer docks. "Won't be easy, considering that I see him and Kaylee right there on the deck of his boat, watching the whole thing. No sign of Brent but he could be below decks."

"You'll get him, RJ. Give it time."

I thought about the incident. It must have taken someone a fairly long time in relatively exposed circumstances to tie all the canoes together. I went to ask around at the boathouse and see if anyone had noticed what was happening, if either of Smythe's people was seen in the area.

Kim headed back to the Inn. I turned again to the dock staring at the big old white boat moored there, trying to figure out what I could do about Mr. Smythe.

One thing I could do was try again to speak to him.

I wondered if it would be worthwhile to put a guard on the boathouse. Maybe.

I went out to the long section of dock where the big boat was tied up, looked around and called to Smythe and to Brent and Kaylee. They were gone. Or hiding below decks, more likely. They'd moved quickly. Everything was battened down and there seemed to be no-one around. Something was bothering me about the picture I was seeing but I wasn't able to figure out what.

I wouldn't go onto the boat uninvited, much as I would have liked to have a look around. It would be just like Smythe to charge me with trespassing!

It was becoming late afternoon and I wondered briefly what I'd do next, then I realized that I was supposed to be cooking the dinner service that evening. Not a good thing for the cook to not show up, especially if he's the owner of the place.

Since I'd not been rooting around in any more trash cans I went straight to the kitchen and, after a wash-up, got into the last of the prep.

Gil and Jeany were with me and had most of the prep done so I looked at tomorrow's list to see if there was anything I could do in advance. Chicken soup was on the lunch menu and I needed to make a new batch of broth.

Bud had removed chicken bones from the freezer yesterday to thaw in the walk-in. I retrieved those and an armload of fresh and frozen vegetables. Fresh onions, celery, carrots and mushrooms were joined by frozen leftover beans, broccoli, cauliflower and corn.

I took half of the bones and browned them in a large pot with some oil and meanwhile rough-chopped the fresh vegetables. Once the bones were browned a bit I put the fresh vegetables in and browned them too.

Then I filled the pot to three quarters with water and put in the frozen leftovers, a couple of crushed cloves of garlic and a couple of tomatoes which had become too ripe to serve in the dining room. Add some salt and pepper, then cover and let simmer for two hours.

As I picked up the lid from beside the pot it suddenly occurred to me what had been bothering me about the yacht as I looked at it after the canoe business. The dinghy was not in its usual place over the stern deck. It was tied up to the dock at the bow of the boat. A small, white outboard.

The dinner service was uneventful and the cleanup was underway when my phone buzzed. I excused myself from the cleanup and went out to the now deserted dining room to answer.

There was a text, telling me that there was a problem at the boathouse and that I should come quickly. I didn't recognize the calling number but there was nothing special about that. Almost all my staff have cellphones and I couldn't begin to keep track of all the numbers, even if I was inclined to try. Odd that the message hadn't come through the switchboard as a phone call. Why a text?

The sky was beginning to darken. A faint breeze ruffled the leaves and a partial moon peeked out from behind a concealing cloud. The growing darkness didn't bother me as I knew every inch of the island's main pathways by now. I went out the back door beside the kitchen, across the short deck and along the path. As I hurried over the saddle of rock that divided the island in two I scared up some bird or other. It squawked once and flapped to a new and safer position as I passed.

All was quiet as I reached the dock. We always keep a few low wattage lights on at the dock overnight, just enough to find your way around. I had no trouble getting to the boathouse in the dim light but realized as I approached that, although there should have been, there were no lights on inside the boathouse, though the ones on the outside wall were on.

Now what? I called out through the large door opening.

"Anyone there? What's the emergency?" The sound of my voice echoed and bat wings rustled high up among the roof trusses.

Nothing. If I'd had 'Spidey sense' it would have been tingling. I'd been in too many dark and potentially dangerous places in my life not to be very cautious, not that that would necessarily stop me doing dumb things. I'd just do them cautiously. I took a couple of steps into the building, trying to get a feel for what was going on. Silence.

The place was almost totally dark inside, now that I was away from the door. You'd think by now I'd have learned some lessons but apparently not enough yet. I went further in, staying as near as possible to the centre of the large opening, as far as I thought possible from the walls. That was what saved me.

Whoever it was had been further from the door than he should have been for maximum effect, a quick and decisive attack. He'd also been holding his breath while I hesitated outside.

Now I heard the exhale and looked toward the sound. He realized that I'd heard him but he had to come farther than he'd wanted to get to me and I heard his movement in the deep shadows, despite his soft shoes.

The old wood floor creaked and he stepped out into the half shadow of the doorway, a two metre length of two-by-four raised above his head, the shadow of his arm across his face. I turned fully to the sound and managed to duck and crouch to the floor as the wood cut an arc over my head and shoulders, smashing hard against the floor. I heard a quiet curse from my attacker as the board missed its mark.

In years gone by I'd have been up and at him in a flash. Now, with a few years on and a still sometimes-wonky knee, getting up from the floor was neither smooth nor graceful but it was just quick enough, just. I was ready for the next swing of the lumber and dodged and twisted sideways as it came at me. The wood brushed past my shoulder but hit hard against my calf, not far below the knee.

It hurt like hell but I refused to give way. I moved in closer and latched onto the two-by-four with both hands as my assailant tried to raise it for another swing and we struggled for possession. Overall we were probably fairly evenly matched for strength and weight but I thought perhaps, with all my kitchen work, I'd have a stronger grip. I hoped so anyway, otherwise I'd be in trouble.

I let go of the board with one hand; not what he was expecting.

His arms were high enough up at the time that I couldn't get a shot at his head so I went the opposite direction. His momentary surprise at my having released the wood allowed me to get in one good punch to his stomach. I made it count.

My grip held as he gasped and his knees buckled a little and then, using both hands again, I wrenched the two-by-four away from him. I should have hit him while I had the chance, but I didn't. He recovered quickly and, finding himself suddenly without his weapon, gave me a hard shove into the door frame then took off running, out the door and along the dock. I'd not seen his face at all since he'd had his back to what little light there was coming in from outside the building.

I tried to give chase but the hit in the leg had been a hard one and I was unable to run. I went to the room which serves as office for the boathouse to see if anyone was there and to ask them to be sure to call me if anyone approached them asking to leave the island. The room was empty. Of course. Had someone been around they would have heard the fight and come to investigate. All the boathouse and dock activities had wrapped up already and there had been no-one to see or hear my attacker.

I threw away the board in disgust and hobbled my way back out of the boathouse. As I went I took out my phone and called the desk and again asked Carole to make a note of anyone returning to the Inn in the near future. It was also possible that, if the person was from off-island, he might have his own boat with which to escape. If it was someone staying here, there were lots of places to hide out in the dark and wait out a search. Again I decided to not call the regular police right away. I decided to call Mike Grant's voicemail so he'd get the message in the morning.

I was beginning to feel that I might need to maintain a security force around the clock – someone to search for attackers in the dark.

As I hobbled on I called and got Mike Grant's voicemail and left him a message about my most recent adventure. When I reached the Inn I was told that, as before, reception had seen no-one returning to the Inn.

I went straight up to my suite and changed into a pair of shorts then went to the freezer to get an ice pack. Funny how often I'd needed one in the relatively short time I'd been here. Well, maybe not so funny. I grabbed a glass of water and took some aspirin and headed for the sofa with my ice pack.

A friend had given me an album of jazz improv by *Nimmons'n'Braid*. I put it on as I went past the stereo. Once I got to the sofa I put my leg up with the pack under it and tried to relax.

I listened to the clarinet and piano and was just drifting off to sleep when a thought jarred me awake. Improv. That's what all this was. All the attacks that had happened in the last few days were so - off the cuff – unplanned – whatever.

I didn't know the true reason why the six people from Winnstar had come to Gilmore but whatever it was, it was certainly not for a peaceful retreat from the stresses of business. It was more sinister than that. As I thought about it I began to see that if the whole thing – the disappearance of Valerie Owens and the teardown of Jason Murdock - had been planned in advance it had not been planned very well. Why would they choose to do this on an island where there were so few places to go and people to provide alibis and there was no ready means of escape? Yes, they had the plane but that would be very noticeable. It would also be noticeable if the four of them just upped and left without a backward glance at the other two. So the plan had to be that the whole thing would be wrapped up neatly within their two week stay. No doubt they were thrown off by the almost immediate police presence, though it was there for reasons not having to do with them. They counted on not having any complications and on fooling the police with their cleverness. But Sergeant Grant was not so easily fooled and I was now getting in the way of the plan's successful completion and they were improvising. And much, much less well than Phil Nimmons and David Braid.

Fully awake now, I decided to get some notes made. The computer in my suite is linked to the one in the kitchen so I opened it up and looked at the file I'd started some days ago; the same one I'd emailed Mike before I went to the County. There was still not much there. I fished in my pockets for the napkins on which I'd made my notes. As usual they were hard to decipher. I did the best I could.

I filled in some blanks with information I'd gathered recently from my own investigations, from Eddie and from the police.

I opened my email and looked at some of the information from Eddie.

There was no record of either Kaylee or Brent in any law enforcement data base that Eddie could get access to and that was most of them. I'd sent him the last names – Smith and Jones - provided by Mike earlier. Eddie said he wasn't done and asked me to see if I could get photos of the two. I'd have to see what I could do about that.

There was lots of stuff about Winnstar.

From what I was reading it looked to me as though the six person executive team from Winnstar had actually split into two groups – four people and two. Internal emails at Winnstar suggested that there was a plan to take over or sell the company and further that four wanted the sale and two did not. I realized that the grouping I was seeing here on the island matched the rumoured boardroom rift.

Murdock and Owens were being moved out, and not gently, it seemed. Valerie Owens was missing and, I suspected, dead. Jason Murdock was being broken down and would most likely be framed for whatever had happened to Valerie. So far that was all guesswork.

The other four were all doing their bit to make that happen. Well, three now. Maybe somehow Dianne Jones had got on the bad side of at least one of the others, maybe all of them, and had needed to be eliminated. Her fall onto the rocks might still prove fatal and even if it didn't she was, apparently, off the team. Hopefully that kind of treatment, by her so-called friends, would make her more receptive to whatever persuasions Mike might choose to employ when and *if* he was able to talk to her at the hospital.

I recalled Mike's description of Suzanne Ellis's reaction to the news that her friend and co-worker had been injured and was gone to the hospital. Mike said she seemed upset and surprised but he thought it had been somewhat superficial. She didn't ask for details and didn't ask what hospital. I typed into my notes my opinion that she didn't ask for details of the accident because she already knew them and that she was upset, not because the attack had happened at all, but because it had not been fatal. Her loose end was still a loose end.

Perhaps I should call Mike and suggest that he put a guard on Dianne Jones, just in case Suzanne Ellis decided to have another go, or get one of the others to do so.

I wondered whether or not confronting one or more of them might shake something loose.

Nimmons and Braid ended and I decided to pack up for the night. I was getting fuzzy and wouldn't accomplish anything more tonight anyway.

Before I turned in I made another quick call to Mike's voice mail, hoping I wasn't treading on toes, but suggesting he might want to put a guard on Dianne at the hospital.

Chapter 23

Winnstar Technologies Messenger   **account wtim0043**

<u>**New Message**</u>   **Tuesday**   **22/07**

From : Spider

To : Hotrod and Geek

Spider – You screwed up. How hard is it to hit someone over the head with a two-by-four in the dark? That Innkeeper is getting to be a major pain in the ass but I think we'd better not go after him again – not yet anyway.

     Geek – You should talk. You had a run at Harrison and you didn't finish him. You said you could handle him.

Spider – Watch your mouth, tech boy. Don't forget who's in charge here.

     Hotrod – This isn't getting us anywhere. Geek. Find out what hospital she's in. I still have the car stashed in Westport. I'll go see what I can do to persuade Flower not to talk. You two get ready to move out, and keep away from Harrison. He's trouble.

Spider – Right. We're almost there. Let's not screw it up now.

———————

I was off the next day so I did a few jobs around my suite. I needed to do a general tidy up and more laundry. The cleaning crew from the Inn would be along today for a thorough cleanup. I had breakfast and took a second cup of coffee to the deck to enjoy the fresh air and the peace and quiet for a few minutes before going on with the hunt.

Today I would try to single out either Washburn or Donaldson. Somehow I thought they'd be easier to get something out of than Suzanne Ellis. Something … no, everything about her bothered me.

I was sure one of the two men had attacked me in the boathouse but I didn't know which. It had been too dark and was over too quickly. Confronting either of them would probably get me nothing other than a denial but it would be the nature and the delivery of the denial that would be telling.

I passed the front desk on my way out.

"Morning, Gwen. How are you?"

"I'm good, RJ. You?"

"I'm well thanks, other than a sore leg. I need a little information, please, if you would."

"Sure, RJ. What do you need?"

"I need to know if Mr. Washburn or Mr. Donaldson has gone out and if so, if they said where they were going. Either one will do."

"They're both out. Mr. Washburn asked if there was an early shuttle to the mainland. I expect he'll be long gone. Mr. Donaldson went out about ten minutes ago, looking like he was going walking maybe. He didn't say anything to me directly but he was mumbling something into his phone as he went by. I think he knew I was there so you'd have thought he would realize I could hear him. He said something about finding you. That's the last I heard before he walked away.

"Speaking of smartphones, how are you adapting to your venture into technology use?"

"Gwen, I think the key to being able to use a smartphone is that you have to believe that on some level you are smarter than it is, that you can master it and not have it master you. In my case, I'm not so sure about that."

"Give it time, RJ. You'll get the hang of it."

"Maybe. Have you seen Kim this morning? I want to see her before I go looking for Mr. Donaldson."

"Yes. She got a call on her cell and went outside to take it."

"Okay. Thanks. See you later."

I stepped out the main door and turned toward the stairs. There, sitting on one of the new Royal Rideau chairs was Kim - hardly her usual place to relax. As I approached she heard me coming and looked up. Her eyes were red-rimmed from crying.

"Kim. What's the problem?"

"Nothing."

"Doesn't look like nothing.

"We found my sister." She stopped and took a deep breath. "My usually totally reliable and predictable sister went away, with a man she had only known a short time, to some minuscule island in the Atlantic Ocean and got herself caught in a hurricane - a really, really early season hurricane. They were only supposed to be gone a few days and then she was coming here. The hurricane knocked out power and communications. Lots of people were missing and the hotel is just about the only large thing on the island. The staff did their best but some people just - were gone. Cell phones couldn't be charged – no power - and the cell tower was gone anyway – I mean gone as in fallen into the ocean and land lines were out too, I guess, if there were any to begin with, so no information was getting out. Somehow someone on another island realized there was a problem and went to investigate. Once help arrived from nearby most everyone was finally found and communications were re-established and the guests started calling home. She wasn't able to let me know what had happened until today. She's okay, RJ."

"Nothing like saving that piece of news for the end, Kim. You had me thinking she'd been hurt – or worse."

Kim jumped up from the chair and threw her arms around me. "Sorry, RJ. I'm just so relieved and I'm not thinking straight."

"That's okay. You've every right to not be thinking straight. Have you told Mike yet?"

She stepped back. "Nuts. No, and I should do that right away so he'll stop looking for her. See you, RJ."

Kim hurried off along the deck but stopped just as she got to the door and turned.

"She's coming next month instead, now. I'm going to reserve a room here for her this time instead of having her at my place. I don't have room for her - and her new husband." She shook her head and rolled her eyes at the incredibility of it all and went on her way.

As Kim hurried away I felt relieved. Her sister was alive and well, and married, apparently. My relief ebbed slightly as I remembered the other thing Kim brought to mind. The gun in her cabinet. I was still not looking forward to that conversation. Wimp.

If Washburn was gone from the island then it was Donaldson who would get my attention today. First I had to find him and I'd have to be careful when or if I did. After last evening's incident in the boathouse I was not one hundred percent.

Another email came through from Eddie so I sat down in the Rideau chair Kim had vacated and I read it on my phone.

"Hacked Winnstar email & some company records … your 6 formed company 10 years ago … Murdock & Owens as driving forces … the visionary & the planner … saw what company could be if they got right people on board … other 4 hired on … became partners – technically junior partners - & fairly short order … each brought something different 2 table … each very focused on narrow field – task oriented – little imagination … usually directed by other 2 … but all 6 functioned well together … company grew & prospered.

"After a few years Washburn, Ellis, Donaldson, Jones got restless - wanted to go on 2 other things … also wanted 2 cash in … board meetings became contentious recently as the 4 tried, unsuccessfully, 2 convince 2 to sell out."

Once he got on a roll, Eddie's attempts at grammatical correctness grew fewer and fewer and the email grew hard to understand.

"wtim s internal message sys. … like BBM … harder 2 hack than email & other stuff … don't know who or what 0043 is yet … Donaldson is good … not as good as me … more later … E."

Eddie was never one to sell his talents short. I knew this was no idle boast.

I was putting my phone away when Kim came back out.

"RJ, Bud needs you in the kitchen right away."

"Now what?" I said to myself as I got up. I went around so I could go in the back door and into the kitchen without attracting attention. Bud was waiting for me at the door.

"Another attempt at sabotage, I think," he said.

He didn't let me go into the kitchen but pointed toward the large panel box in the hallway. We went to it and Bud pulled open the door. Inside was a wide array of breakers of various sizes, all of which were in the "on" position at this time of day. A strip of plastic, cut from an old vinegar bottle, hung loosely over one group of breakers. I had, before our opening, printed on the plastic the words "DO NOT SHUT OFF THESE BREAKERS – <u>EVER</u>".

"About fifteen minutes ago I went into the freezer to get a package of smoked salmon. I thought it felt warmer than usual in there so I looked at the thermostat. The thing was up five degrees from where it should have been. My first thought was that it was on the fritz and I was headed for your desk to find a number to call for service, but then I thought this is a pretty new piece of equipment to be doing this – not that it's not possible."

"So you checked the breakers," I said.

"Yup. Almost all of these under the sign were off. Freezer, walk-in, outdoor lighting, the works. All but the emergency systems."

I thought about that. "Whoever did this knew that a power failure in the emergency systems would trigger an alarm at the front desk and we'd be alerted. There was a possibility that, if no-one noticed the gradual rise in temperature in the fridge and freezer during the day today, we might not have discovered the tampering until tomorrow morning. By then we might have lost a lot of stock – a lot of money."

"My thoughts exactly," said Bud.

"Suggests someone with inside knowledge," I added.

"Yup. Hard to believe one of our people could do this but you never know."

"How about someone with not so much inside knowledge as prior knowledge," I suggested.

Bud was as aware as any of the staff here of the history of Gilmore Island.

"You're thinking of maybe some previous owner – someone who's been making a pain of himself recently?"

"That's *exactly* what I'm thinking. Keep this to yourself for now, Bud, but I think he's been up to no good in more ways than you may have realized. You and I both know there was nothing wrong with that salmon he ate here. What I also suspect is that he's been involved in the two small fires in the trashcans, the boat damaged and sunk and the mass release of our canoes. Now this. All minor stuff but all calculated to be annoying to the guests and, especially, to discredit me, as the owner."

"And he thinks if he makes things uncomfortable enough for you you'll take whatever lousy offer he makes and leave the place to him."

"Something like that, maybe."

"He'd be wrong, though."

"Yes. He would."

"I'd better get back to work. Holler if you need help with anything. I swing a mean skillet."

"Thanks, Bud. I'll let you know. And, Bud, good catch on the temperature rise."

Bud went back into the kitchen and I went out the back door to begin my search for Harvey Donaldson, just to see what he was up to.

As I went out I got a surprise. There at one of the outdoor dining tables were Brent and Kaylee. I had seldom seen them here. I got my new phone from its holster and got the photo app open and went inside again. Eddie wanted pictures and here was my chance, but I wasn't sure these two would just sit still while I photographed them.

In the dining room I corralled a couple of staff.

"I need your help, please. This is going to sound pretty weird but humour me. We're going to take some pictures on the deck, ostensibly as part of a publicity package for the Inn. What I'm really doing is getting photos of those two young people from the yacht.

"There are two tables occupied out there. I want you both to go out there and tend to your tables. I'll follow and take the pictures and leave the dining area, continuing to take pictures of other things so hopefully they won't notice that they've been singled out. Maybe they won't even care."

As plans went, this one wasn't much but it would have to do on short notice.

We three went outside and I followed the two wait staff to their tables, first to the pair from the yacht, then the other couple. I mumbled something about publicity for the Inn as I went to each table then headed off down the stairs. In thirty seconds it was done and no-one seemed to have cared.

Chapter 24

It didn't take much searching to find my quarry even though he'd had a head start. Too easy? Maybe.

Harvey Donaldson may have been a computer genius but he wasn't so hot as an assassin. I saw him almost as soon as I went out the door. He was watching from a short distance up the path, trying to hide behind a tree and I was careful not to look in his direction. From where he was I knew he couldn't see the dining room door and he wouldn't have seen me taking my pictures. I called out to an imaginary staff member that I was going for a walk to Loon Point. As soon as Donaldson heard my plan he hurried off in that direction. I turned off my phone and followed. Sort of.

I didn't take the same path.

I walked quickly along a leaf-littered interior trail which ran relatively parallel to the shoreline path, being careful to be quiet and remain out of his sight.

The chattering of squirrels and chipmunks paused, then resumed as I passed and jays squawked overhead.

If it had been Donaldson last night, he'd got the better of me in the boathouse but that was in the dark at the end of a long day.

Moving slowly through the trees and watching carefully I saw him setting up for his attack before he saw or heard me coming. He seemed to be taking a page from the Suzanne Ellis playbook, ready to attack from behind, hiding in the bushes at the edge of the path, crouching down and out of sight. He thought.

I was in no hurry. I guessed that this would be new to him. He was out of his element here and the idea of attacking someone might make him jumpy. When I didn't show up as expected he'd get even more anxious.

I waited about fifteen minutes, letting him cramp up, letting him visit with the spiders and mosquitoes, letting him stew. I decided it was time to move and was about two metres from him when his phone buzzed. He fumbled nervously at his pocket, trying not to stand up, withdrew the phone and answered in a hoarse whisper.

"What? … I'm doing what you said, Richard. … out in the damn woods with all the bugs waiting for him but he's not here. … I have the sap – blackjack – whatever you call it. I didn't have much luck with the two-by-four last night. … Yes. I can do it. You do what you need to do at the hospital and I'll do what I need to do here. … I know that bitch doesn't believe I belong here and doesn't think I have the balls for this but I can smell that money and I'll do what I have to … ." He ended the call and fought the phone back into his pocket.

He sat there, head bowed, looking at, apparently, nothing, listening to the sounds of nature, but perhaps not enjoying them very much.

He was camped in a small tangle of bushes, presumably hidden from the path but there was a small clearing directly behind him. I crossed it in three steps, with no effort at stealth. He heard me coming but it was too late.

Donaldson rose as quickly as he could, given that he hadn't moved in twenty minutes or so, and drew the sap from his pocket as he turned to face the noise. I was ready. I grabbed the weapon and tore it from his left hand before he knew what was happening and dropped it on the ground behind me. I blocked a big, clumsy roundhouse swing of his right with my left arm and hit him one short sharp jab in the throat with the knuckles of my right, just hard enough to cut off the air temporarily without doing any serious or permanent damage.

He gasped once and his eyes got very large and round and he sat down hard on the leaf-covered ground. "That was just the beginning of what I can do to you if you don't behave yourself," I said.

"That was a nice speech you made to your friend Richard. I think, though, that Suzanne Ellis – the bitch? – was at least partly right about you: you don't belong here. You should have stuck to your computers, Mr. Donaldson. You're not cut out for close combat – or murder. First the two-by-four, now the sap. No luck with either."

He was still unable to respond but his breathing was a little easier now.

"You just sit there, keep your hands where I can see them and listen carefully for a minute before you try to talk, okay?" He didn't respond so I gave his boot a kick to get his attention. "You hearing me?" This time I got a nod.

"Harvey. Here's the way it looks to me and unless I'm very much mistaken, the way it will look to Sergeant Grant when I turn you over to him. If I turn you over to him." The eyes got big again with that.

"You're going to be charged with attempted murder – twice. Once for what you just tried to do to me and once for what you tried in the boathouse last night. You'll also be charged as an accessory to the murders of Valerie Owens and, if she dies, Dianne Jones."

He found his voice, a little hoarse still but there.

"What do you mean 'if you turn me over'?"

"No-one knows you're out here and no-one knows I'm out here. I got my training in Europe during the cold war. Use your imagination, Harvey."

He did.

"Have you got your driver's licence with you?"

A frown and a nod.

"If you haven't signed your organ donor card, now would be a good time."

I let that settle a bit as I turned quickly and picked up the sap.

"Time to start talking, Harvey, and no bullshit. Remember I heard your conversation with Richard a few minutes ago."

I saw in his face the brief and desperate battle he waged within himself. He didn't know what I would do if he didn't cooperate. He didn't want to prove that Suzanne Ellis had been right about him and he didn't want to rat out his friends but in the end he did both. No doubt his imagination showed him scenarios that were far worse than anything I might have actually thought of doing. It came out in a rush.

"I never wanted any of this to happen." He croaked out the words … stopped … started again. "It sounded like a fairly simple plan when I first heard it. Discredit Jason and get Valerie to cave. Easy. But there was another variation of the plan that only Suzanne and Richard knew. That was obvious soon after we got here but by then it was too late.

"Richard and Suzanne hatched the plot to take control of the company by getting rid of Jason and Valerie. The assumption was that Jason would be easier to manipulate than Valerie and so it was decided that she would be got rid of. Naïve of me maybe, but it didn't occur to me that she would be killed. Jason would be drugged, disgraced and, I realized later, framed for the murder. Suzanne took the lead, doing the planning and bringing me and Dianne along. She laid out the jobs we would all have to do. She also found a buyer for the company and she had paperwork ready for Jason to sign off on the sale before he was arrested.

"Dianne would find a place for our annual two week retreat, part vacation and part work. Suzanne told Dianne that she needed to find an out of the way location where the plot could evolve without anyone interfering. She found Gilmore Island and made our reservations and all the arrangements for the two week stay. She was also to work at getting closer to Valerie who was the strongest voice against the sale. There wasn't supposed to be anyone here to get in our way."

"Guess you picked the wrong island. You were using some kind of drug to induce Murdock's mental deterioration?"

"Yes. Richard supplied the drugs. I don't know where he got them or what they are. The plan was to make Jason appear to be a druggie and to mess him up to the point where he didn't know what he had or hadn't done. He would be disoriented by the effects of the drugs, by the loss of Valerie and by the police pressure, though there wasn't very much of that. Mostly just that Sergeant and you, poking around everywhere we looked. Jason wouldn't know what was happening to him or why his life was being turned upside down. He would be framed for the murder. Richard was also the pilot of the company airplane so he would have control of what went into it for the trip to Ontario."

"Explain to me the nature of the frame–up," I asked.

"The drug use was part of it but Richard was going to plant the actual drugs in Jason's room. I was going to plant phoney texts in Jason's phone and emails on his computer to make it look as though he was planning Valerie's death in advance. There's even an online search for a hitman. One of us would convince Jason that it was a good idea to let the police search our rooms as part of the investigation. We had nothing to hide, after all, right?"

"All right. Go on with the story."

"I'm the primary tech guy for the company. I created the Winnstar Technologies messenger system which was used throughout the company. It's very secure – hack-proof. I adapted it to be used, under a different account number, by the four of us for our as-needed communications which were not to be seen by the rest of the company and especially not by Jason and Valerie. I shared the process of creating a separate account with Suzanne Ellis who used the information to link herself with someone called Sailor-man. She didn't want me to know who he was.

"I also got a couple of body bags for Suzanne to bring."

He stopped talking then so I leaned over and gave him a poke with the sap he'd tried to use on me.

"Did you not think it was odd that they'd have you getting body bags? What did you think they were going to use them for?"

He continued to stall.

"Get on with it. You're not done yet."

After another moment's hesitation he continued.

Chapter 25

"Within a couple of hours of our arrival at the island Valerie had been killed by Suzanne. I had nothing to do with that. I swear. I talked to Richard the next day as we were coming out of our rooms. Tried to make him rethink, but he wouldn't."

"Sure. Go on." I didn't tell him that I'd heard part of that conversation.

"Valerie had changed clothes soon after we arrived and had gone out for a walk, saying she needed to stretch out a bit after the long plane ride. Both the other women watched to see what she was wearing and had gone out also, with identical outfits stashed in large purses.

"Suzanne had earlier, while we were still on the plane, taken Valerie's phone and when Valerie was looking for it as they were checking in, had told her that she may have seen it on one of the seats of the plane but had assumed that Valerie would have picked it up.

"When Valerie went for her walk she made straight for the plane to look for the phone and Suzanne was not far behind. No-one was nearby as she reached the plane and entered behind Valerie. On the pretence of helping her look for her phone Suzanne was able to get close enough to Valerie to hit her from behind with a climbing hammer she had brought along for the purpose. Suzanne told us all this. She likes to brag about this stuff. To keep us in line. It works.

"Valerie was zipped, hammer still embedded in her head, into first one then a second body bag.

"Suzanne then cleaned up any evidence she could see, changed clothes, into ones the same as those worn by Valerie, put on a short dark wig and went out to continue Valerie's walk around the island.

"At some point Suzanne went back to her room, seen as Valerie in the lobby by several people, and changed clothes again. She folded the clothes into a drawer and went out, putting the wig in her bag.

"As they passed in the lounge, Suzanne slipped the wig into Dianne's bag and went on. Dianne carried on out to the beach change room and came out wearing the wig and yet another identical outfit. She went walking around the Inn and grounds for a good while, being seen by lots of people, then returned to the change room and reverted to her normal self."

I interrupted briefly. "That would be why the canine team followed a trail right to the table where Suzanne Ellis and Dianne Jones were sitting.

"Somewhat later five of you were seen together in the lounge and later still at dinner and after that, back in the lounge. Valerie was supposedly out walking or taking a nap or something. I talked to you while you were having dinner," I said.

"We thought we had you fooled."

Then came the beginning of the police interviews about the woman in the lake.

"As good citizens will, the group of you volunteered to get your interviews over with that evening. It was masterfully done," I said. "Sergeant Grant was interviewing staff so they could go home for the night. His two guys were talking to any guests they reasonably could without being too intrusive."

"The five of us were back in the lounge by then and were asked if we'd mind doing our interviews. We all agreed to be interviewed. Jason and Dianne went first, one with each of the officers. I think the Sergeant was talking to staff at that time. Jason went straight to his room after that, presumably to look for Valerie, or probably just to sleep. Richard had given him drugs at dinner and later in the lounge. Suzanne and Richard went to be interviewed next.

"At some point after Jason left, Dianne said she would try to find Valerie and get her to come for an interview too."

The penny dropped.

"So, while the second group was being interviewed," I said, "Dianne went back to her room, changed her make-up a bit, changed clothes and donned the Valerie wig. She was ready and waiting when the second group came out of the interview room and breezed into the room to the table of the officer who hadn't seen her before. So she was interviewed as Valerie Owens. And Jason didn't see her at all during that time because he'd gone upstairs.

"Since none of you," I continued, "had anything at all to do with the woman who had been found in the lake you were all able to tell the truth in response to all questions asked and neither of the officers had any real reason to disbelieve what had been told to them. I remember one of them saying that he had a feeling that there was an undercurrent of uneasiness in all of you but put it down to being interviewed by police." Donaldson went on. "I thought for a while that Suzanne might have been the one who did-in the woman you found in the water. She was an acquaintance and might have seen Suzanne near the plane that first afternoon. Turns out Suzanne didn't have to deal with her after all. The husband took care of that problem.

"We were all nervous, even Suzanne, I think," said Donaldson. "But we knew we were in the clear at that point because you weren't looking for Valerie because she'd been there, as far as you were concerned. Until Dianne screwed up by not getting rid of the clothes properly, as planned."

"That also explains a couple of other things I've been wondering about. All this clothes switching. We've covered why Max tracked the scent from the bundle of clothes we found in the trash right to the table where your two friends were having lunch. One of those two had been wearing them. It also tells me why they both visibly relaxed during a conversation with Sergeant Grant when they should have been getting more nervous. They had confirmation then, from what he said, that at least part of the plan was working. We believed – *we knew* - that Valerie Owens was still alive late in the evening."

Donaldson said nothing. His attention had drifted, as though he was listening to something I couldn't hear.

"There's still one question about clothes that we haven't answered. Jason told me that Valerie had changed as soon as you arrived but when Sergeant Grant went to him to get something for the tracking dog to use, there weren't any worn clothes in the suite. What happened to the clothes Valerie wore on the plane trip? How were they disposed of?"

"Easy. One of your housekeepers got rid of them for us."

"What?"

"Suzanne went into Valerie's room and just threw them in a trashcan. When the housekeeping person came to tidy the room she emptied the trashcan and – gone."

Too easy.

I carried on to see if I could prompt another flow of talk from him.

"You were greedy, and in a hurry. Once you started to think about the idea of becoming very rich, not that any of you were hurting before, it became an obsession and although the nuts and bolts of the plan were sound you didn't take time to think about contingencies. What if something went wrong? What if one of you got cold feet? What if … anything.

"You were arrogant and overconfident, not to say ruthless. You'd been so used to having everything go your way. You were a winning team, could do anything, have anything you wanted. Your skills as a group were amazing and had propelled your company to phenomenal success in a short period of time. You expected that this scheme would go as smoothly as everything else you planned and executed."

"So what went wrong?" asked Donaldson, his head once more bowed so that his chin rested on his chest.

"Two things went wrong, basically speaking," I said. "First, you failed to realize that your superb team consisted of six people, not four. There was a reason why Jason Murdock and Valerie Owens were the CEO and CFO. All the others of you were expert in your fields but Murdock and Owens were the visionary and the planner respectively. In your brainstorming sessions all the rest of you threw in good ideas but it was Murdock who tweaked those ideas, adapted and refined them and made them viable. Valerie Owens refined them further and made them part of the corporate strategy and figured out how to make them make money. Murdock and Owens focussed you."

"So," interjected Donaldson, "we four came up with the most audacious idea we'd ever had but couldn't make it work properly because we didn't have our two best brains."

"Right," I said. "The whole thing came apart for you because you hadn't planned for the unexpected. How could you know what would happen? You couldn't really but then, in life, one never can really. But we can speculate, imagine, conceive. We do not go blindly into tomorrow without some belief in what will happen, what we'll do – that sort of thing.

"But *you* did. You thought up this seemingly brilliant idea and set about making it happen without reckoning for the unexpected, and when those things happened, those things you had not planned for, you reacted hastily, without consulting each other, each believing in your own brilliance and invincibility and each doing what they thought should be done and without foreseeing the consequences."

"But we were good at what we did," said Donaldson, pouting now. "We were used to thinking on our feet and making important decisions."

"But under normal circumstances," I said "you would've had a whole team of people backing you up. Here you made decisions and implemented them but they were hasty decisions, not thought out and without the team for back up. Nevertheless some of them nearly proved fatal to each other and to some of us."

"Yes," said Donaldson. "When the plan started to go south we didn't sit around waiting for you to zero in on us. We did something rather than nothing but I guess we didn't do it well enough."

I realized I'd been lecturing instead of asking questions.

"How did you know I was going away to that winery thing?"

"I was going around cloning any phones I could get access to. I couldn't get to yours, which surprised me. It was the one I really wanted, but I got a few others. There was a text from one of your staff to another saying that you and your girlfriend were going away to something called the County. Just gossip really but it came in handy. That was the morning of the day you were going."

"So you passed it on to the other two and they followed us, sabotaged my car and almost killed both of us."

He was quiet again. Listening to that inner voice.

"You say you were against all this violence, so why didn't you rebel, leave, talk to the police, anything?"

"You don't know Suzanne. She's dangerous. Once I knew that she'd killed Valerie I went along with the rest because I figured I'd end up in one of those body bags if I didn't. That's the truth of it."

Having looked into the eyes of Suzanne Ellis at the winery reception I recognized that this might well be true.

"You don't seem to be very broken up about what happened to Dianne Jones. She's your girlfriend, isn't she? Suzanne damn near killed her. You just let that slide?"

He had no response to that.

My cell rang. It was Mike, calling me to say that he'd had a run in with Richard Washburn at the hospital in Ottawa. We'd been right to think that one of them might try to have another go at Dianne Jones. Washburn had stolen a lab coat and had sneaked up on Mike in the hospital room. He tried to hit Mike over the head with a crescent wrench – apparently his weapon of choice for use on cars and people – but Mike had heard him move. The blow went wide and struck his shoulder instead of his head but sent him sprawling anyway.

His fall to the floor had been accompanied by a lot of crashing and smashing of hospital equipment and the noise immediately brought a number of people running. Washburn hit the road without doing any more harm to Dianne Jones.

Mike had a badly bruised shoulder but would be fine. He had made a call to the OPP right away to get them onto Washburn even though he hadn't got a really good look at his attacker. He had not called me until after the doctor had checked out his shoulder, twenty minutes or so after Washburn had gone.

"So if he's on the run will he come back here, do you think, or will he just vanish? He may think he got away without being identified."

Mike seemed to think that he would return to the island to get Suzanne Ellis and Harvey Donaldson – and most importantly, the plane – though I couldn't believe they could actually think they would get away. I decided that I'd better get back to the dock as soon as possible. I'd need to make sure Washburn wouldn't be able to pick up my new friend here. I gave Grant the short version of Donaldson's confession and said I'd get him back to the Inn and locked up somewhere to wait for Grant and his constables.

Washburn had left the hospital a while ago. It would take most of an hour, perhaps more, to get here from Ottawa but by the time Mike and I finished talking perhaps twenty to thirty minutes had already passed. Washburn would not be sparing the horses. He was a weekend racer and as such was comfortable with high speeds and with taking risks as he drove.

Time to cut short my chat with Harvey.

Just then I heard a sound. Donaldson looked up and turned. I realized then that it was not something he had been listening to but something he had been listening for.

The distinctive roar of the Twin Otter's engines starting up.

"That'll be Suzanne, getting the motors warmed up. Richard must be on the way back," said Donaldson. His facial expression had undergone a change from dejection to - what – hopefulness?

"It's been nice talking to you, Mister Innkeeper, but now we should be going. You can't prove anything we talked about. I'll deny everything. We're going to win, just like Suzanne said we would and you're going to lose."

I knew I had to get moving and it was a sure bet that Donaldson was not going to make that easy. I wasn't going to be taking him back to the Inn to await the police and I was not about to just let him go – even if he was probably going the same way I was. I looked around for some way to hold him here while I went away.

Donaldson struggled to his feet. He nodded toward the sap. "You didn't think I'd come after you with nothing but that little thing did you?"

If he'd kept his mouth shut he'd have been successful, but he hadn't.

We moved at the same time. I didn't know what was in the deep pocket of the cargo pants he was wearing but I wasn't going to wait to find out. I covered the two metres separating us by the time the pistol cleared the pocket.

As the barrel was coming up to firing level I swung the sap down hard on his wrist. We both heard the bones break. I felt bad about hitting him so hard but I didn't feel as bad as he did. He was screaming blue murder by the time the gun hit the leaves, and clutching his damaged hand to his chest. His little show of bravado was over. I waited a moment, looking him over.

"Lost some weight recently, Harvey?"

Now it was his turn to wait. "Yes. How the hell did you know that?"

"Your pants fit pretty well but your belt is way too long."

He was quiet again, looking down at his belt buckle.

"If you cooperate I won't have to hurt you again. Come over here."

I led him a short way along the path to where there was a tall tree with a strong-looking branch about two metres up. On the way there I stopped and picked up the gun. It was a small, gunmetal grey .22 semi-automatic pistol. I'd seen it before.

"Where did you get this gun?" I asked as I slipped it into my pocket.

"Richard brought it with him."

"But I've seen it before, in the filing cabinet in the office at the Inn."

"We didn't think it was likely but it looked like maybe a possibility that the police would search our rooms, when they were investigating that woman that was found in the lake. Richard didn't want to take a chance that the gun would be found in his room so he hid it in the office. It was a necessary risk. Someone might have found it there but it couldn't have been traced to any of us. I picked it up earlier today. We made a couple of tries to get it earlier but there was always some reason we had to stop. I think you saw us once. Today Suzanne distracted the desk girl and I went in the office and got it."

I should have just taken the damn gun when I first saw it. Now I wouldn't have to have that conversation with Kim.

"Undo your belt and take it off."

"My pants'll fall down."

"That's going to be the least of your worries if you don't do what you're told. Get on with it." Still he didn't start.

"You can do this yourself or I can hit you with your sap, and do it for you. You have any idea how much damage this thing can do to your head?"

I guess he believed I'd do what I threatened.

It took a minute to get it unbuckled but he managed it.

"Now give it to me." He did. "Put the damaged hand inside your shirt and your good hand behind your back."

This took some time, too, but eventually he got the shirt unbuttoned a bit, put the broken hand carefully inside.

"Now come over here and stand under this tree. Re-button the shirt around your arm then put your hand back behind you."

Meanwhile, I slipped the belt through the buckle and made a small loop. This I slid over Donaldson's hand and tightened until it was just snug enough that it wouldn't slide off.

I quickly took hold of his arm and lifted it up in front of him and, at the same time, threw the end of the belt over the branch. I pulled it until the arm was almost straight up and tied it off.

"I don't guess that will be very comfortable but you won't be there long. I hope. If you don't struggle too much it shouldn't be too bad. I'll send someone along for you soon."

My comment was rewarded by a torrent of curses, which I chose to ignore.

I started on my way to the dock. After a couple of steps I stopped and turned back to him, pulling my phone from my pocket as I did so. I waved it at him. He stopped yelling.

"By the way – did I mention that I've recorded our conversation?"

The litany of whines and curses gradually faded as I made my way over the centre of the island to the dock. Much as I didn't like Donaldson, I'd need to make sure I sent someone to rescue him soon so he wouldn't come to too much harm.

As I reached the top of the saddle my phone alerted me to a text. I stopped to catch my breath and opened the message. There didn't seem to be any great hurry. Ellis may have been warming the engines but it was a fairly sure bet that she was not going to fly the Otter away from the island.

"news ... found 0043 & others ... account # 4 your 4 ... they're bad ... Owens dead ... plan coming unglued ... last message from Hotrod to Spider ... ? ... 'get the plane moving – wait for Geek if possible ... ? ... will meet you out on the lake' ... . RJ ... watch out for Geek ... ? ... has orders to 'finish you off' ... . also got your fancy boat crew pegged ... used facial rec. ... age prog. technology ... not who they say they r. ... E."

Better late than never for that bit about 'Geek' but hopefully in time for stopping the plane. Confirmation from a second source that Valerie had been killed was good to have, if not comforting. But where was the body? The Otter?

Chapter 26

I jogged across the island as quickly as I could, taking care not to end up in a tangled heap among the exposed roots and fallen branches on the forest floor. My banged-up leg slowed me down a lot. The sound of the aircraft motors had not changed that I could tell, so I assumed that it was still tied up at the dock waiting for Donaldson.

As I went I wondered what Eddie had for me about Smythe's crew.

I stopped for a quick breather and called the Inn. I asked the receptionist to contact the police and tell them where to find Donaldson and then asked to be connected to the kitchen. I wasn't making very good time and I didn't want the plane to get away so I needed to bring in reinforcements. Bud picked up after a couple of rings.

"Bud. Listen carefully, please. I need your help. You hear the airplane engines? Go to the dock, please. If it starts to move, do whatever it takes, short of getting yourself injured, to stop that plane from taking off."

Bud was gone.

This was something I'd not expected. We knew that Washburn was the pilot but now it appeared that he had shown Suzanne Ellis how to at least start up and taxi it. Hopefully she couldn't fly it.

As I broke through the trees beside the boathouse I heard a change in the engine noise. I came around the south end of the building and as I ran to the dock I could see that the plane was well away from its mooring. It was taxiing out into the lake. Bud was on the dock where the plane had been.

"Sorry, RJ. She pushed off when she saw me running to the dock. I couldn't stop it from leaving but I may have slowed them down."

"Meaning?"

"I don't know how well it will fly after being hit with two thirty centimetre cast iron frypans. One made a good dent in the engine cowling and bounced back onto the dock. The second hit the prop on the starboard side. Didn't break the prop but may have thrown it out of true. The sound changed some but it kept on going."

I motioned for Bud to follow me and we hurried to where we could get a runabout to give chase.

"Go on. What else."

"After you called I looked around for something to use to disable the plane. As you probably remember from earlier in the year, my weapon of choice is a forty-five centimetre frypan."

We reached the place where the boats were tied up and Bud pointed to the Port Carling Seabird.

"That one will catch them, long as they're not moving too fast. It'll go maybe 30 miles an hour and the Otter taxis at a lot less than that." He continued as we untied the lines. "The Otter will need about 60 to get in the air so we have to get to it before it throttles up too much." As we climbed aboard he continued with his story. It occurred to me that, when this was all over, I'd have to razz Bud about his use of miles-per-hour instead of kilometres-per-hour.

"The big iron pan is good at close quarters but I thought I might have to throw something at the plane so I took two smaller ones instead."

Bud, knowing my deficiencies as a boater, took the port seat and started the engine. I climbed in on the starboard. One of the staff untied the lines and Bud expertly pulled away from the dock, steered around a couple of other boats and when he was in the clear pushed the throttle ahead.

Over the roar of the motor he shouted. "As I said, the plane was already moving by the time I got to the end of the dock. I tried to hit a prop but miscalculated the speed with the first shot. I threw both pans, one after the other. One bounced off the skin of the engine cowling. Who knows how much damage it caused, if any, but the other one must have."

I pointed ahead. "I'm seeing a lot of smoke coming from the starboard engine. Looks like good shooting to me."

Bud concentrated on getting us caught up with the plane while I tried to figure out what we would do if we did. We skirted around a couple more small boats and then Bud pushed the throttle to the wall. The old boat responded.

A moment later, Bud swatted me on the shoulder with the back of his hand. I looked at him, then at where he was pointing. Another, larger boat was on an intercept course and coming fast.

I hoped briefly that it was the police boat, but no.

The engines of the Twin Otter wound up and we found we were not gaining as fast. I wondered how fast Suzanne Ellis was capable of safely running the Otter. The other boat was faster than ours and would get to the plane before we did.

Bud was pushing the old boat as fast as it would go. We were still gaining but not as quickly as the other boat.

About a hundred metres separated Bud and I from the plane when the second boat roared past. Richard Washburn was at the wheel, steering with one hand, the other holding his phone to his ear. I guessed that he was talking to Suzanne Ellis in the plane. He must have practically flown from Ottawa. He saw us and swung in front of us, not close enough to hit but close enough that we had to contend with his boat's huge wake. Bud corrected and we splashed through the wake at right angles, slowing slightly.

Suddenly the Otter slowed as well and we were gaining again. Washburn roared up alongside it, dangerously close. He cut his speed to match that of the plane and climbed over the gunwale onto the port side pontoon. He climbed in the door and almost immediately the Otter was speeding up again. I felt as though I was in the middle of a *James Bond* movie. I still had no idea what I would do if we caught up with them. The prospect of hanging off a pontoon high over the lake did not appeal. Washburn's boat veered off away from the plane to end up who knew where.

Luck was with them. The lake was calm and they were headed into whatever small breeze there was. Wouldn't take long to hit the magic 60.

Bud and I had been gaining, then we were even, then we were losing ground. The Otter's motors roared, the pontoons hydroplaning, giant rooster tails of water flying. The Otter skipped once, twice and was finally airborne.

That was when the starboard side motor came apart. It didn't so much explode as disintegrate, in a cloud of smoke and oil, taking with it a large portion of the skin from the starboard side of the plane, part of the wing and some of the tail. Bud immediately backed off and veered away so we wouldn't be injured by the flying debris.

The nose dropped and the once graceful Twin Otter plunged, like some ungainly water fowl, into the lake. It hit pontoons and nose first, killing the second motor, and came instantly to an almost complete stop. There was utter silence suddenly as the forward momentum carried what was left of the tail up and over like an over-fat caber, until it splashed down gently into the lake – upside down.

Bud and I looked at the mess, then at one another. We both shook our heads.

"Guess we'd better see if they're alive in there," I said.

Bud only nodded. As we moved toward the stricken aircraft we began to hear more boats coming at speed to the scene.

By the time we reached the plane both Washburn and Ellis were out, standing on the bottom of the upturned wing. Neither had taken the time to put on safety harnesses so they were both beat up and bleeding.

Bud pulled the boat along-side and cut the engine, and I threw Washburn a line which he tied loosely to a spar.

"Are you seriously injured?" I asked.

Washburn shook his head 'no'. Suzanne Ellis just stood, hands at her sides, fists clenched and her flat, black eyes staring at me.

"Come aboard and we'll get you back to shore," I said.

Bud had stood up near me to lend a hand getting them onto the boat. Other boats were now only fifty metres or so from us.

Bud reached out to give Suzanne Ellis a hand to board. She took the proffered hand then pulled hard, hauling Bud over the gunwale and into the water. I looked back at Washburn only to see that he had a gun pointed at me.

Ellis was making her way to the driver's seat of the old boat. Washburn motioned for me to come out onto the wing of the now slowly sinking airplane. As he waved the gun I got a good look at it. It was a model I was familiar with and I could see at a glance that the safety was off. I didn't know whether or not he'd racked the slide in advance of exiting the damaged plane but I couldn't take any chances.

I made as if to step out of the boat, putting one foot on the gunwale, as Ellis restarted the engine. I pushed off hard with my uninjured leg, lunging over the gunwale at Washburn. I caught hold of his arm and pushed the gun aside as he fired.

The bullet went wide and all at once I was standing in front of him on the wing of the plane, still holding his arm. It was hard to keep a grip on his wet sleeve. He tugged his gun hand free and tried again. In one swift motion, which I would not have believed I'd remembered, I took the gun from his hand. Surprising that I didn't break his finger in the process.

Still not ready to quit, he took a swing at me. I'd had enough now. After the disarm, the gun was in my left hand. I blocked his swing with my left arm and stepped back so I'd have full reach with my right arm and closed my right fist. I hit him once, hard, right in the middle of the sternum. It didn't stop his heart but it got his attention. Still holding his right arm I pulled him off balance and used my left leg to sweep his feet out from under him. He went down hard onto the wing, sitting stunned in ten centimetres of water.

I heard Ellis screech behind me and turned to find her coming back over the gunwale after me. She didn't get far.

Bud reached up from between the boat and the wing, grabbed a handful of pant leg and hauled her down into the water. He held her in the water while she struggled to reach me, screaming and cursing, hardly paying attention to why she was unable to do so, until she ran out of energy.

"RJ. You all right?" Sergeant Grant had arrived with the cavalry. The police boat slid into place on the other side of the now well-submerged wing. "We'd best get you off there. The launch has some floatation gear aboard that we can attach to the plane to keep it from sinking. We have blankets over here too. Come on."

Mike had stepped carefully into the antique boat. His left arm was in a sling.

He and I bent to lift Bud out of the water and help him into the police boat. There was a significant bruise and bump forming on his forehead. We sat him down and wrapped a blanket around him.

"Who's going to get our boat back?" he asked.

"What. You don't think I could do it?"

He was saved from having to answer when one of the marine officers pointed over the aft end of the boat. "One of them can do it."

Idling about ten metres away was another of our antique runabouts, a 1934 Ditchburn lapstrake, triple cockpit, with three Gilmore staff aboard.

While these interactions were going on other officers had secured Washburn and Ellis.

"Mike. Washburn could probably do with a check-up. I hit him rather hard and there may be residual effects."

"I saw that. That was some shot. And quite the disarm too. Didn't learn that stuff in cooking school, did you?"

"No. Not in cooking school."

"Someday you're going to have to tell me where and why you learned stuff like that."

"Maybe."

One of the marine officers called out that the floatation gear was good. We transferred Bud into the second, larger Gilmore boat and moved one of our guys into the smaller one we'd been using to chase the plane.

"There seem to be a lot of police here at the moment," I said to Mike.

"Yeah. I radioed ahead when I left the hospital. I didn't know what Washburn would be driving but it was a fairly safe bet that he would head back here. A couple more cars ended up at the Westport dock at the same time I did. The place was in an uproar because some tourist had had his boat stolen just moments before we arrived.

"Reynolds and Conroy responded with their boat. They were doing spot checks of boaters not far from Westport at the time the call about the theft came through. We all piled into their boat and here we are. I'll send somebody over to the island to pick up Donaldson."

The police boat would have to stay with the plane until a barge with a crane came from Morrison's. Mike, along with the two patrol officers and Ellis and Washburn boarded a large cruiser that had stopped to watch the action. They would go to Westport and then take the prisoners to Smiths Falls. Mike said he would see me later at the Inn and get a formal statement from Bud and from me.

I climbed aboard the second Gilmore boat and sat beside Bud.

"We'll get Michelle to have a look at your head when we get back, unless you think you want to go to the hospital."

"No. That's okay. I just need to dry off and warm up. Michelle can patch up the damage. I may take tomorrow off, though."

"Not a problem. We'll find someone to cover. Thanks for your help today."

"Sure. Let's don't make a habit of this kind of stuff though, okay? Oh. We lost the second frypan too – the one that hit the prop. Sorry."

"No problem. We'll get some new ones soon enough. If anyone finds the ones in the lake, maybe we should get them bronzed."

The Gilmore staffer driving the boat did a tight circle around the partially submerged aircraft and as we passed close by I was able to see through some of the small round windows.

There, floating in the cabin, was a body bag.

We found out later that Suzanne Ellis had dragged it out of the storage compartment before she started the engines. The plan was to fly to another lake and dump it as soon as possible as the trio made their escape.

We were quiet for a few minutes as the old boat bounced over the water.

Shortly we passed the Morrison barge coming the other way.

"You know Bud, this may be the first and only time in history that a plane's been brought down by a couple of frypans."

––––––––––

The day had come and gone in a blur of activity. By dinner time I decided I was too tired to be bothered cooking for myself so I had dinner in the dining room. I couldn't remember whether or not I'd eaten lunch but I thought not.

I ordered a Bud's Best Burger, this time not prepared by Bud. Michelle had patched up his head wound and he'd gone home. Kim had called someone in to fill the spot in the kitchen for the evening.

While I waited for my meal I sipped from a glass of Pinot Noir and replayed the day. It was almost too much to take in.

Kim's sister had been found, alive and well. A murderer and two accomplices caught, a boat chase, a plane crash, Mike and Bud both injured and it was not even seven o'clock. My only ongoing aggravation was that I still had to deal with Smythe. I'd still no good idea how I was going to do that but I sure wasn't going to worry about it tonight.

My burger and fries arrived along with vinegar and a small container of home-made ranch dressing in which to dip the house-cut fries.

Since Bud had not made the burger and since I am who I am, I lifted the top bun to examine what was underneath. All was as it should be: toasted bottom bun with leaf lettuce, thin shaved red onion, one-third pound beef burger, a pile of shredded medium cheddar, thin slices of tomato and avocado covering the whole surface and a toasted top bun with Bud's own house-made burger dressing.

I enjoyed every bite.

I ordered a second glass of wine and sat quietly trying to think how I would deal with Smythe.

About nine thirty I left the dining room and went up to my suite.

I called Cam and filled her in on the events of the day. We talked for a long time about the Winnstar group and about Smythe. Finally I had to hang up. The day was catching up with me and I needed sleep. Cam and I agreed to meet for dinner at The Cove later in the week.

Chapter 27

Next morning, early, long before sunrise, my phone rang.

"RJ. Sorry to wake you so early. It's Carole, on the desk. Sorry, but it's important."

"Don't worry about it, Carole. I sort of assumed that you wouldn't have called me at this awful hour just for fun. What's going on?"

"It's that Kaylee person, you know, from the big yacht."

I was fully awake now.

"So, what's she up to now?"

"I went out onto the deck to get some fresh air a few minutes ago and I saw her come along the path from the direction of the dock and turn off behind the Inn."

I was out of bed now and rifling through my wardrobe to find something to wear.

"Have you seen or heard anything since then?"

"No. I came back in and thought about if I should call you or not. I figured you'd want to know, so I called."

I was dressed now. "It's good that you did. I'm hanging up now. I'll be there in a minute."

I practically flew down the stairs and was at the desk in a lot less than the predicted minute.

"Keep an eye on the main door please, Carole. Call my cell if she comes in. Better yet, if you don't mind, take your headset and go sit outside. That way you'll be able to see the door and the pathways as well. Don't do anything to get yourself hurt if anyone comes along. And lock the office door before you go out, please."

"Okay, RJ."

"I'm going to go through to the dining room and see if I can see anything from there. If not I'll go outside and look around."

"Be careful, RJ."

"Right. Is there anyone else around?"

"No. Just you and me."

I seemed to be spending a lot of time sneaking through my dining room recently to peer out into the dark. Here I was about to do it again. I decided not to. Instead I would walk the perimeter first and see if anything was amiss.

I retraced my steps and went out the main door, saw Carole sitting in one of the Rideau chairs to my left and went down the front stairs. I then went right on the pathway, across the front of the Inn and around the corner and along toward the back.

Loons called out on the lake, as the first faint lightening of the sky began over the hills to the east.

I went past the dining room stairs, moving as quietly as I could, past the kitchen and around to the east side of the building. Half way along was the storm cellar hatch. As I was passing the double doors, something caught my attention. Actually it was half of something.

One side of the double door was clear of trash and of the leaf litter that accumulated whenever there was any kind of rain.

Upon closer inspection I found that the lock had been removed – opened, not cut – and was standing on the ground leaning up against the raised door frame.

I reached to open the door but stopped. Odds were that it would make a lot of noise as it opened and would alert whoever was most likely still inside – most likely Kaylee.

As quietly as possible I placed the hasp back in place over the crown and slid the shackle of the lock through, leaving it unlocked because that might have made enough noise to alert whoever was down there, but leaving the door unable to be opened from inside. Now, even if I was heard by my intruder, there would be no escape – not that way at least.

I hurried along the rest of the east side, around the corner and up onto the front deck. Carole was there, wearing her headset. She jumped and cried out as I mounted the steps.

"It's okay, Carole. Only me. You can come back inside now."

We went in and to the main desk.

"I'm sure Kaylee is in the cellar. I don't know what she's up to but I'm going to find out. I'd like you to stay by the phone and be ready to call the police if necessary."

I left her there and went to the door leading to the basement stairs. It opened silently. My monthly tours of maintenance had paid off. It occurred to me that I should have been a little more specific with Carole about what constituted 'necessary'. Too late now.

The stairwell was dark and the old top step creaked as I put weight on it. I moved to the very edge of the steps and continued, more quietly, down. I stood a moment at the bottom to let my eyes adjust to the darkness and to listen. There were several rooms down there but from where I was standing I could see no light outlines around any of the doors.

As I moved along the hallway I remembered another door, around the corner of the concrete block structure that stood almost in the centre of the basement. The elevator maintenance room. It should be locked but the storm cellar doors should have been locked too.

I heard a thump. Then another. I rounded the corner to see a light outline around the door. It was closed but the lock was on the floor. I should have just flipped over the hasp and put the lock back through the crown and gone back upstairs and called the police. Would have been the bright thing to do so, of course, I didn't.

A series of short, sharp taps came to me through the door and I figured whoever was in there was busy doing damage to my elevator so it was as good a time as any to move. The knob turned without sound and I slowly opened the door of the maintenance room. The ceiling of the room was actually the bottom of the elevator.

In the centre of the room was the oil-filled ram which raised and lowered the old hydraulic elevator. The tapping continued as I crossed the small room, staying on the opposite side of the ram. I saw that it was indeed Kaylee who was kneeling at the base of the ram. A bright work light shone above her head and I cast no shadow in her direction. The saboteur laid aside hammer and chisel and stood slowly. I stepped a little to one side to where I could be seen. The movement caught her eye and she looked at me for the first time.

"Hello, Kaylee. What's this, then?"

She was quick. She retrieved the hammer from the floor and in one smooth motion threw it at me. I ducked to one side of the ram and she went around the other and was gone out the door before I could grab her. But she went the wrong way. Had she gone for the main stairs she probably would have escaped but she went the other way, towards the storm cellar stairs. I heard her crash against the secured doors. Of course they didn't open. She was in a blind hallway and there was no way out except back the way she'd come. And past me.

We stood there, each barely able to see one another in the near darkness. I had the small amount of light that came through the door opening of the elevator room behind me so I could see her face. She could not see mine.

She stood stiff, fists clenching and unclenching … waiting … deciding. Her face showed fear … desperation. No malice. Then she charged.

I think she planned to just run over me and run away.

Not happening if I could help it.

I didn't want to get into a scrap with her here in this narrow hallway but my options were as limited as hers. I waited until she was almost on me – two, maybe three seconds – then I stepped to the left side of the hall, flush against the wall. She must have thought I was letting her go and put on a burst of speed.

As she neared me I turned quickly to the left to face the wall then the rest of the way around and, as she passed I flung my left arm out, catching her high across the chest, dropping her to the floor.

She landed hard on her back but had the wherewithal to keep her head up. She was winded, likely bruised, but not seriously hurt and luckily for me, the fight was gone. I looked down at her, watched her slowly recover her breathing.

"We can find a more comfortable place to talk or you can stay right there. Your choice, but we are going to talk."

"Why would I want to talk to you?"

"Either me or the police. Doesn't matter to me, one way or the other."

She was quiet so I let her be for a minute.

"I locked that storm cellar door before I came down here. I knew you were here and I could have called the police. I found you in the elevator room and the lock outside. I could have locked it with you inside and called the police. I didn't. Despite all the nasty shit you've pulled since you arrived here I'm trying to give you a break. You going to stay down on the floor or are you going to get up and talk to me?"

After another moment's hesitation she decided.

"I'll get up."

"No more rough stuff. I don't want to knock you down again but I will if I have to. Being a mechanic has made you strong but you're not a trained fighter. I am." I didn't add that that training had been a long, long time ago. I reached out a hand and she took it, got to her feet.

"Why?" she said.

"Why what?"

"Why are you giving me a break? And how far does it extend?"

"The 'why' is my business. The 'how far' depends on what you have to say."

She was a little unsteady on her feet so I took hold of one arm and we made it up to the top of the stairs without incident. There was still no-one around except Carole. The sun was not yet up.

"I need you to make a call please, Carole. There is a file marked 'elevator' in Kim's office, in the file cabinet, second drawer. Pull it and call the repair company. You'll need the file because you'll need to be very specific when you talk to them.

"They will need to be told who we are, where we are, what type of elevator it is and how old it is so they send the right service person. Everything you need to know is in the file. And please ask them to put a rush on it."

Carole looked at Kaylee then back at me.

"Is the elevator broken?"

"Maybe. Please put an 'OUT OF ORDER' sign on it, just in case. All three floors."

Carole went to do as requested and I took Kaylee into the empty dining room.

"We don't have a lot of time before people start arriving for work. You and I need to get some things cleared up before that happens. If you waste my time I'll just turn you over to the police. We clear?"

She nodded.

"I know that you and Brent are responsible for a lot of annoying and potentially dangerous things. I want to know why."

"What's going to happen to us?"

"I told you before that that will depend on what I hear from you and whether or not I believe you. You're wasting time."

"We did what we did because Mr. Smythe told us to."

"And you just complied, even though you knew that what he was telling you to do was wrong, dangerous, illegal. You did recognize that, didn't you?"

"Of course we did. But we didn't have a choice."

"There's always a choice, Kaylee."

"No. Maybe. It didn't seem like it to us. You don't understand. He knows things about us, things from a long time ago. I don't think he knew when we first signed on to work for him on the boat and I don't know how he found out but he did and he threatened to tell."

It occurred to me that Smythe might have access to an 'Eddie' who could find things out. I let that sit.

"So what could he know about you that's so bad?"

"We were accused of something a long time ago – something we didn't do. We couldn't prove our innocence and we were young and we were going to be separated. Brent is my brother, older brother by one year."

Despite the similarities in their appearances that hadn't occurred to me.

"So what were you accused of?"

"I don't want to say. Please. I don't want to relive it, again. It wasn't true. We've been hiding for years, running from that situation."

Her eyes were moist but she didn't cry. Maybe she was past that.

"All right. We'll leave that for now. How did you end up working for Smythe?"

"We were living in Kingston, doing piece work for day cruises and like that, and we had some experience running quite a variety of boats. We heard that he was looking for a crew for the yacht. We applied and after a few days got the call to come to work. Smythe's actually a decent boater. He knows the boat quite well – he's had it a long time - and drives it fine. It's just too big for one person to run alone, especially through the Rideau, with the locks and all."

"Was there a third person – Andrea – on the boat?"

"Yes. She signed on at Kingston when we did, to double as crew and as Smythe's office assistant but she bailed part way up. Smythe kept hitting on her and she wasn't interested and he wouldn't quit. How did you know about her?"

"Smythe asked for her when he first landed, forgetting momentarily that she was gone."

"Tell me all the instructions you got from Smythe and what you did, and who did what."

For the next fifteen minutes, Kaylee ran through the list of events: day, time, place and which one of them had done what. I was glad to realize I knew about them all - no booby-traps left to go off.

"Who's the film buff? That thing with the cigarette and matchbook is straight from a 1960s movie."

"Mr. Smythe showed Brent how to do it. There were going to be more of those but we didn't get to them."

We were quiet for a couple of minutes, Kaylee looking down at the table and I looking at her. At last she looked up.

"So, what now?"

I'd already made my decision. I hoped it was the right one.

"Do you like working for Smythe? Does Brent?"

"No, neither of us does. We've been trying to think of a way to leave but it's like he's psychic or something. Every time we get close to going he seems to know and reminds us what will happen if we even try. He owns us." She stopped briefly then went on. "Kind of ironic, us working on a boat called *Serenity*. Not so serene for us."

I thought a bit. "Maybe not for him either."

"I have a question which may seem to be unrelated but bear with me, please. The woman from the Winnstar group – Suzanne Ellis - has she ever been to see Smythe?"

"Oh yes. They're quite friendly, or seem to be. She spent a night or two on the boat. I have the feeling, though, that she's playing up to him because he's in a position to help her somehow or that he had something on her and that she doesn't like it one bit, not owing him or being threatened by him. She's scary."

"We agree on that." I considered my options.

"I think your fortunes are about to take a decided upturn."

I looked at my watch. Six fifteen. I took out my phone and called a lawyer friend, at home. His wife answered sleepily, saying he was in the shower but would be free shortly. I told her who I was and that I needed my lawyer friend to come to Gilmore Island right away, now. He would be taking sworn statements and should bring any appropriate paperwork along. This all had to be accomplished as soon as possible, so he'd better hurry. I think she didn't like my tone - perhaps found my request somewhat bizarre but she did recognize my name and she did promise to relay the message.

"You need to go back to the boat now. Be there when Smythe next looks for you. If he asks, tell him that the damage has been done to the elevator. Later on, nine o'clock or so, find Brent. Think of a way to get him and yourself off the boat, without Smythe knowing, if possible. Then come back here. There is an empty room on the second floor, where the police were conducting their interviews. Room 201. You and Brent wait there until the lawyer comes – he might even be here when you arrive - then you each give him a statement about Smythe's coercion and threats, just as you gave it to me. Sign the statements. He will seal them in an envelope, and will hold on to them, at his office in Smiths Falls, in case they're ever needed."

My mind was racing. "As soon as you've finished with the lawyer, go back to work. I'm going to have a package delivered to you, probably at the boat. Make sure Smythe doesn't see you receive it. It will have enough funds to get you away from here and keep you going 'til you can find work again. I'll probably have one of the boathouse staff deliver it so there'll be no chance of Smythe seeing me before I'm ready."

We both stood. "You need to know that Brent feels really bad about the business at the stable. Up to then everything had been annoying and troublesome for you but that was dangerous, potentially fatal. He's glad you weren't hurt, or anyone else."

"Tell him not to worry about it any more." Now she was crying.

"Go now. I've got work to do. I'll be at the boat later in the morning to deal with Smythe. I'll do my best to make him see the folly of pursuing you. Get packed and be ready to leave while I'm there keeping him busy."

She hugged me then left to go back to the boat. I went to make my own arrangements.

It occurred to me that, once this last meeting was over, I'd be able to get the bedroom furniture back into the interview room before we needed it for a new guest.

Chapter 28

I knew a lot more than I could prove about Smythe's involvement in the events at the Gilmore but I wasn't willing to keep wasting my time trying to figure it all out. Time to act.

It was now or never for my showdown with Smythe. I had a lot of ideas running around in my head, only some of which made more sense now that I'd had it out with Kaylee. Some things I could prove and some not. The trick was going to be in not letting Smythe know which was which. This was going to be, largely, a bluff.

I had come to the conclusion that Smythe was a rich, arrogant bully, used to getting his own way, throwing money or hired rabble-rousers at situations to steer them in any direction he wanted them to go. But I also believed that, as with most bullies, Smythe was, most likely, at heart, a coward. As such he would be susceptible to someone who would stand up to him. I planned to do exactly that. There was, of course, some chance that I was wrong but I had to risk a confrontation and see what happened. He'd made a lot of money at his various ventures and so I knew he was not stupid.

I spent the next while organizing the package I'd give to Kaylee and Brent. I got an envelope from the office, put everything inside and sealed it. Carole was still there but ready to leave and Gwen was there to take over. Carole told me my lawyer friend and the two kids from the boat were upstairs.

"Carole. Would you please do me a favour? You're going off soon. When you're ready to head for the boat to the mainland, please wait until you see Kaylee and Brent leave here. Walk with them and give this to one of them as you go." I handed her the envelope. "Do it early on so that Smythe doesn't see you doing it. You okay with that, Carole?"

"Sure, RJ. No problem."

"Thanks."

I went to the dining room for a late breakfast. I was just finishing up when my lawyer friend, Jim Long, came into the dining room.

"Jim. How's things? Thanks for coming out."

"No problem, RJ. We're all done and the kids have gone back to work, as you instructed." He hoisted his briefcase into view. "The statements are in here and I'll hold onto them at the office. I'll send you my bill."

"Great. Don't forget to include the gas. You have time for coffee?"

"No thanks. I need to get moving. I have a client meeting at one. Another time?"

"You bet. Drive safe."

Jim left and I sat a while longer and finished my coffee, priming myself up for my confrontation with Smythe.

I walked along in the bright sunshine, past most of the docks, to where the Twin Otter had been and where the yacht was now, tied up at the very outer end. It had been moored a little closer-in until recently, in a slip that was perpendicular to where it was now, at the outermost possible location, as if Smythe was anticipating the possibility of a hasty departure.

The yacht, I had found out, was a 1956 Chris Craft, Salon Motor Yacht; 58 feet long and about 15 feet wide, in the imperial measures she was built to. It was one of only seven hulls built in that style. Powered by twin diesels, it was totally original on the outside and looked original on the inside, too, but any and all nautical and comfort conveniences had been added and most were artfully concealed.

Brent watched me approach from his perch on the outside of the fly bridge windshield which he was cleaning. I called up to him.

"Ahoy, *Serenity.* I need to see Mr. Smythe. I know he's on board and I'm not taking 'no' for an answer, so you might as well go tell him I'm here." I tried to sound annoyed in case Smythe was within hearing.

Brent hesitated only a moment then climbed over the roof of the fly bridge, dropped, catlike, onto the open deck, then disappeared below decks. I waited patiently, watching the sun on the water.

A few minutes later Brent reappeared on the main deck. "Come aboard," was all he said, and he disappeared again.

I stepped onto the stern deck and was met by Kaylee. "This way."

I followed Kaylee down a short flight of stairs. At the bottom we encountered Brent.

"You received the package I sent you?" I asked.

"Yes," said Kaylee. "Thank you. The lawyer has the paperwork you wanted from us."

"Yes, I know. I saw him before he left. Hopefully none of this will come back to bite you but I can't guarantee that."

"Doesn't matter. We'll be gone and free of him," said Brent.

I hugged Kaylee and shook hands with Brent.

"Now?" he asked.

I nodded and he turned along the gangway toward the staterooms. I followed Kaylee.

She led me along a companionway to the centre of the boat, to the main salon which looked like a smaller, shinier version of the lounge at the Inn – this one all teak and brass and glass rather than oak and stone.

As I entered from one door, Smythe was entering from the other end of the room. He ignored me and went to the bar and selected a bottle of champagne and a jug of orange juice from a small fridge there. He opened the champagne and brought it, the juice and a couple of glasses to a small round lounge table. He drew out a chair and sat down. His eyes flashed to Kaylee and she left the room. Good. She was free.

"Sit, Mr. Harrison. Have a Mimosa. We might as well be civilized."

I sat – he poured. Smythe sat opposite me, his hands, thin like the rest of him, fingers laced, resting on the table.

We sat there in silence for a moment or two. Sun poured in through the large windows and the polished surfaces sparkled.

"It's your dime, Mr. Harrison. You have something to say?"

I was looking into Smythe's eyes – had been since I entered the room. They were grey and a little small for his head, with slightly drooping lids and thick, bushy white eyebrows.

"I want you to stop playing whatever game it is you're playing. I know you're responsible for the – incidents – shall we say, that have been happening ever since you arrived here: the fake food poisoning, the boat damage, the thefts, the fires – those and more – all you. As you are no doubt aware I can't prove any of that … yet. But, proof notwithstanding, I know and you know that *you* are responsible. I want it to stop."

Smythe hesitated a moment, deciding how to proceed. Arrogance won out over prudence. He made no effort to deny my allegations.

"I am going to win this little contest we are having, Mr. Harrison. I have more money and more resources – more of everything in fact. You cannot compete with me and you know it."

I continued looking at Smythe. "No. You're not," I said calmly.

Smythe frowned briefly, then, realizing that I was responding to the beginning of his speech and not the end, he went on.

"I can continue this campaign of harassment for a long time and let me be frank – if you hold out too long I will simply arrange for you to have a fatal accident."

I didn't let my surprise show. He'd jumped to the big threat sooner than I'd expected. I wondered briefly if he had the guts to try it. He seemed to be assuming that the threat of death would impress me. Been there – done that.

"You'd kill me – or find someone else to kill me – just to get this island?"

He was on a roll. Fired by greed and arrogance he continued.

"Of course I would, Mr. Harrison. I'm used to getting what I want. This will be no different. If killing you is what is required then that is what I shall do."

"Did you actually have this in mind, retaking possession of the island, when you first came here or did it occur to you later? I know that you came at the invitation, more or less, of Suzanne Ellis, formerly of Winnstar Technologies. Your role was to divert attention, provide a distraction while Ellis and her cohorts completed their own murderous plot, which makes you an accessory, by the way."

Now I had his full attention.

"You were to be the buyer. 'Sailor man' wasn't it, that Ellis called you?"

I'd practiced and used the so called "dead eye stare" a lot in past lives and had never had it fail me when I needed it to work. I'd not taken my eyes off Smythe's since we sat down at the table. My face remained expressionless. His almost so. I sipped my Mimosa. It was very good.

"I said that I'm not able to prove that you are responsible for the current spate of unfortunate incidents. That was ... untrue. I can prove that you're responsible and maybe prove some other things that could turn out to be much more damaging."

"You can't prove anything or you would have brought the police with you today."

Despite the bravado I could tell that Smythe's resolve was beginning to slip. His eyes darted around the room now and then and a few small beads of perspiration appeared on the perfectly tanned forehead. He hadn't wanted this personal confrontation. Certainly he'd avoided meeting me for long enough. Probably thought he could intimidate me; thought I'd fold up and go away. Wrong.

"I have written depositions stating that you gave Brent and Kaylee orders for all the nasty things they did. I had a lawyer friend come here early this morning and take statements from both of them. They were very thorough, very forthcoming. You know ... they don't like you. You've forced them to do your bidding with threats and coercion. They did what they did for fear of exposure of past misdeeds, real or otherwise, and once they started, fear of arrest. Small wonder their loyalty to you was a bit thin."

Smythe's colour began to drain and he looked less and less sure of himself.

"I also have documents showing your involvement as the potential buyer of Winnstar – emails dating from several months ago, right to this week. In and of themselves they are not incriminating except from a business ethics perspective, but, and I refer now to your threat to *kill me* a few moments ago, it might be suggested that you were in on the plot to kill Valerie Owens and destroy Jason Murdock right from the beginning. Perhaps you even planned the whole thing."

Smythe was now quite grey and his breathing was growing ragged.

"I think you should reconsider your plan to retake ownership of Gilmore Island, Mr. Smythe." I took a long slow breath. Smythe seemed unable to speak.

"This is my - third life - so to speak, and I'm liking it a lot. I like this place; I like the Inn-keeping business and I like the people I've got to know since I came here. I'm not about to let you take that away from me."

Time to finish letting the wind out of his sails.

I drained my drink and set the glass firmly on the shiny table top then leaned forward and spoke very softly.

"Let me recap. I know you're the secret buyer for Winnstar Technologies. I know Ellis contacted you some time ago and I know she's been in touch with you on a regular basis over the last ten days or so, before, during and after the murder of Valerie Owens. That's the important bit, by the way."

I stopped for a moment to let that sink in. His face lost, if possible, even more colour under his tan.

"I don't know whether or not you really want Gilmore Island or whether you're just doing this to provide a diversion for Winnstar; perhaps it's some of both. Doesn't matter. One person is dead and another seriously injured and you're in a position to be charged as an accomplice or an accessory to both crimes.

"You need to pack up your fancy boat and leave. I don't know if Suzanne Ellis will throw you under the bus or if she'll take the fall with the rest of them and leave you out of it but I'd guess the former. I don't guess she was happy at being coerced into sleeping with you. She doesn't seem to me to be a person of any great compassion or empathy. If I were you I wouldn't want to be hanging around here to find out which way it will go. You need to be where your lawyers are."

I leaned back a bit and relaxed.

"You can't prove any of these allegations, about Winnstar or anything else," said Smythe.

"You know that's what guilty people often say: not 'I didn't do it' but rather 'you can't prove it'. Besides, I can prove at least some of it but I probably won't have to. Suzanne Ellis is the lynchpin. My accusations, made in public, will get you a lot of unwanted, negative publicity but probably won't get you charged with a crime. Probably. However, if Ellis decides to give you up you'll have a hard fight to stay out of jail. She could suggest that you were the instigator of this whole take-over mess and she would be the one whose word will be listened to first. You decide. You may be as innocent as a new born babe relative to the murder of Valerie Owens, or you may not be. Whatever. It's your life. Do you want to spend the rest of it trying to stay out of jail?"

I let that sit. He wasn't blustering anymore. He was weighing his options.

"Oh, I almost forgot to tell you. Kaylee and Brent are gone. I gave them each a little something to tide them over and sent them on their way. I wouldn't have told you about their ratting you out if they were going to still be here for you to abuse."

Smythe yelled, loud and clear, for his two crew members. There was no response.

"You thought I was kidding?"

Now he was sputtering again.

"And I wouldn't make any effort to get back at them. I'm quite willing to take you to court if necessary and I have their statements to use if I do. Them and the Winnstar stuff."

"One last thing," I said. I leaned forward again so that I was as close as I could be to him with the table between us.

"Think very carefully before you consider trying to kill me; tougher and smarter men than you have tried and all of them are either in jail or dead." I let the silence stretch out a bit. "Which group do you want to join?"

I watched as one side of his face began to twitch and his gaze shifted to the remnant of cocktail in the glass before him.

Without another word I stood and walked out of the room, off the boat and down the dock. I didn't say thanks for the Mimosa.

Nothing to do now but wait and see what his next move would be. I wondered if he would fight or turn tail and run. It also occurred to me that he might have been running from some local threat when he left the island the first time. An old adversary of mine had indicated in his diary that he'd made efforts to hurry the departure of some previous owners and residents of Gilmore Island. Perhaps Smythe was one of those.

As I returned to the Inn, I saw my Picnic Launch being returned. One of Andy Morrison's service boats was giving escort and would, no doubt, take the driver of the picnic boat back to their shop. On a whim I called Cam. Her voicemail picked up.

"Cam. It's RJ. I have a little surprise for you. I'd like you to please come to the island tomorrow at about one o'clock – for lunch – if you can. If you can't make it, please call me. If you can, just show up. Lunch outside."

After that I went inside to make arrangements to test out my newly repaired picnic boat.

Chapter 29

A couple of days later Cam and I were sitting with Mike and Kim in the living room of my suite. We were sipping drinks and coming to grips with the depths to which some people will sink in order to get what they want.

"How was the lunch yesterday, Cam?" asked Kim.

"It was lovely. Perfect weather and a peaceful setting."

"And what did you think of the new name?"

"I like it."

"I think RJ was probably relieved to hear that."

Looking at Cam I said, "Yes, I was. Renaming the picnic boat *"Lady Cam"* was a gamble – something I don't often do. I'm glad you approve. And yesterday's lunch was an excellent test run. It's good to have that part of the business up and running again," I added.

"So," said Kim, "we all know the big boat left yesterday, finally, but I just heard something else. Apparently Smythe's crew took off and left him alone on the boat a couple of days ago. He was in a big rush to get away. I wonder why. He scrambled around locally, trying to get some help so he could leave that afternoon but couldn't find anyone. He had to send to Kingston. A new crew was driven up in the evening."

"They're finally all gone," said Cam. "And they were all in on it together, or most of them anyway, from both groups?"

Mike shrugged gently, stretching his injured shoulder. "Seems so. The fearsome four wanted to get rid of Jason and Valerie, and take over the company so they could sell it. They'd rounded up a backer but couldn't move on the sale, not without Valerie and Jason's approval or removal. Smythe was the backer. Brent and Kaylee were Smythe's minions, doing his bidding relative to his proposed takeover of the island and not involved with the Winnstar thing."

"But murder? That seems a pretty drastic step to take to get control of a company," said Kim.

"Yes. But they were ruthless, Suzanne Ellis in particular. They came here to kill Valerie Owens and frame Jason Murdock. They started immediately, killing Valerie almost as soon as they arrived. Then the women went about impersonating her, out of Jason's sight.

"We all thought Murdock was crazy when he started his ranting about Valerie going missing in the afternoon the first day because we all *knew for certain* that Valerie Owens was alive late in the evening. Washburn had started that same evening giving Murdock small doses of drugs to make him a little dopey and disoriented."

I took up the story.

"When I got involved with the search and started asking a lot of questions it made Suzanne Ellis uneasy. She took a run at me on the shoreline and was almost caught at it by a couple of walkers. No plan, no forethought. She saw me on the path and decided then and there to try to get rid of me. Did the same with Dianne Jones, though with a little more forethought. Jones had become a liability, changing the plan without consultation, not disposing of the wig and the phone and the clothing as planned, and using the phone to send a message from the dead woman.

"Later, Harvey Donaldson was able to intercept a tweet or something that one of the staff sent about our trip to the

County. Washburn and Ellis put together another quick-fix plan to dispose of me. You, Cam, were to be nothing more than collateral damage."

I stopped briefly and took hold of Cam's hand.

"Washburn rented a car and he and Ellis followed us to the County. He was an expert mechanic and knew how to do just enough damage there in the parking lot of the winery that a few high-speed kilometres would shake things loose. It almost worked."

"When do you get your new car?" asked Kim.

"Mike's driving me into Ottawa tomorrow to pick it up. I'd been looking and had primed up the dealer for the possibility of a change. Didn't happen quite the way I'd planned, though."

"All right," said Cam. "What made you sure enough of their plan to start putting things together?"

"No one thing in particular, but a lot of little things.

"The accident with the car – that wasn't an accident. Washburn was a weekend racer and did his own mechanical work. That, and the fact that they were there at the winery at all said something was up. We thought they'd gone back to the Inn the previous day but I saw them drive slowly past the wreck, not looking as though they were seeing what they wanted to see.

"Cam, do you remember what was on TV when I came out of the shower that morning at Wellington?"

"That old movie? 'The Prisoner of Zenda', I think."

"Right. One of the primary things people remember about that movie is that Ronald Coleman played two parts. He spent a lot of time as a man pretending to be someone else.

"It didn't register at the time, the one person playing two parts thing, but after the wig was seen in the suite where it didn't seem to belong, I started to get that feeling that there was something that I should know but couldn't quite grasp. You and I talked about the fact that all the women were similar in size and colouring. Later when we found the wig on the rocks where Ms. Jones had been injured I put it together. The clothing found in the boathouse trash which resembled those of Valerie Owens but which led Max right to Suzanne Ellis and Dianne Jones and the wig that looked like Valerie's hair found in Dianne's possession. Those things all pointed me toward the idea that Ellis and Jones had both been playing Valerie. But I didn't know why at the time."

Misdirection.

Mike took over.

"Dianne Jones filled in some background when I saw her in the hospital after the attempted escape by Ellis and Washburn. She's going to testify against them, by the way.

"That one particular outfit was to be in evidence only in the first few hours after the group arrived. All three women had the same outfit, on purpose. Suzanne Ellis had been shopping with Valerie Owens a week or so before the trip. She saw the three new outfits Valerie bought for the trip and went back later and bought two identical versions of all of them. It was a calculated risk, but Ellis expected that Valerie would change into one of her new outfits when she got to the island. She did. Ellis and Jones then arranged to have that same outfit in their large bags. There was only one wig. Originally both Ellis and Jones had had a wig to match Valerie Owens because the three of them had gone to a Halloween party the previous year done up as triplets. Maybe that's where they got that part of the plan. Jones had lost or thrown out her wig so they had to trade off the one remaining, depending on who was playing the part. We later found other sets of clothes, three different outfits, in Owens', Ellis' and Jones' suites."

I took over again. "You know, as investigators we are told that coincidences don't exist. But they do. You just have to take a very close look at them to be sure you're not being fooled. I, for one, was distracted by the sheer coincidence of all the women in this case having chosen to wear similar clothing on that first day. The woman in the water – denim and white, the boat crew – navy and white and the two and/or three women from Winnstar – dark purple and pale mauve. Similar enough to associate them all in the mind even though they weren't really associated at all."

Mike continued. "We couldn't trust the timeline we'd established for the comings and goings of Valerie Owens. If the other two women were playing Valerie, as we suspected they were, how long were they doing it and when had it started? We realized that Jason Murdock was probably right. Valerie had gone missing almost as soon as the group arrived."

"I remember hearing that Valerie was seen on the dock and around the island after that first evening. What about that?" asked Kim.

Mike answered. "Both sightings were on the morning of the day we finished the interviews and pulled the guard off the dock. Suzanne Ellis and Dianne as Valerie were seen together and a little later Dianne as Valerie was seen on the dock, maybe boarding a shuttle boat to Westport. At the hospital Dianne told me that she did go to the mainland, browsed around a few stores as Valerie then changed clothes and took off the wig. She returned to the island as herself later in the day. Later she dumped the original outfit into the trashcan in the boathouse but kept the wig and the phone. Her Winnstar Messenger message as Valerie, after Valerie had supposedly left the island, had exactly the desired effect on Jason and on the investigation, but got Ellis riled because Dianne was improvising." Mike hesitated a moment. "She also told me when I asked, that she's the one with the oval-shaped birthmark on the back of her leg.

"I'm annoyed with myself because I had a search of the plane on my list for later that same day but priorities got rearranged when we thought Owens had left. Besides we didn't think it was possible for her to be there. She'd been seen on the island and there was a constable on the dock, keeping people away."

I excused myself for a few minutes. The four of us were going to have dinner together in my suite so I went to the kitchen to get things started. Pork Chop Parmesan was on the menu tonight and I had a bit of setup to do, though most of the prep was done. As I was pulling the various items out of the fridge I heard the other three come into the kitchen. They arranged themselves on the tall chairs at the work island and prepared to carry on the conversation while they watched me work. I had no problem with that. Seems most gatherings at my place end up in the kitchen eventually.

"So, Donaldson's attacks on you - planned or another of those off-the-cuff things?" asked Kim.

"Ellis and Washburn put them together between them but I'm not sure you could call them very well planned," I said, "as with the car thing. Since the car sabotage didn't work and since they didn't see how they'd get another similar chance they threw together a couple more ideas to slow me down then they told Donaldson what he had to do.

"The first plan was for Donaldson to attack me in the boathouse and when that didn't work, to lure me into the woods where he would try again to kill me. He was reluctant he says, but they bullied him into it. As that attack in the woods was going on, Washburn would be driving back from killing Dianne, Donaldson would join Ellis in the plane, they'd pick up Washburn on the lake then fly away, first dumping Valerie's body somewhere, in some other lake. All neatly leaving Jason to face the music alone. With their deepest regrets, no doubt." I thought a moment.

"I'm not sure what the thought process was at that point, or if there even was one. They could not possibly believe that they were going to just go back to Winnipeg and carry on with their plan. There was too much evidence, some of it circumstantial to be sure, of their complicity in Owens' disappearance and of their very definite involvement in the attacks on me. They couldn't have possibly thought that they would get away with what they'd done despite their efforts to lay it all on Murdock."

Mike carried on as I seasoned the pork chops and set the pre-cooked potatoes to brown in a little olive oil. He leaned forward so he could see both Cam and Kim.

"Turns out RJ was harder to kill than Donaldson expected. The other fly in the ointment was that Washburn didn't get away as cleanly as he hoped. He was not there to fly himself, Donaldson and Ellis away to dump the body. He was tied up at, and then escaping from, the hospital in Ottawa where I was trying to interview Dianne Jones. We know the end of that story."

"A good ending, thanks to Bud," I said.

"How's your shoulder now, Mike?" asked Cam.

"Still sore but a lot better, thanks. No golf for another couple of weeks."

"We haven't heard the end of Donaldson's story," said Kim.

"Donaldson," I said, "managed to escape from my little backwoods lock-up. He couldn't get the belt undone because I'd rigged it too high. He apparently bounced up and down under the branch until it finally broke off. It took a while but he got himself free and made it back to the dock, to try to get away. He said later that he was going to take a boat and go if Ellis and Washburn weren't there ready and waiting for him. To tell the truth, I'd forgotten all about him for a while, what with the boat chase and the plane crash and whatnot. Bud and I had just made it back to the dock when Donaldson came crashing out of the woods beside the boathouse, only to find the place was swarming with people – police, Inn staff, guests.

"As you know, there's a perfectly good path to follow across the island but he ignored it, thinking it would be faster to go across country, so to speak. When he emerged from the woods several of us looked around at the noise. His face and arms were cut and bleeding from being whipped by branches as he ran through the trees and he was bruised and battered from several falls along the way. He also had a badly broken wrist, where I'd hit him with the sap. He took one look at the crowd at the dock and promptly sat himself down on the boathouse steps and started to cry.

"I made sure one of the police officers knew that Donaldson was someone who needed to be rounded up. Last I saw he was being led away to await the return of the police boat. Bud and I came inside to get Bud's injuries seen to."

The potatoes were browning nicely so I started the pork chops in another pan. The oven was pre-heated and ready. I used some pepper, salt, and granulated onion and garlic then browned the chops on both sides.

"How is Bud, by the way? I haven't seen him for a couple of days," asked Kim.

"He's good. He took some time off and was back to work today."

"And Jason Murdock? What's happening with him, Mike?" asked Kim.

"After a day in the hospital in Perth to make sure there were no nasty leftover effects from the drugs he'd been given he went back to Winnipeg. We got his statement while he was in the hospital and he'll be back to testify when the case gets to court. Word was that he spent most of his brief stay in Perth on the phone, organizing the rebuilding of his company."

"Do we get to keep the plane, RJ?"

"No. Sorry. It would have made a nice addition to the place, even just as a decoration but the expense would be terrible, even to make it look decent, never mind get it flying again."

"What about Smythe? He disappeared very quickly," asked Kim. "Did he have anything to do with all the rest of it? The murder? Whatever?"

Mike answered.

"Unknown, but we think not. There's currently nothing that we can charge him with. He still could be charged relative to the Winnstar stuff, as an accessory to murder, if Ellis or Washburn roll on him and with mischief, coercion maybe, at best, if Kaylee or Brent speak up. Not likely in either case.

"Ellis and Washburn have lawyered-up and are saying nothing to anyone. Donaldson is much more talkative. He'll be testifying against the other two, in return for future considerations but he says he didn't know about Smythe, as Ellis' buyer or as our saboteur."

"Kaylee told me," I said, "that Smythe was forcing both of them, herself and Brent, to do what he wanted. He had something on both of them – something damning from their past - and they felt trapped, unable to resist. He dreamed up the ideas and set them to work. I'm glad they got free of him finally, made their great escape.

"I went to Smythe's boat and confronted him the morning after the boat chase. Brent and Kaylee left while I was with Smythe."

"Once his new help arrived he lit out in a big hurry," said Kim. "One of the boathouse staff said he'd seen the big white yacht sailing off into the sunrise yesterday morning."

"Smythe won't be hard to find if we need to," said Mike.

I put the browned pork chops on a wire rack over a sheet pan and assembled the rest of the dish: a scoop of pizza sauce, some mushroom slices, more pizza sauce and a mound of shaved parmesan and last a sprinkle of chopped fresh oregano. I put that in the oven and the browned potatoes on another sheet pan along side. As they came out of the oven they would get a little salt and pepper and a shake of grated parmesan on top. I turned the heat on low under the steamer pot holding the green beans.

"Dinner in thirty minutes."

Kim, after a moment of silence, asked, "You said there were two reasons that they weren't successful, the Winnstar bunch. Okay, they didn't have their visionary and their best planner, having killed one and framed the other. So, what's the second reason?"

"Us."

"Pardon?" asked Kim.

"We four," I said. "We talked together, kicked around ideas and observations. You did some research for me. Cam gave ideas for me to think about. Mike did what he does – got his people to dig, made his presence felt, led the investigation. Sometimes it's the most important part of an investigation – the collaborating and the sharing of ideas. We listened to what the staff told us. Between the four of us, we sorted through all the random bits of information, sifted out the good stuff from the trash and solved a murder. They might have got away with it, despite the fact that they were not well equipped to handle this kind of thing, if we hadn't been here to stop them. It never made any real sense to me that they picked a relatively isolated island. They chose the wrong place to roll out their little plot."

We were quiet briefly as we thought about that idea. I uncorked a bottle of Pinot Noir from the County then opened the fridge to retrieve the last of what we would need for dinner: a fresh-made cole slaw and a jar of home-made red pepper jelly. I searched around and found that I was missing something.

"Nuts!"

"What's the matter, RJ?" asked Cam.

"I wanted to have some olives with this dinner but apparently I've forgotten to buy any. Maybe I'll go borrow some from the main kitchen."

"That leg of yours is still giving you trouble. I'll go," said Kim.

"I'll come too - keep you company," added Cam.

"Main walk-in – right side as you go in – top shelf near the door. I think."

"We'll find them."

"Thanks."

They went off down the hall toward my recently repaired antique elevator.

I checked the beans and then wandered over to the large window. Mike followed.

"Quite the storm."

We stood at the window, looking out at the violently waving trees, at the rain lashing against the glass. It reminded me briefly of another big wind and rain storm, the results of which had brought us to work together for the first time, to solve our first murder.

"Brent and Kaylee? I think you know more about them than you're saying," said Mike. "Care to share?"

I glanced at him then back to the storm.

"If it becomes necessary that you know I will certainly tell you all I know. I told them I'd keep their real names and histories to myself if I could and I'd like to stick with that."

"I guess I shouldn't ask how you found out about them when I couldn't."

"Probably not."

Mike thought a moment.

"Fair enough." Then, "So, some of your staff are wondering about you now, RJ, wondering how you can do some of the things you do and know the things you know. Not things that are part of the past they attribute to the RJ *they* know. What are you going to do about that?"

I looked at him – shook my head once. "Nothing."

He raised his eyebrows and waited for me to go on. I turned back to the window as a particularly bright flash of lightning slashed across the sky.

"I can't imagine that any of them will come right out and ask questions and I'm going to ignore the inquiring looks and go on as before. The curiosity will fade." I thought a moment. "It's possible that if these people ..." here I hesitated, looked into Mike's eyes then back again out to the storm ... "if they knew some of the things I've done they might not like me so well. Or not. It's not that there was anything particularly horrific or anything I'm ashamed of having done. What went on then was coloured by the times and circumstances, but might not look so good to some people today. Or, perhaps it wouldn't matter. I don't plan to find out. My past is well buried and I want it to stay that way. Every once in a while it claws its way, unbidden, to the surface, but I don't let it see the light of day for long. It gets reburied. As it should. No-one needs to know, and I don't need them to know."

"Not even Cam?"

Thunder rumbled, close and loud, shaking the old building.

"Ah. That, as they say, is the question. I don't like having secrets from her, especially if we're going to be together for the long haul, which looks like it might be a possibility. But I'm not sure that she would react differently from what I fear of others' reactions, if she knew all there was to know about me. Same applies to you, actually."

Before he could respond the door of the elevator rattled open and Kim and Cam re-entered the room, Kim carrying a large jar.

"Damn thunder went off just as the door was closing. I thought the old beast was going to croak with us inside. Ugh." Kim gave an exaggerated shudder.

"Looks like we interrupted a serious conversation here," said Cam.

"Not really," said Mike

I turned and started toward the kitchen, stopping to put on Phil Nimmons' *Atlantic Suite* as I passed the music system. One of my favourites.

"Thanks for getting those olives. Everything is now ready. Let's eat."

Readers:

Thanks again for looking at the story. I hope you've enjoyed your second visit to Gilmore Island.

What follows this time is a copy of the Gilmore House Inn lunch menu.

Also appearing are a few more of our recipes.

Try them out and see what you think - play with them and make them your own. As before some are original to the Inn, either Bud's or mine, usually, and others are adaptations of meals I've had and enjoyed. I'm not always sure where they came from, but I wouldn't be using them at the Inn if I hadn't thought they were really good. Bud and I put our own little spin on everything we cook at the Inn but we try to be consistent, always using the same spin. These recipes are as close as possible to what is actually served here, scaled down for home use. I hope you enjoy them and that they bring back pleasant memories of your time with us.

The Gilmore House Inn Recipe Book is still in the works but is taking longer than expected because I seem to be spending a lot of time trying to solve mysteries.

In the recipe for Bud's All Canadian Fruit Cookies from *Old Bones,* I made an error regarding flour substitution, so a correction is included here.

As before, I've included some floor plans, a road map and a topographical map believed to be made by Alexander Gilmore. The floor plans don't seem to be professional but were among the papers stored at the Barrhaven real estate office.

We hope to see you again.

R.J.Harrison

The Gilmore House Inn
Gilmore Island, Westport, Ontario, Canada.

Lunch Menu

Starters *(changed daily)*

Soup du Jour - *Please ask your server to tell you about our soups of the day. Each is made right here, using fresh, local and organic ingredients wherever possible.*

Shrimp Crostini - *Six large Shrimp seasoned and pan seared to order, flavoured with garlic and butter. Served over house-made Garlic Crostini and topped with fresh scallions.*

Garden Salad - *Made to order — just for you, with your choice of house-made Dressing.*

Mains *(changed daily)*

Smoked Salmon Sandwich - *Your choice of fresh made breads, Ciabata roll or bagel, toasted, with Havarti cheese, lettuce, sliced cucumber and smoked salmon. Served with a salad.*

Buds Best Burger – *1/3 pound burger of beef and pork seasoned with onion and garlic, flame broiled, served on a fresh-made bun with cheddar cheese, red onion, tomato and avocado and Bud's secret dressing.*
Double if you dare. Served with house-cut fries and our own Gilmore House Cole slaw.

Open-faced 6 oz. Rib Eye Steak Sandwich - A 6 ounce Rib Eye Steak grilled to your specifications on toasted Calabrase bread. Served with house-cut fries and a salad.

Florentine Quiche - A vegetarian quiche, heavy on the spinach – light on the pastry. Served with a salad and roll.

Please note that salads and breads are available at no additional charge with all mains.

<u>Desserts</u>   (changed daily)

Ice Cream - Please ask your server to tell you about the flavours of the day.

Amazing Brownies - We have them with or without nuts: deep, rich, dark chocolate – with or without ice cream.

Fresh Baked Pie - We have at least two types of pie available every day. Please ask your server for today's selections,

----

We provide bag lunches upon request. These include a sandwich of your choice, fruit and a Great Canadian Fruit Cookie. Canned soft drinks and bottled water are also available. Please arrange for this with your server if you would like one for tomorrow.

correction to the recipe for:

Bud's All Canadian Fruit Cookies from *Old Bones*

A reader brought it to my attention that I had made an error in my handling of flour substitutions as they pertain to gluten intolerance.

Spelt and Kamut are both ancient grain wheats and as such <u>do</u> contain gluten. Some people with mild gluten intolerance find these easier to handle than other wheats, hence their inclusion as substitutions for all-purpose flour.

For those with gluten intolerance the best bet is to substitute a non-gluten flour blend. Sometimes these are problematic for breads and cakes but will work fine in a cookie. And remember to lose the wheat germ.

With my apologies, hopefully this will clear up any confusion I may have caused.

RJH.

a recipe from

The Gilmore House Inn
Westport, Ontario, Canada.

Gilmore's Smoked Salmon Sandwich

Ingredients: *serves 1*

4-6 oz   smoked salmon   sliced thin   thaw if frozen
*   use at room temperature*
6-9 slices   English cucumber   sliced very thin
(number will vary by size of cucumber and bread)
2 leaves   iceberg or other fairly mild lettuce   crisp
1 slice   creamy Havarti cheese
1-2 tbsp   mild red onion   raw   sliced very thin
(almost shaved)
1 tbsp   Tartar sauce   (more or less to taste)
2 slices of your favourite bread or a Ciabatta roll or bagel
(something that can be toasted)
salt and pepper to taste

remove the smoked salmon from the refrigerator ½ hour ahead and allow to come to room temperature   you don't want it cold but don't heat it either - that changes the flavour

build the sandwich filling on a plate or board   without the toast in this order
sliced Havarti   lettuce   smoked salmon   sliced onion sliced cucumber

toast the bread or Ciabatta roll or bagel butter one or both sides
spread one side with Tartar sauce
add salt and pepper to taste

lift the filling with a spatula onto the side without the Tartar
sauce   cover

cut and serve while the toast is still warm

———————

substitutions are <u>recommended</u>   change it up – it's your sandwich

use a Panini maker to toast the bread or roll
use smoked trout or other mildly smoked fish
use a stronger cheese if you like – Emmenthal or Gruyere - not too
strong though or you overpower the fish
substitute the cucumber for thin sliced radishes or tomato or use
all three
I like a mild lettuce for this but feel free to use a stronger or a
bitter green or baby spinach

Enjoy.   RJH

a recipe from

The Gilmore House Inn
Westport, Ontario, Canada.

Roasted Lemon-Thyme Chicken

Ingredients: serves 4

4 chicken breasts   bone in   skin on
2 lemons
4 tbsp   olive oil
2 tbsp   thyme leaves   fresh   (or 1 scant tbsp dried)
Salt and pepper to taste

preheat the oven to 350° F   rack in centre position   spray a baking sheet and rack

zest both lemons   cut one in half for squeezing (save the other half for another time)

heat the oil in a fry pan   medium heat   salt and pepper the chicken – both sides

lightly brown both sides of the chicken breasts   2-3 min each side

place the chicken on the sprayed pan with the rack   skin side up

evenly distribute the thyme leaves and the lemon zest over the four breasts give each a light squeeze of lemon juice   don't wash off the thyme and lemon zest

roast at 350° F for 40-45 min (depending on size)   uncovered

let stand, tented with foil, 3-4 min to rest before serving

we serve this with mini roast potatoes and fresh green beans

(Note: As I write this recipe it seems appropriate to mention the spray. Various commercial, non-stick sprays are available but for home use I have a pump-spray bottle which I fill with light olive oil. It works fine.)

Enjoy   RJH

a recipe from

𝒯he 𝒢ilmore 𝐻ouse 𝒥nn
𝒲estport, 𝒪ntario, 𝒞anada.

Garlic Lover's Steak

Ingredients: *serves 2*

2 Rib Eye steaks   4-6 oz. each   1 -1 ½ " (2-3 cm) thick
2-4   cloves of garlic   whole   peeled
1/4 tsp   granulated garlic
1/4 tsp   granulated onion
salt and pepper

garlic-chive compound butter   (compound butter recipes included)

———————————

pre heat the oven to 350° F   rack in middle position

pre heat grill or grill pan if cooking indoors (use a fry pan if you
like)   use a shallow pan with a rack or trivet if cooking indoors
spray the pan / rack / trivet with non-stick spray

unwrap the steaks and pat dry with a paper towel   (wet steaks
take longer to brown)

cut 2 largest garlic cloves lengthwise to expose a large flat surface
use the rest as needed

rub the garlic cloves over the surface of the steaks   both sides and the edges   wait 5 min and repeat

season the steaks with granulated garlic and granulated onion and salt and pepper

grill the steaks   both sides   3-4 min each side   rotate ¼ turn at half time each side

remove the steaks to the rack and place in oven if cooking indoors or to a place of indirect heat on an   outdoor grill

depending on thickness allow 7-10 min for rare, 10-12 min for medium rare, etc

remove from oven or grill and tent with foil for 5 min before serving.

when you plate the steaks top with a slice of garlic-chive compound butter

we serve with home fries or restuffed baked potato and a steamed vegetable

Enjoy

a recipe from

The Gilmore House Inn
Westport, Ontario, Canada.

Rainbow Pickerel

Ingredients: *serves 4*

2-4   pickerel fillets   about 1 kilo raw weight   deboned and skinned
6-8 c   baby spinach   raw
1   each red, orange, yellow, purple mini peppers   sliced into very thin rings
6-8   mushrooms   sliced very thin
1/4 c   red onion   sliced very thin
12   mini grape or other mini tomatoes   red   quartered lengthwise
2 tbsp   parsley   fresh   chopped fine
2 tbsp   butter   softened   substitute margarine if necessary
salt and pepper   (optional)

you'll need a sheet pan with parchment paper   sprayed with non-stick spray

pre heat the oven to 400° F   rack in centre position

in 1/4 tsp dollops distribute half the butter onto the parchment smooth it out with a spoon or spatula

spread the spinach over the parchment

lay the fish in a single layer onto the spinach

distribute the pepper rings, mushroom slices, red onion and tomatoes evenly over the fish

in 1/4 tsp dollops distribute the remaining butter over the top

add salt and pepper if using

bake at 400° for 15 min

serve hot with multigrain rice and Tartar sauce

(okay so it's not all the colours of the rainbow but colourful none the less)

Enjoy   RJH

a recipe from

The Gilmore House Inn
Westport, Ontario, Canada.

Pork Chop Parmesan

Ingredients: *serves 4*

4 pork chops   bone – in   fat trimmed   pat dry with a paper towel
3-4 mushrooms   sliced thin
1 c   pizza sauce   commercial or home made   spicy or not
1/4 c   parmesan cheese   shaved   (use a vegetable peeler to shave curls off a wedge of Parmesan)
2 tbsp   fresh oregano leaves   or   1 tbsp dried
2 tbsp   olive oil

———————

pre heat the oven to 350° F   rack in the middle position

foil and spray a sheet pan and a rack   preheat a frypan   add the oil

salt and pepper the chops and sear both sides until golden and slightly crusted   remove to the rack

apply 1 tbsp of pizza sauce to each chop
distribute the mushroom slices on each chop
apply another tbsp of sauce to each

add curls of parmesan to each
top each with a sprinkle of oregano leaves

put the assembled dish in the oven for 30 – 40 min depending on the thickness of the chops

remove and let stand, tented with foil, for 5 min before serving

we serve with Italian seasoned (oregano, basil, granulated onion and garlic) roasted potatoes and a vegetable.

Enjoy

RJH

a recipe from

The Gilmore House Inn
Westport, Ontario, Canada.

Eggplant Parmesan with Spinach and Zucchini

Ingredients: *serves 4*

1-2   eggplants   1 large or 2 med. depending on size available sliced 1/4 " (1/2 cm)
1   zucchini   8 inch or so   (20 cm)   sliced 1/8" (1/4 cm)
4 c   baby spinach
1/4 c   red onion   sliced very thin
2 tbsp   fresh herbs   chopped fine   assorted basil, oregano, parsley
2-3 tbsp   olive oil   for frying

2 c   Italian seasoned bread crumbs   commercial or home made
1   egg   beaten   with 2-3 tbsp cool water
1/2 c all purpose flour (substitute gluten free flour mix if necessary)

4 c   meatless pasta sauce   (marinara)
1 c   white cheese blend   (we use parmesan, asiago, provolone, mozzarella)
1/4 c   parmesan cheese   grated

pre heat the oven to 350° F   rack in centre position   sheet pan below for drips

you'll need three pie plates or the like: 1 for the flour, 1 for the beaten egg and 1 for the crumbs, a baking sheet with parchment paper, a frypan and an oven proof casserole dish - sprayed

heat the frypan with the oil

dredge each slice of eggplant in flour then egg then crumbs
fry in a single layer   3-4 min per side or until golden   remove to the sheet pan   fry remaining slices

cover the bottom of the casserole with sauce (each layer gets 1/3 of the sauce, herbs and cheeses)
layer spinach, zucchini, eggplant, onion, herbs and cheeses   add more sauce and repeat
top with remaining sauce, herbs and cheeses

bake for 30-40 min covered and 10 min uncovered to brown the top

let stand 10 min before serving
we serve with garlic toast and a salad

Enjoy   RJH

a recipe from

The Gilmore House Inn
Westport, Ontario, Canada.

Restuffed Baked Potato

Ingredients: *serves 4*

4   med to large Russet baking potatoes   scrubbed   dried
holes poked to allow steam to escape
1/4 c   old cheddar cheese   shredded
3 tbsp   butter or margarine
3 tbsp   sour cream
1 tbsp   chives   chopped to 1/4" (1/2 cm) or smaller
1 tbsp   roasted red pepper   minced fine   place on a paper
towel to absorb excess liquid
1 tbsp   roasted garlic   smoothed
Salt and pepper to taste

pre-heat the oven to 400° F

bake the potatoes 45 min to 1 hour depending on size   check after
40 min

let cool slightly then cut lengthwise as near the centre as possible

with a soup spoon carefully scoop out the potato from all 8 of the
skins

place the chunks of potato in a large bowl
add all the other ingredients except the red pepper

stir the ingredients together until well mixed   do not mash   you want texture

add the roasted red pepper and give it one final mix

spoon the mixture into 4 of the potato skins   mound it higher than the skin

place on a baking sheet or pie plate in a warm oven until ready to serve

(if you like, place the potatoes under a broiler for a couple of minutes to brown before serving)

Enjoy   *RJH*

a recipe from

The Gilmore House Inn
Westport, Ontario, Canada.

Multi-Grain Rice

Ingredients: *serves 4*

1/2 c   each white, brown, red and wild rice
5 c   water plus 1 c
2 tsp   butter of margarine   divided in 4
1/2 tsp   salt   divided in 4

the objective here is to get a finished product which has four distinct colours visible
at Gilmore House we do each rice in its own pot – 4 pots going at the same time
you can do any variation you like using 1, 2, 3 or 4 pots as long as each rice cooks separately

I'm laying out the method using 4 pots

1 pot gets   1 c water   1/4 tsp butter   1/8 tsp salt   1/2 c white rice
1 pot gets   1 c water   1/4 tsp butter   1/8 tsp salt   1/2 c brown rice
1 pot gets   1 c water   1/4 tsp butter   1/8 tsp salt   1/2 c red rice
1 pot gets   1½ c water   1/4 tsp butter   1/8 tsp salt   1/2 c wild rice

as the water heats add the butter to each   when the water is boiling add the salt to each add the rice to each pot   stir to be sure nothing is sticking on the bottom of the pot

when the water returns to the boil time as follows: white 20 min, red and brown 40 min each and wild 60 min   test for doneness 10 and 5 min ahead of these times (al dente   chewable with firmness)

remove from heat and leave covered for any remaining water to be absorbed   not cooking

when you're sure there's no water left mix all four together in a large pot or bowl

this can be made hours ahead or the previous day   keep sealed and refrigerated

reheat in a microwave-safe container   bring to room temperature 2 hours ahead   add 2 tbsp of water

we serve this with our Rainbow Pickerel and other fish dishes

Enjoy

a recipe from

The Gilmore House Inn
Westport, Ontario, Canada.

Tartar Sauce

Ingredients: *serves 4*

1 c   mayonnaise or salad dressing
1 tbsp   sweet green relish   or chopped gherkin pickles
1½ tsp   chives   chopped to 1/4" (1/2 cm)
1½ tsp   capers   chopped fine
1 tsp   lemon juice
1/4 tsp   white pepper   fine

in a large bowl mix all the ingredients together until well blended

transfer to a smaller stainless steel or glass bowl and refrigerate at least 2 hours, preferably longer – even the day ahead

stores well in a sealed container, refrigerated, 2-3 weeks

———————

add more capers or more chives if you want to change it up a bit by using dill relish or finely minced dill pickles and add some fresh dill

———————

use a stainless steel or glass bowl because it will chill faster in the refrigerator than in plastic   don't use aluminum   it's okay to store the leftovers in plastic

Enjoy   RJH

a recipe from

The Gilmore House Inn
Westport, Ontario, Canada.

Compound Butter

compound butters can be used for lots of dishes and can come in a great number of flavours and flavour combinations can be stored frozen several months

we use this one for the Garlic Lover's Steak

Ingredients: *serves 4 (with leftovers)*

1/2 stick butter   (1/2 c)   softened 1 hour at room temperature

1 tbsp   chives   chopped to 1/4 " (1/2 cm)
2 tbsp   garlic   finely minced or grated

mix the ingredients thoroughly in a bowl

place the mixture on a piece of plastic wrap and shape into a log about 1-1¼ " (2-2½ cm) diameter
roll up the log in the plastic and seal the ends
place the log in the freezer to firm up
remove to the refrigerator 6 - 8 hours before you'll need it   frozen butter doesn't slice well
slice in discs of 1/4" – 1/2 " (1/2 to 1 cm) and place on top of hot meats or fish

here are some more possibilities to try in your ½ stick of butter

1 tbsp   cilantro   fresh   chopped fine
1 tbsp   lime zest   grated fine
1/2 tsp   lime juice   be careful adding liquids – too much will
deter the re-hardening of the butter

2 tbsp   roasted red pepper   minced fine   dry up excess liquid
on a paper towel or mixture will be pink
1 tbsp   chives   chopped to 1/4" (1/2 cm)
1/8 tsp   white pepper   very fine

2 tbsp   blue cheese   crumbled small
1 tbsp   red onion   minced very fine

Enjoy   *RJH*

a recipe from

The Gilmore House Inn
Westport, Ontario, Canada.

Gilmore House Cole Slaw
(from Bud's sister's mother-in-law)

Ingredients: *serves 4*

3 c green cabbage   shredded   small
or
2 c   green cabbage and 1 c   red cabbage   shredded   small
2 tbsp   red onion   sliced thin   chopped small
2 tbsp   celery   sliced thin   chopped small
2 tbsp   carrot   shredded   chopped small
1/4 c   mayonnaise or salad dressing
2 tbsp   ranch dressing
1/4 tsp   celery seed
1/4 tsp   mustard seed
1/4 tsp   black pepper   fine
1/8 tsp   salt

———————

place the vegetables and the dry seasonings in a large bowl   mix well

add the ranch dressing and half the mayo   mix well

now you decide when the mixture is moist enough   add the remaining mayo a little at a time and mix well   stop when you reach the consistency you like once the salad is thoroughly mixed transfer it to a glass or stainless steel bowl and refrigerate at least 2 hours

don't make more than you need for 1 day because the mayonnaise will break down (the salad will get watery fairly quickly)

Enjoy   Bud

a recipe from

The Gilmore House Inn
Westport, Ontario, Canada.

Classic Peach Pie
(recipe from the Osgoode Bakery)

Preheat oven to 425° F   rack at one position lower than centre

You may wish to prepare the crust before preparing the filling, so that the filling does not stand too long … if the filling is made ahead of time, the sugar will pull water from the fruit, making the filling too runny … for a juicier filling, allow the filling to stand at room temperature, stirring gently occasionally

Crust
Ingredients and instructions: makes 1 pie   serves 6-8

2 c   cake and pastry flour   unsifted
3/4 tsp   salt
1/2 c   lard   plus   2 tbsp   cold butter
3 or 4 tbsp   cold water   (approximately)

sift the flour and salt together into a bowl

cut the lard into 1" (2 cm) chunks and drop into the flour, keeping the pieces separate.

use a pastry blender or a pair of knives to cut the lard into the flour until the mixture resembles fairly course oatmeal.

cut in the butter until it is the size of peas
stir gently with a fork and sprinkle in the water 1 tbsp at a time
until the flour is evenly moistened

gently form a ball by pressing the moistened bits together until
the flour mixture cleans the bowl ... add more water sparingly if
needed. Gather into a firm ball.

divide the ball into "a larger half and a smaller half" ...
approximately 2/3 and 1/3.

set 1/3 of the ball aside for the top crust, and roll the remainder
for the bottom crust.

cut a circle bigger than the diameter of your pie plate, and transfer
the bottom crust to the pie plate ... trim the edges even with the
rim of the pan.

rub approximately 1 tsp of flour on the bottom crust before adding
the filling.

roll out the top crust so that it is bigger than the pie plate.

Filling
Ingredients and instructions:

3½ to 4 cups fresh ripe peaches, peeled and chopped into medium
sized chunks (approximately 16 pieces from each peach is usually
a good size)

2/3 to 3/4 c sugar ... the amount depends on the ripeness ... use
more when the fruit is less ripe ... too much sugar will make the
filling runny ...if you prefer a sweeter pie add more sugar and

increase the amount of thickening

4 tbsp   flour   OR   2 tbsp   cornstarch   OR   2 tbsp   tapioca ...
(for thickening)

(this filling is for an 8 or 9 inch (20 cm) pie plate ... for a bigger
pie, add more fruit, sugar and thickening)

combine the sugar and thickening ... sprinkle it over the fruit ...
stir gently

pour the fruit into the bottom crust

Assembly and baking

moisten the top edges of the bottom crust with water, and transfer
the top crust ... trim the top crust to approximately 1" (2 cm)
beyond the rim ... fold the extended edge under the moistened
edges of the bottom crust and press together ... crimp the edges

cut generous gashes in the top crust ... this will allow steam to
escape during cooking and prevent the creation of an empty space
above the filling ... cut a hole in the centre to allow you to see
that the filling is bubbling

bake at 425° F for 20 minutes ... reduce the temperature to 350°
F ... continue baking for approximately 20 minutes ... the filling
should be bubbling

Enjoy   Sandi and Liz

About the Author

Brian Lindsay has recently retired after ten years of operating a personal chef service. He spent numerous years in food service, as a food and beverage manager and a kitchen manager. Before that he was, for a few years, in retail security. He has now turned his focus to writing crime, with an epicurean garnish.

He has two grown children, a son and a daughter, and lives with his wife in Kitchener, Ontario.

Brian's first book, *Old Bones* – A Gilmore House Mystery, was short-listed as a finalist for the 2016 **ARTHUR ELLIS AWARD** for Best First (Crime) Novel.

To contact the author please visit www.brlindsayimagist.com